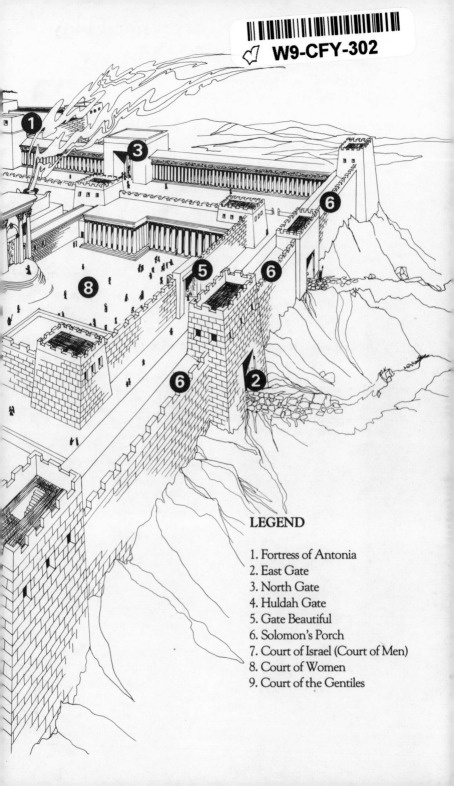

W9-CFY-302

LEGEND

1. Fortress of Antonia
2. East Gate
3. North Gate
4. Huldah Gate
5. Gate Beautiful
6. Solomon's Porch
7. Court of Israel (Court of Men)
8. Court of Women
9. Court of the Gentiles

THIEVES

T.A. NOTON

THIEVES

T.A. NOTON

impact books

A Division of The Benson Company
Nashville, Tennessee

THIEVES. ©Copyright 1979 by IMPACT BOOKS, a division of The Benson Company. All rights reserved. Printed in the United States of America. No part of this book may be used or reproduced in any manner whatsoever without written permission, except in the case of brief quotations embodied in critical articles and reviews. For information, address: IMPACT BOOKS, The Benson Company, 365 Great Circle Road, Nashville, Tennessee 37228.

Library of Congress Catalogue Number 78-67232

Hardback
ISBN 0-914850-41-5
MO569

Paperback
ISBN 0-914850-48-2
MO550

First Edition

TABLE OF CONTENTS

PREFACE

Thieves has created a dramatic change in my life as a writer and as a natural man striving toward the godly characteristics in I Corinthians 13. As the words of this book began to link themselves together, I found I was growing in love—not only for God and my fellowman—but for the characters that sprang full-blown from my imagination. As I continued, it became increasingly difficult to remain emotionally detached from events in the life of Marcus.

Of the many questions I am asked concerning the writing of *Thieves*, the question "Where did the idea originate?" seems to occur more frequently than all others combined. The answer has not been a simple one, for if I say the book was divinely inspired, I am met with skepticism and uneasy silence. Yet being candid, I will have to stand with an answer bordering on that very premise.

My wife, Bobbie, will attest to the tears of joy which followed the reading of each completed chapter of the raw manuscript. Along with the growing awareness of supreme intervention and my wife's encouragement, the work went on. It has been nurtured in the physical and mental crucible of my own life and has come to fruition in God's own time.

Within these pages, we have mingled accounts from God's Word and characters devised for the purpose of telling the story as it may have happened . . .

T. A. NOTON
January, 1979
Mulberry, Florida

CHAPTER
I

During these days of Roman occupation, Jerusalem was filled with a cross section of seething humanity. Greeks had taken refuge within the great walls to study their philosophies, their gods, and the Roman women brought in for the pleasure of Caesar's army. Men from the tribes of Israel, every sect, wandered the streets in search of another of like kind.

These masses milling about the streets did not go unobserved. The occupying hordes of Roman troops surveyed every gathering and subsequently scattered those who seemed destined for trouble. They were especially watchful of the Zealots. That group of Jews dedicated to insurrection constantly needed to be watchdogged. To the Romans the teacher called Jesus was of little concern, yet the fanatically religious Jews continually urged the captain of the guard to take the man before Pilate.

This night, however, seemed *too* calm to one young

Jew easing his way into an alley. He moved quickly, stopping only once to look back down the darkened street. His thick, black hair fell across his forehead, down into his eyes. He brushed it back and squinted. No one followed him, but he listened carefully to make certain. As he stood there in the darkness, the distant sounds of hooves clattered against the streets of the upper city. The smell of trash burning outside Jerusalem's walls caught in the young Jew's nostrils and almost brought a sneeze. He quickly covered his mouth and nose, and stifled the sneeze.

With only a sliver of moonlight piercing the night, the darkness hung thick as he turned and made his way deep into the narrow space between the buildings. Feeling along the rugged stone walls with his fingertips, he was filled with warm relief, easing the tension in his spine and in the knotted muscles between his shoulder blades. A smile tugged at the corners of his mouth. No one had seen him. He was sure of it.

He stopped once more, his keen ears attuned to any deviation from the normal sounds of the night. All was quiet—nothing to cause the young Jew alarm. He felt the metal object beneath his tunic and breathed a deep sigh. He had succeeded in stealing the Sacred Goat of Kahl, and the danger of discovery was well past. He could sell this treasure to Nadab, the trader, for quite a goodly sum—enough to provide food and warm clothing for his mother for some time.

His sense of well-being was shattered by a noise from the blackness. He stopped abruptly, his eyes straining into the depths of the alley. He froze, forcing his body hard against the wall. Again he squinted, hoping to make out the source of the disturbance. Focusing by squinting into the dark was an art he had perfected during his few short years as a beggar and thief. He shivered. Whether it was from the chill night air or the icy fingers of fear that ran the length of his slender body was hard to say.

Something moved just ten or twelve feet away. His body oozed with cold perspiration, beginning with his palms. His tongue felt thick. Cotton formed in his mouth. He listened—there it was again—scratching. Mustering all his courage, he thrust his body toward the movement—better to see and determine his course of action. One of his sandals slapped the stone pavement. It cracked like thunder in his ears, yet whatever awaited in the darkness had taken no notice of the sound. His eyes were slowly making their adjustment. Pursing his lips, he hissed lightly. The scratching stopped. He hissed again. A low growl met his ears. He pushed against the wall, braced for an attack.

The small dog had been so intent on finding a meal in the garbage that the movements of the young man had eluded its sensitive hearing. Now, however, the sight of the man raised the little animal's defenses. The hair on its neck bristled and it crouched as if to spring.

Sensing the dog's fear, the young man slid down the wall until his knee touched the hard surface of the alley. The rough cobblestone bruised the flesh, but he bore the dull ache quietly hoping not to startle the little dog further. Now he began to hum softly, extending his hand slowly, fingers folded under. His mother had taught him the value of these gestures to gain the confidence of small creatures. It was working. The little one was responding. Slowly, softly, he began to talk to the mongrel. The smile on the man's face broadened as he made out the contours of the body. He could see that the dog was a female, near time to drop her puppies.

The little dog lifted her floppy ears and cocked her head to one side. The voice seemed kind, unlike any she had ever heard. She was confused. This human didn't kick or curse with loud shouts. The hair on her back settled. Tentatively, she lifted one foreleg. But years of hard experience with man had taught her to be wary, and she tucked her tail.

Noticing her hesitation, the young man began to speak in a low, easy manner. "The Lord has provided you well, little one." The voice was filled with tenderness. "We can be friends?" he asked. His fist unfolded and the fingers stretched forth in a friendly motion. The dog, still apprehensive, stood her ground.

"The God who watches over us has prepared a feast for you." The young Jew gestured toward a large bone at the edge of the garbage heap.

The soft laughter in the young man's voice dispelled her fears. The dog moved her tail slowly between her legs, her head now fully lowered in submission.

"Oh, ho!" the young man exclaimed. Then he quickly slapped his hand over his mouth, glancing back toward the entrance of the alley. The dog darted away.

"Oh, little one," the young man whispered, "I did not mean to startle you, but" (his voice became barely audible) "we must be quiet. Even at this late hour, the *Roman* dogs are marching in the streets." The young Jew's mouth became taut. "Little one, will you forgive me? I have insulted you by linking your kind with that of the Romans." He moved his hand to stroke her, but she was still beyond his reach. "I am truly sorry," he pleaded. He eased his body into a sitting position, his hand still extended.

The little female, tail between her legs and body twisted sideways, inched forward until she could lick his fingertips. After a few seconds, she moved another step closer, still wary.

He stretched his hand its full length until he could

scratch her ear. "In all my boyhood days on the hillsides of Judea, I dreamed of a dog for myself." He patted her belly, then caught her face in his hands. "If you will stay with me," he whispered, his nose almost touching hers, "I may have my dream tenfold!" He patted her swollen sides.

The minutes ticked by as he spoke. The gentle stroking eased her foreboding and soon she lay beside him, her head resting lightly on his thigh. Even the cold night air filtering in from the street could not penetrate the warmth they shared.

Forgetting the problems of the present, the young Jew allowed his mind to drift up and out of the blackness of the alley, back into the brightness of boyhood, where laughter—long spent—resounded in some chamber of his mind.

Only two or three years back (or was it four now?) he recalled a birthday; he presumed it to be his fifteenth. Reflecting on his anticipation of that day, he could hear his mother calling him somewhere in the distance of time.

"Marcus, Marcus, where are you?"

He stepped around the corner of the little house on the hillside near Bethany. "Here I am, my lovely mother."

"Such flattery," she smiled knowingly. "Your gift was purchased days ago and plying me with your compliments will not change it."

"Is it a dog of my very own?" He had attempted to suppress the excitement in his voice. After all, he was now a man grown. "If it is not, I will not be upset," he lied.

His mother turned away, covering her soft smile. He remembered the sweetness in her voice as she said mysteriously, "You will see . . ."

The dog lurched in the boy's lap, interrupting his reverie. Some sound in the distance had caused the little dog to prick up her ears, her body poised for flight.

"What is it, little one?" he whispered. Then he, too, heard the commotion. The sound of soldiers from the Fortress of Antonia echoed in the narrow streets. Marcus pulled the dog into his arms and rose to his feet. "You have heard the distant buzz of the Roman wasps. You have keen ears and eyes," he whispered. "Good fortune has smiled favorably on me. I will keep you always at my side."

Then the young man grew quiet. Horses' hooves tapped their staccatoed cadence on the stone streets of the lower city. Sharp commands were issued. Without warning, foot soldiers ran by the alley's entrance, causing Marcus to tighten his grip around the dog in his arms. In the distance someone screamed in agony. A dog barked, then another.

Responding to the familiar presence of fear, the little female lifted her head, growling deep within her throat. The young Jew placed his hand gently on her muzzle. "No, little one," he warned, "please, not now." As he spoke, the sound of footsteps drew ever nearer. The dog lurched in his arms, and he pulled her closer to his chest, nuzzling his face against hers. He pressed hard against the wall. "Be still," he whispered. The footsteps were louder now. The boy slid back a few more steps, sinking deeper into the darkness. Someone was close to the entrance. He heard the swish of clothing and the scraping of sandals.

The young Jew strained to hear. Whoever was near the alley's entrance had stopped there. Was someone hiding from the soldiers' whip, as he was? He frowned. No movement stirred near the alley's mouth. Perhaps he was mistaken.

Relief was short-lived. Suddenly an alarming sequence of sounds broke the silence. A large figure hurtled into the alley, rolling deep into the darkness and coming to rest just a few feet from the young man and his frightened dog. Instantly, the clapping of hooves was heard. A quaternion rode by at full gallop, shouting and cursing. As they clattered down the street, a man's voice cried out in pain, cursed in Greek, then fell silent.

Marcus' eyes focused on the man who lay motionless near his feet. His ears, however, remained tuned to the fading voices in the narrow streets. The atmosphere was now charged with tension. The dog's ears twitched in the strange silence—waiting.

Finally the man spoke. "The curs!" He rolled over and sat up, wiped blood from his lips with the filthy sleeve of his coat, cursed, and spat. His thick beard was matted with blood. "They shall pay," he muttered, wiping again.

He was unaware of company in the shadows. Instead, his attention centered on the mouth of the alley through which he had made his hasty entrance. A sneer contorted his leathery face and his bushy eyebrows turned down in furrows toward the bridge of his nose. "Dogs!" he spat again. "Dogs!" Exhausted, he leaned back against the building, his eyes still blinded by the darkness.

He took a deep breath and pushed his back against the rugged wall, trying to arrange his legs under him. He took another gulp of the stale air and heaved. About halfway up, his legs gave way and he crumpled in a heap on the stone pavement. He muttered to himself, cursing the contemptible darkness! If he could only see to gain his footing.

Marcus felt the dog jerk in his arms. He gripped her more tightly, which made her struggle all the more. She whimpered.

The unexpected sound startled the injured man. For the first time, he realized he was not alone in the alley. His eyes flashed as he searched the darkness. Gathering new strength, he was on his feet in one swift motion, dagger drawn. The fine steel glistened as a ray of moonlight struck its curve. He squinted into the blackness, skillfully maneuvering the blade back and forth, slowly and deliberately. "Who's there?" he growled. His voice was like gravel, but a cruel edge sharpened his words. "Step out, or I quarter you now!" He sliced the air with the blade.

Marcus swallowed hard. "Have mercy, my lord," he pleaded.

"Step forward!" the man demanded.

The young Jew moved hesitantly, the dog secure in his arms.

As the boy emerged from the darkness, the grizzled man frowned. "A boy? Only a boy?" He laughed aloud. Looking again, he added, "An—and a mongrel." He placed his hands on his hips and twisted his mouth. "And what, stupid one, are you doing in the streets at this late hour?" Before Marcus could reply, he demanded, "Your name! And be quick to answer."

"M-Marcus, sir."

"And?" The man waved the blade impatiently.

"And?" Marcus repeated, genuinely puzzled as to what more the man might want of him.

"And, what are you doing here? Can't you answer even the simplest of questions?" The gruff voice grew louder. "Young and stupid," he growled.

"I-I'm . . . ah . . . ." he glanced at the dog, "I'm gathering some food scraps for my dog," he lied.

"Ha!" the older man responded. "You call *that* a dog?" He laughed again, then searched the young man's face. "Yes," he shook his head, "*you* would consider this mange-filled mongrel a dog." He reached out to touch the animal, but drew his hand back at the sound of the deep throaty snarl.

Turning toward the street, he tucked his knife into the folds of his garment. He crept to the alley's entrance and leaned against the wall in silence. Several minutes passed. The man turned back into the darkened passageway. He looked the boy over, assessing his value. *Youth is stupid*, he mused, *but youth is quick and strong*. Maybe he could teach this one the specialty of his trade. Yes, he might prove to be an asset.

"Marcus, is it?" The bearded man sat down on the stone pavement and leaned against the building. "Let the mongrel go eat her scraps." He motioned toward the garbage heap. "You—sit here with me," he commanded.

Marcus shrugged his shoulders and obeyed.

The pair sat in the darkness for a few moments while the little dog found the bone and began gnawing greedily.

Without warning, the older man turned and grabbed Marcus' cloak at the throat, snapping his head backward. "You idiot," he spat. "Do you think I am stupid, like you? Now, tell me the truth! Why are you hiding in this alley?" He tightened his grip on the young man's clothing. "If you lie to me again, I shall cut out your tongue." He cursed prolifically. "*Now, tell me!*" Each word was punctuated by a powerful yank.

The violent movement sent Marcus' hidden treasure spilling to the stone pavement. Instantly the older Jew reached in the direction of the sound and muffled its piercing clang. Based on his years of plundering, he calculated that the thing he touched was indeed an object of value. The weathered hand caressed the cold metal curves. His fingers moved across it, finding the embedded jewels. He released Marcus and scooped it up, concentrating fully on the metal sculpture.

A lone cloud skimmed the moon's surface, freeing the faint ray of light that now illuminated the object. The older man was amazed to see the figure of a goat carved in silver, with golden wings outstretched and great emerald stones studding the eye sockets.

He turned slowly toward Marcus, visibly shaken. When at last he spoke, his voice was tremulous, "It is the Sacred Goat of Kahl." He knew the value of this precious work of art. He eyed it speculatively. Though the light grew dim again, he could still make out the lines. He was sure it was worth at least three thousand shekels. Amazement vied with anger in his voice. "How could such a stupid one get away with stealing a . . . a . . ." he coughed, "this?" He shook the goat in Marcus' face.

Marcus swallowed but kept silent.

Then, smiling for the first time, he shoved the goat into Marcus' hands. "I'm sorry," he said in a sudden change of mood. "It is not my affair, nor right for me to question you about it. I, too, am a thief." He was certain this confession would do the trick and catch the boy off guard. "Our little band attempted to besiege and rob the house of one Theodius, a rich cousin of none other than Caesar himself." He chuckled under his breath "How were we to know it was the night of an orgy?" He laughed uproariously.

As his smile faded, he studied Marcus' reaction. He shook his head and slapped his palm against his forehead. "How stupid I am." He smiled again. "We have been talking some time now, and I have not so much as told you who I am." He bent his head in a mock bow. "Your humble servant, Barak. A lowly thief, even as yourself."

"My lord," Marcus countered, "I have never before

stolen." He lied, for he had lived as a beggar-thief since the days of his early youth. It was necessary to support his widowed mother. Honest work afforded barely enough to pay the tax, so he was forced to turn to more convenient methods.

"Liar!" Barak bellowed. "Liar!" He looked into Marcus' eyes. The two faces were mere inches apart. Suddenly Barak grinned, then broke out in riotous laughter. "Stu-stupid, stupid liar!" he sputtered.

Suddenly Marcus raised his hands in warning. "Shhh . . ." Marcus put his finger to his lips.

Both men froze. The dog scratched at the garbage a few feet away. Moments passed. The darkness hovered around them, bringing the smell of impending danger. Barak leaned close to Marcus' ear. "I hear nothing," he whispered.

"Horses!"

Barak listened. "Ah," he whispered again, "the Roman dogs are back."

The two sat motionless. Now the dog had caught wind of the Romans nearby. She moved closer to Marcus, cautiously skirting the older man.

Out on the street, a quaternion rode past the little shops. As the four horsemen cantered by the alley's entrance, one of them reined up. Sensing something in the alley, he turned his mount around and nosed the big animal into the dark separation between the buildings.

From within, the two Jews could see the foreboding silhouette towering over them. The big horse blocked the only exit. The centurion listened intently. A glint of armor flashed now and then. The pair remained frozen against the wall.

Catching a scent of the dog, the stallion snorted and scraped a forehoof nervously. The horseman leaned into the darkness, listening. He thought he heard some activity—a faint rustle, some scratching. He called to the other soldiers, who had moved down the street. "We have cornered our prey!" he shouted triumphantly.

Marcus could hear the quickening click of hooves as the others turned back to move in on the alley. A paralyzing fear seized him. Except for the Romans, all was quiet. Marcus closed his eyes. Blocking out the shouts of the horsemen, he reached for the dog. The hair on her back bristled and her muscles tensed. He tried to pull her into his lap, but the restraint was too much to bear and she lunged forward instinctively, barking and snapping at the horse's legs.

The great stallion reared, eyes wide. In spite of her advanced pregnancy, the little dog managed to dodge as the sharp hooves crashed to the pavement. The horse stumbled and fell against one of the buildings as he attempted to back out of the narrow alley. Pressing her advantage, the little dog ran wild at the stallion's feet, nipping at its fetlocks. The other horses moved nervously, bumping into one another. The street was in momentary confusion as the four animals kicked and reared, nearly throwing their riders. The dog darted around under the big armored mounts. Suddenly a hoof shot out, catching the little animal in the back leg. She yelped in pain.

Marcus leaned forward. The older man grabbed his arm. "Don't move! Let her go!"

The dog got to her feet and, crying in pain, limped around the corner out of sight. Only her whimpering could be heard as she dragged herself down the street.

Marcus tensed and nearly stood. The older Jew pulled him back. "If you make a move, I will cut your throat," he warned in a deep whisper. The two melted into the darkness and waited. The dog was still whimpering, but by now she had made her way into the depths of the city.

They heard the soldiers' angry voices, still near the entrance. One had obviously been thrown from his horse and was shouting obscenities at the "little scoundrel." As the quaternion regrouped and turned off into the night, the three ridiculed the lead soldier for calling them back to capture a stray dog. Marcus and Barak waited until the sounds had faded and all was quiet once again.

"Now," Marcus said defiantly, "we owe our lives to her."

Barak looked at the younger man in disbelief. "That dog be cursed," he snarled. "I could have turned that filthy squad of pigs with my bare hands."

Marcus looked at the big man and shook his head. "An empty wind," he mused, turning away.

Barak lashed out and caught the young man's clothing, whirling him around. He drew back his other hand, prepared to slap the boy.

Marcus merely smiled. The overwhelming fear he had experienced earlier reduced this threat to a mere trifle. "Go ahead," he scoffed, "if you must prove your manhood to *me*."

The pettiness of the issue angered Barak; even more the boldness and calm assurance with which this mere child faced him. Marcus possessed a bearing and demeanor that even the crusty old varlet could not easily miss. It was a puzzlement to Barak how a youth of Marcus' obvious breeding had fallen into the life of a common thief. It was all very baffling.

He stared at the boy. Dropping his raised hand, he released him. "You're a weakling," he muttered.

"But," he gestured with open hands, "do we not all have some weaknesses?" He chuckled, trying once again to win the young man's confidence, for he remembered the valuable Sacred Goat of Kahl, still clutched in Marcus' hand.

"My weakness," he admitted, "is money." He laughed. "There is *nothing* I wouldn't do for a handful of shekels." He laughed again. "*Nothing!*" He cuffed the young man's shoulder. "Come, we will go find your stray." He knew Marcus would not be able to resist the offer.

"Barak is not as you think," he smiled. "I, too, have feelings for animals," he lied. He stuck out his hand. "We will be friends," he said. Marcus hesitated, then shook the extended hand. Barak held the young hand tightly. "Not only friends," he offered, "but brothers. If one is in trouble, the other will come to his aid." He gripped the hand tighter. "Brothers?"

Marcus looked into the lined and leathered face. Barak's mouth turned upward in a smile, but the bloodshot brown eyes remained cold. *Still his handclasp is strong and sure—something like my father's might have been,* Marcus thought. *It will be well to have this man as my ally.* He smiled slightly. "Brothers," he agreed.

Barak squeezed Marcus' hand as he swore sternly, "This vow shall be forever. We shall be brothers unto the death."

Upon that oath, they released their grip and the two left the narrow alleyway. "Follow me," Barak ordered and eased into the street, Marcus close behind.

For nearly two hours they searched, backing into dark doorways to miss the Roman soldiers patrolling the streets. Marcus whistled lightly as they moved from place to place. Barak had genuinely attempted to search out the animal, for he knew it would strengthen the boy's confidence in his new compatriot. Finally, he had his fill of looking. He cursed. "Enough of this womanish nonsense! Let the dog go. She will be better off for her freedom."

Marcus looked up to see the older Jew turn toward the

east wall, near the pool of Bethesda. The young Jew stepped up his pace and soon caught up with the other. He knew Barak was right. The dog would survive. Her instincts were sharp and sure, and the blow from the horse's hoof had not been fatal. He shifted his concentration to their movement toward the great wall that encircled the city. "Where are we going?"

"The sun will be coming up soon. We must leave the city now." Suddenly he pushed Marcus back against a building. The pair stood silent as a lone soldier walked by, headed toward the east gate. The gate was closed and secured for the night. The guard standing watch there called out as the soldier approached. The two engaged in conversation, and Barak and Marcus moved on.

Within minutes, the two arrived at the base of the wall where a building stood so close by that a donkey could barely pass through. Barak put his back to the wall. He placed his feet against the building and began inching his way upward. Marcus followed. Upward they pushed until they were almost at the top. Suddenly they froze. The soldier they had encountered near the east gate had returned. He sauntered by, humming softly. As he strolled through the narrow passage, he was directly beneath the pair, poised so precariously above. Barak began to perspire from the physical strain. His forty-odd years had taken their toll. Marcus braced himself easily and prayed the soldier would not look up. Moments later the Roman moved on, and the pair climbed over the wall—then dropped lightly to the ground on the other side.

Marcus unhesitatingly followed Barak as they moved out into the hill country, away from the walled city. "Where are we going?" Marcus asked again.

"To see how the others have fared," Barak answered.

"Others?"

"You blockhead," Barak chided. "I have already told you of our band of men. Only a stupid jackal like yourself would be without friends to help him."

Marcus didn't like Barak's reference to jackals, but kept his silence. They moved on into the hillsides of Judea.

Barak babbled on about a number of unrelated subjects. "A strong man has wisdom as his guide and numbers as his strength," he quoted, attempting to impress his young protege. "When our band goes out to loot and rob, a quaternion is no match for us."

Marcus wondered about the problems of the night just past, but said nothing.

Barak was babbling on. "You shall soon see," he laughed. He shook his fist, then slapped his palms together in anticipation.

The two figures cast long shadows across the slopes as the sun pushed its way over the edge of the Judean hillsides. The brown limestone ridges became perfect stepping stairways up into the secret fortresses of the craggy hills. The two trudged on through the morning haze. Up, then down, then up again. Large patches of greenery broke up the dull brown earth, forming a patchwork pattern across the lumpy landscape.

Marcus wasn't really listening to Barak who continued his philosophizing and bragging, alternating one with the other. Instead, he was interested in the path they were following. The wooded area atop the steep hill in the distance now seemed to be their destination. His thoughts were interrupted by a question from his companion.

"Enough of my life," Barak said. "What of yours, Marcus?" The big man smiled. "Tell me about yourself."

"Until tonight, I have not had so much as one exciting event to relate to one of your background," he said apologetically.

"Well, tell me what you have to tell, even if you find it dull. I want to know," Barak insisted.

"I don't know where to begin," Marcus laughed, embarrassed.

His childishness irritated Barak. "How old are you? Where were you born? Begin at the beginning!" He waved his hands impatiently.

Marcus could see Barak's temper flare in the curled lip and narrowed eyes. For a moment the young man wished he had never agreed to come with this stranger. He had given his pledge to be "brother" to a man he scarcely knew and liked less. Well, as his mother had always taught him, he would make the best of it. He cleared his throat. "In four days I will be nineteen years of age."

Barak lifted his eyebrows and nodded approval. "You are older than I thought. When I was your age . . .," he hesitated. "Never mind," he chuckled, secretly amused with the memory of some boyhood mischief. "I am over twice your age," he added proudly.

Marcus continued without expression. "I was born in Bethany," he said, "just south of these hills." He pointed in the general direction. "My father was a tanner. He was sick of the fever when I was small and died when I reached five years." The thought disturbed him, and he hesitated.

Barak thought to himself, *This one has never known the firm hand of a man. He shall learn the ways of men in the days to come.*

Marcus was remembering the mist that gathered in his mother's eyes when she spoke of his father. He was a good man, highly respected in their village. The young Jew remembered the secret of his *grandfather* as well. The old man was of Roman parentage, but had been proselyted and escaped the Roman life, all for the love of a beautiful Jewess. From that union, Marcus' father was born.

Marcus thought of his father often. A lump formed in his throat. He turned away before Barak should think him weak. He swallowed. "My mother still lives in Bethany. I go there every few months to take her money and goods. I am her only means of support. When I was last there, I saw the one they call 'The Nazarene'." He watched for Barak's reaction, but there was none. "I saw him heal many." Still the older thief trudged on. Marcus made one last comment. "They say he is the Messiah."

"Bah!" Barak stopped, looked into the young face, turned and spat. He put one foot ahead of the other, then stopped again. "And you?" he questioned. "What do you say of him?" He looked deep into Marcus' eyes.

Marcus thought a moment. It was true. He had seen the man perform miracles. Blind eyes had been made to see and old men who had never walked had risen to take their first halting steps. People wept and some fell to their knees in the dusty road and worshipped God openly. He remembered the leper who had spent his days as an outcast, calling out the warning prescribed by law, "Unclean! Unclean!" Choked with emotion, he bowed before the Nazarene in gratitude for his healing. Marcus recalled his mother's reaction the day *she* saw him. Her face was alive with an unnamed emotion, and she prayed much in the weeks immediately following.

"Well?" Barak demanded. "What do *you* say?"

Marcus knew that he was subject to ridicule if Barak suspected that he wavered in his appraisal. "I think," he paused, considering his words carefully, "that he is a . . . a magician," he choked. His throat suddenly felt very dry.

"Oh, ho!" Barak was jubilant. "You have stolen my very words." he said. "Indeed, you are a thief after my own heart." The big man smiled broadly, patted Marcus on the back and slid his arm around the young shoulders, turning him up the pathway. "You will do nicely," he laughed. "Ah yes, Ben-Elah will be delighted that I have brought you." They continued up the hillside, following the serpentine path. Barak jabbered loudly.

Marcus wasn't listening to the ramblings of the big man, but had retreated into another realm. He fingered the jeweled object still secure in the folds of his coat. For all that was within him, he couldn't make himself believe this "healer" was the Messiah, yet he felt strange in professing the man to be a magician. He sighed and dismissed the troublesome thought. Barak's bragging droned on as they neared their destination.

CHAPTER

II

Near the top of a large hill, heavy foliage and an abundance of tall trees concealed the opening to the thieves' refuge. If one drew near, he would not see the hideout artfully cut into the hillside near its crest, but he would surely hear the noise. There was continuous laughter, shouting and cursing, mingled with the high-pitched chatter of women.

The damp morning air filtered into all eleven chambers, hollowed out by time and the expertise of certain of the present occupants. A thin fog reclined lazily on what the women referred to as the courtyard—a level area perhaps thirty feet long and some twenty feet wide. It jutted off the main feasting "room" overlooking the southern hillsides. Forming the floor were flat stones of varied shapes. An elevated section overlooked a pool in the center. The design was suggestive of the more lavish Roman courtyards.

Inside, the domed ceilings, hand-carved, supplied an

air of elegance to the cold stone. Colorful murals covered the rugged walls—an incongruous study in art and design to house a humble band of thieves!

The main room was more like a hall, as it was much longer than it was wide. A low table ran down its center and plush pillows lined either side.

Nine of the ten remaining rooms contained sleeping pallets. The sleeping arrangements were awkward since there belonged to the band of thieves twelve men and only five women. The final room at the end of a long passageway was used for laying plans and conferring. It held only a table, three chairs, and a bench.

The morning's rays streamed through the window-like opening of the main room and into the eyes of one man sprawling on pillows spread at the low table. (Dining while lying around the table was a pleasure the thieves had acquired from the Romans.) He cursed loudly and slapped one grubby hand over his eyes. "Ahhhh!" he mocked. "The god of light has blinded me." He fell heavily on his side, his foul body pressing hard against the pretty girl seated at his right. Everyone laughed, except the girl.

At that moment, a deep voice resounded through the room. "Jehiel!"

The man was laughing so loudly he did not hear his name. As the joviality subsided, he rolled his eyes to gaze upward at the young woman. He slipped his filthy hand into the tumbling, dark tendrils of her hair. Jerking her head back, he kissed her throat. His breath was heavy with the odor of too much wine, and his body reeked of filth and perspiration. He pulled at the wineskin in his free hand and offered her a drink. She wrinkled her nose and turned her face away, struggling to free herself. The man put his thick lips to the spout and allowed the ruby liquid to run freely.

"Jehiel!" This time the booming voice reverberated through the hall, bringing all activity to an abrupt halt. At the crack of it, Jehiel snapped to attention. Shoving the girl aside, he sat up and blinked. Instantly sober, he allowed the wineskin to slip from his hand to the littered floor.

There, in the doorway leading to the other rooms, stood Ben-Elah. His head was wrapped turban-like and his muscular frame blocked the passage. His arms were folded across a massive chest. A Roman tunic, cinched with a wide leather belt, and the boots of a centurion gave him a god-like appearance. His jaw was set ominously; a bushy, reddish mustache concealing the thin line of his lips.

He glared at Jehiel with granite-gray eyes. "You like my woman?" His voice was now lowered threateningly.

Stepping out of the doorway, he swaggered to the center of the low table and stood like a mountain over the one who cringed cross-legged on the other side. Ben-Elah's eyes were glazed.

The young woman rose quickly, her bare feet pattering as she made her way around the table to fall on Ben-Elah's arm. "Have mercy on him, lord! He is drunk," she begged. Her voice was shrill with fear. She knew the look in Ben-Elah's eyes. Men had died for less than the hatred he felt at this moment.

The muscular arm flexed, shrugging the girl away. Without a word, the big man uncoupled his leather belt. The metal studs of decoration caught the morning sunlight as he began to wrap the buckled end around his hand.

Jehiel looked at him in terror. His eyes widened. "No!" he shouted. He stumbled to his feet. "Please, lord, no!"

"Amalek!" Ben-Elah barked orders. "You and Garth will have to hold this slimy pig while I skin it!" His eyes blazed and a smile parted his lips.

Amalek, seated near one end of the long table and Garth near the other, rose slowly.

"No!" Jehiel pleaded. "I meant no harm!" He began to shuffle his feet and look from side to side as the two approached him. He pointed to the table. "It-it was the w-wine! I swear before the gods, I was . . ."

Amalek grabbed his wrist with a firm grip, while the man's words choked in his throat. Inflicting pain at his master's bidding always gave Amalek peculiar pleasure. He twisted the flesh cruelly while Garth quickly captured the other flailing arm and shoved Jehiel against the rough stone wall.

It was useless to expect clemency. The unfortunate man was at the mercy of his fellows—barbarians like himself. Yet their very lives depended upon a crude code of honor. Those violating the unwritten laws invited death—or worse.

Ben-Elah stepped across the low table, crushing the abandoned wineskin with the heel of his heavy boot. The sharp metal studs lining the thick belt aroused Amalek's lust for blood. He moistened his lips.

Ben-Elah tightened the belt around his hand and glanced at the white-faced girl pleading silently with him. A tear formed in her dark eyes. He looked back to the sniveling man before him.

Amalek had pulled his knife and skillfully slipped the point into the neck of Jehiel's garment. He drew it downward slowly, splitting the robes and baring the filthy skin.

Jehiel was crying now, praying Ben-Elah's mercy and begging to do anything in atonement for his misdeed.

The huge man noticed Amalek's glittering eyes, then

turned to look at the others waiting to witness the beating. They sat silently as the tension mounted. His eyes first met those of Justus. It was plain to see the priest felt pity for the poor wretch who pleaded for mercy. Ben-Elah's gaze swept the room observing the variety of expressions registered on the faces of his band. The women had mixed emotions. Scarcely any of them had escaped humiliation at Jehiel's filthy hands. Yet, while they detested him, bloodshed was another matter.

The leader paused, studying the matter, then turned to those whose eyes remained fixed on the grisly scene. He placed his hands on his hips and spoke. "I want all of you to see what a true leader you have in Ben-Elah," he said. "When the need arises, you will see how a man of great wisdom settles a problem. The great leader will weigh the question in the balances of justice." He glanced at Amalek then back to the people as he continued. "I have taught all of you the art of thievery, save Justus. He was a wretched scoundrel long before I." He laughed, then his voice rose with intensity, "All of you are as children to me."

Jehiel whimpered in the background.

"I have shown you my wisdom and my strength in times past," he boasted. "It is time you knew the meaning of *true* leadership."

Amalek frowned. He gripped the oily wrist tighter as Jehiel squirmed to be free. Amalek sensed a change, yet he wouldn't allow himself to consider its meaning.

Ben-Elah's intent was unmistakeable. He looked straight into the flint-hard eyes. "Let the wretch go free," he said firmly.

Neither Amalek nor Garth could believe their ears. It was unthinkable! How could Ben-Elah allow this pig to escape his just punishment? What of the others? They would soon lose all respect for leadership. Had not Ben-

Elah himself decreed the penalty for such conduct? It was he who had instituted rule by fear and appointed Amalek to enforce his commands.

"*He wanted your woman!*" Amalek screamed. "He must be scourged!"

Ben-Elah's face grew fiery red. "You forget your place. I will have mercy!" Turning quickly on one heel, he shouted, "Release him!" His belt spun through the air, slashing across Amalek's forearm, then recoiling to come down hard on Garth's.

Both men cried out in pain and dropped their hold on the quivering victim. Amalek cursed loudly, searing the air with his oaths.

Jehiel fell at Ben-Elah's feet and kissed the Roman boots. "The Lord shall remember you, my wise and merciful leader," he whimpered.

Ben-Elah looked down at the sniveling wretch in disgust, then at the solemn faces ringing the room. Justus alone seemed pleased with his leader's decision. A smile broke out on Ben-Elah's face. "Eat! Drink!" he ordered. "Justus, you ungodly priest—music!"

The preceding events were forgotten for the moment. Conversation and laughter resumed on command, and Ben-Elah seated himself at the head of the low-lying table. The young woman ran to his side.

Amalek, however, removed himself from the others and leaned against an outer wall petulantly, rubbing his forearm. Blood oozed from a small puncture at the wrist. He sucked the warm blood, then spat it on the wall. Turning, he noticed Garth already seated, gnawing at a goat rib as though nothing of great importance had transpired. "Jackal!" he muttered. He looked around the room. Everyone was bowing to Ben-Elah's wishes, especially the young one, Timaeus. The old priest was playing his instrument. "Fat pig." He sucked the puncture again.

Recalling the morning's beginning, he wished Barak had been here to witness all of it. Barak. His eyes narrowed in deep concentration, and absently he sucked the wound once more. It had stopped bleeding. "If Barak had been here . . ." He snorted, shaking his head. "Bah! He, too, would have bowed to this god, just like the others!" His eyes darted from one laughing face to another. "They are all pigs!" The hatred that twisted his rugged features sprang from a deep sickness of soul.

Ben-Elah noticed that the golden glow of the morning sun had grown brighter. "It must be the second hour of the morning," he remarked. The room grew quiet. "Where is that rascal, Barak, and the two scoundrels at his side?" he shouted.

As if on cue, Barak and Marcus appeared through the narrow entrance from the mountain path. "I am here, lord!" Barak called in feigned reverence. Two of the women squealed and ran to greet him. He kissed each of them soundly, then pushed the older one toward Marcus.

Justus stopped his strumming and every eye turned toward the newcomer.

Marcus shifted his feet uncomfortably, pulling away from the woman. His face flushed.

"And who have you brought from the bowels of Jerusalem, Barak?" Ben-Elah asked.

"Whoever he is," the woman giggled, "he belongs to me." She pressed her body against Marcus and ran a slender hand through his thick, black hair. "He is bashful," she teased.

Everyone roared with laughter while Marcus pulled his head away and glanced down at the pretty female making a fool of him.

"Easy, Shua," an older man shouted. "One so young has not yet felt the claws of a tigress."

As the jesting subsided, Barak offered a salute. "The

house of Theodius sends greetings." Then he looked directly at Ben-Elah, still seated on a large pillow at the head of the table. "But . . . no spoils." The room hummed softly at the declaration.

Ben-Elah stared at Barak for several seconds, searching his face. The muted voices grew silent. The big man shook his head affirmatively, biting his lower lip. He glanced at Marcus, then back to Barak. "So be it," he acknowledged. He gestured toward the smooth-faced youth. "And where did you find this lad?"

"Tell us, please!" Shua begged, bringing a ripple of laughter.

Barak reached over and grasped the woman's arm, jerking her away. Marcus stood alone. Barak motioned him forward toward the center of the room. He moved uneasily to the place Barak indicated and stood mute. "His name is Marcus," Barak said. "He is a thief."

"Stone him!" someone shouted, bringing laughter from all parts of the table. Some of those reclining sat up, sputtering on their food and drink.

As the laughter died down, Barak lifted a hand. "Wait. He has brought something with him." Barak looked secretively toward the head of the table. "A gift," he announced. "A gift for our mighty captain." Then he turned and stared into Marcus' eyes. "A gift," he repeated clearly, "of hope that Ben-Elah will receive our friend with mercy into this lowly band." He paused to allow the words to sink in. "For well we know, that anyone who has seen the cover of our hiding place must be accepted by our lord, or . . ." He drew his index finger across his throat.

Marcus swallowed hard. He reached into his coat and withdrew the silver goat. The room buzzed with excited whispers as he moved to the end of the table. He bent his knee in homage, placed the statue on the table in front of Ben-Elah, then backed away.

The big man picked it up. Everyone strained to see. The morning sun sought out the sparkling depths of the emerald eyes. The silver body with its golden wings shone splendidly. The object filled one of Ben-Elah's massive hands to his fingertips. He held it high for all to see. The sheer beauty of the piece brought gasps of delight.

Barak stepped around Marcus to Ben-Elah's side. He bent low, near the big man's ear, and spoke softly. "The Sacred Goat of Kahl could bring four thousand shekels," he exaggerated. "This youth is not as stupid as some. He was able to steal the goat and it seems no one was the wiser. His clean looks are in his favor. I feel he is trainable, my lord."

Ben-Elah looked up at the young Jew. His eyes narrowed in deep thought. He pulled at his mustache. Tilting his head to one side, he appraised Marcus with a smile, "But, Barak, he's only a boy."

"I shall *mother* him." Shua's enthusiastic offer caused some to snicker, but Ben-Elah wasn't amused, and the snickering died rapidly.

"Timaeus," he said at last, "it seems you shall have a companion your own age." He extended one hand toward Marcus and other toward the young man reclining in the lap of a beautiful girl.

Timaeus lifted his head. "He is not my type," he quipped, then returned to the invitingly cushioned restingplace.

"Can this youth speak?" asked Justus. He strummed the strings of his lute to accentuate his question.

Marcus stood rigid. He took a deep breath, then shifted his weight. Perspiration formed in little beads on his forehead.

"Timaeus," Ben-Elah called, "stand and introduce yourself. Then take our new friend . . . Marcus . . ." he paused. "It is Marcus, isn't it?"

Marcus nodded. "Yes, my lord. My name is Marcus."

A cheer went up at the sound of the young man's voice. "He has found his tongue," someone yelled. Marcus shuffled his feet and shrugged his shoulders nervously.

Ben-Elah raised his hand for silence. "Introduce Marcus to the other scum of this devil's household," Ben-Elah commanded and rose from his place.

Marcus looked up at him as he towered to his full height. The young Jew was glad he hadn't made the fatal mistake of withholding the treasure.

"Barak and I have important matters to discuss," Ben-Elah continued. "But before we go . . ." He stretched forth his big hand and grasped the young man's wrist in an act of friendship. His other hand lay heavy on Marcus' shoulder. "I welcome you, Marcus," he said, patting the lean shoulder. "Treat him as a brother, all of you," he waved his hand commandingly over the group.

Turning to Barak, Ben-Elah said, "Come, I want to know where Darkon and Zia are and what took place in Jerusalem last night." He turned to look at Amalek, still leaning against the wall. He motioned to him, "Come, Amalek. We have business."

Amalek hesitated, glancing at the wound on his arm. He looked at the two men already moving out of the banquet hall. Suppressing the hatred within him, he fell in behind them. He looked back at the new member of the band. He had always hated Timaeus, and now it appeared as though there would be *another stupid child* to nursemaid.

Marcus caught the look on Amalek's face. He leaned near Timaeus. "Who is the mean one?" he questioned, nodding toward Amalek's retreating figure.

Timaeus grimaced, then replied reassuringly, "Don't worry about Amalek. Although he and Barak vie for second-in-command, Ben-Elah keeps both of them in line. I dread to think what would happen to us all if Ben-Elah were not harnessing those two." He smiled, "In fact, Ben-Elah is mighty enough to keep all of us in line." His wry smile broadened as he looked down at the young woman Jehiel had molested. "That is, all but Tamara. She allows him to think he controls everyone, but this little vixen really pulls the strings." He looked for Marcus' response out of the corner of his eye. "Do you know what I mean?"

Marcus nodded, smiling, but there was much he did not know nor did he wish to reveal this ignorance to his new comrade.

Justus began fingering the lute he played so well. Though his fat fingers barely touched the strings, melodic music flowed freely. He continued playing as Timaeus began the introductions.

"This is our own priest," Timaeus taunted. "Justus is his name." He motioned to the double-chinned man, his round face fringed with tufts of white hair that refused to grow on top of his head.

Marcus looked on while the old man played a lilting tune. "And why do they call you 'priest'?" he asked.

Justus laid his hand against the strings to stop the vibrations. He looked at Marcus with a broad grin and whispered, "Because once I studied in the Temple under Caiaphas." He strummed the instrument once more. "But *they* don't like to hear about it." His chins shook as he gestured toward the others with his round head. "I left," he continued, "because the sect of the Pharisees was worse than any band of thieves, and the Sadducees were rude and self-righteous." He tilted his head. "Yes, a mean crowd they are." A smile played across the dimpled folds of his face. "Now, perhaps, I have a better chance with the Lord God. Do you agree?" He laughed at his own joke and looked around the room. "Even this mob is more godly than our Temple leaders." He poked a stubby hand at the young Jew. "Welcome, my boy. Do forgive an old man who finds no fault with these scoundrels."

Marcus clasped the chubby hand warmly. He liked Justus and hoped to sit at his feet and learn from him. Such tales as he could tell! "I should like to hear more on another occasion," he said, as he and Timaeus moved away.

In the dark counsel room, in the far reaches of the mountain hideaway, a single candle burned in a shallow plate. At the wooden table, Barak was relating the night's activities.

He was nearing the end of his tale when Amalek interrupted. "Why bring that son-of-a-sow up here?" he asked. Without waiting for the answer, he cursed and raised a fist toward the banquet room. "He is as Timaeus—another sniveling girl whose nose will need wiping."

Barak looked into the scarred face. "The sacred goat, for one thing," he growled. "And . . ."

"What!" Amalek yelled, interrupting again. He spat in the air contemptuously. "Your mouth is filled with deceit! You *like* the child," he growled. "You could have had the goat and left your blade in his weak ribs."

Barak pushed back his chair in disgust. He turned to Ben-Elah. "My lord," he begged, "why do we keep this barbarian's brain in a locked chest?"

Amalek jumped to his feet, his knife drawn and raised in one smooth motion.

Barak didn't move, but rather leaned back in his chair. He knew how to handle his treacherous enemy. He smiled confidently. "Sit and listen to all I have to say," Barak said easily. "If, when I finish, you feel the same way, *then* quarter me, but first sit and listen."

Amalek relaxed his tense body, his eyes still burning brightly. He slammed the point of his knife into the table top and sat down. He folded his arms across his chest and glared at Barak. His chest throbbed with the heavy pounding of his heart. Perspiration formed under his arms and his palms were wet. The hatred he felt for everything and everyone had taken its toll. His face was lined beyond his thirty-six years, and he had a nervous habit of stretching his neck by leaning his head to one side and lifting his chin.

Barak leaned forward. "As I was saying," he continued, "I know the boy is young and stupid, but he did manage to get his hands on the goat. If he was daring enough to break into Lucius' private collection without discovery, I thought he might be of value to us."

Ben-Elah nodded his head in agreement. He pulled Amalek's knife from the table and began to clean his fingernails. "What did you have in mind?" he asked.

Barak leaned on the table. The candlelight cast shadows around the windowless room. "As I mentioned, I am sure Darkon and Zia have been caught or even killed. We will need replacements." He looked deep into Amalek's eyes. "The reason Darkon and Zia are not here now," he added, "is the very fact they were *too old* and *too slow*. When the Roman pigs surprised us at the house of Theodius, we fled. I drew away from them easily, but I heard the screams of our comrades and feel assured they were run down by the centurions." He leaned back, "Of course, I don't like the boy *as he is*, but we can whip him into shape. He can be very useful." He turned to Ben-Elah. "Even I know we need youth to survive. The old one, Justus, is too fat and aged to do anything except play that accursed lute and ogle the women. We must have youth!"

"Perhaps you are right," Ben-Elah nodded his approval. Amalek remained silent.

As the three men continued their serious discussion in the dark little room, the sun brightened the main hall where laughter still prevailed.

"Marcus," Timaeus said, "this is Rhoda, *my* woman." Timaeus put his arm around the soft shoulders of the young girl. "She is beautiful, is she not?"

Rhoda smiled. "Do not embarrass him," she reprimanded Timaeus and put out her hand to greet Marcus.

The young Jew had never been with such women as these. The women of his acquaintance were quiet and modest, like his mother, while these women chatted easily with the men. Though it made him uneasy, there was something strangely reassuring in their friendly, open manner. Perhaps, as outcasts, they had sought refuge of a different sort here with these men of the hills.

Timaeus whirled the girl around and called out over the soft sounds of the lute and the hum of voices. "I want you all to meet Marcus."

Everyone looked up. The music stopped, along with the chatter. All was quiet.

"That is Jehiel," Timaeus said, pointing to the filthy man grawing at a bone. (He reminded Marcus of a dog.) Jehiel nodded, the bone still held to his mouth.

"Next to him is Bunah, keeper of the stores."

The small man frowned at Marcus, but acknowledged the greeting sullenly.

"He views you as another mouth to feed from our meager provisions," Timaeus smiled. "The two women who greeted you on your arrival are next." Everyone snickered. "The small one is Eve. She is the same age as Rhoda—eighteen." He glanced slyly at Marcus. "Now

Shua, her sister, is older and will be able to teach you many things." Coarse laughter filled the room. "The man near the end of the table is Garth. He says very little, but when he speaks, his language singes the ears."

Garth muttered into a cup of wine. He cursed loudly, then nodded to Marcus.

"Did I not speak the truth?"

Marcus smiled.

"Next is Vashni," Timaeus said.

The man didn't look up from his eating.

"Next to him is the lovely Dinah. Watch out for her," Timaeus warned. "She can steal anything with her light-fingered touch." He leaned toward Marcus and feigned a whisper. "They say she can steal your undergarments without so much as undressing you."

Everyone roared.

Timaeus looked down near his feet. "And here at your service is Phinehas. He actually belongs to the band of Barabbas, but he frequently shares his talents with us." Timaeus leaned close to Marcus. "He likes our women."

The man stood and shook the young Jew's hand. He held his grip and turned to address the others. "Lift your cups, my friends," Phinehas said, "Let us welcome our brother together."

Everyone stood, raised their cups, and in unison toasted Marcus. "Hail, Marcus! Welcome!"

CHAPTER III

Several weeks later, under Barak's watchful eye and careful tutoring, Marcus was rapidly learning the finest points of his craft. Moreover, he seemed to be losing some of the gentle and courteous ways that had marked him as a weakling in the eyes of the seasoned thieves. He was acquiring a sturdy manliness that puffed Barak with pride.

Marcus' development was Barak's prime accomplishment, and he lost no time in goading Amalek about his young student's aptitude. This fact served only to increase the enmity between the two veterans.

Today was no different. Before Barak and Marcus left the hidden refuge, Barak had managed to get in another jab, boasting that Marcus had even knocked a woman to the ground during one of their recent escapades. Of course, Barak conveniently forgot to mention that the boy had stopped with the intent of helping her up. Barak himself had pinned the woman's shoulder to the ground with his foot as she tried to rise, screaming, "Thief!" They had then melted into the milling crowd with Marcus looking back only once—another portion of the episode left untold. Barak merely said that young Marcus had come a long way under his instruction. "Do you not agree?" he had prodded Amalek. The man only growled in reply.

This day in Jerusalem was another created for teaching the boy the ways of the streets. Barak and Marcus were there to observe, not to steal. As the sun moved directly overhead, Jerusalem's marketplace teemed with hot, smelly bodies pushing each other about in the pursuit of buying and selling.

With Marcus close at his side, Barak ambled through the narrow streets, pointing out shops that would be easy to rob or warning of protective measures taken by some shopowners. At times he motioned with his chin toward a passerby. "One of our kind."

They moved along slowly, making their way into the wide bazaar which was lined with portable carts, shops, tents, or other makeshift stalls. Merchants hawked their wares to the crowds milling through the street with chants much like those of priests calling the people to worship.

No one seemed to mind the stench of the donkeys and other animals moving freely about the streets; nor did they take notice if the flies landing on the freshly hung meat of the stalls had just tasted the street dung left by the animal population. They merely waved the insects away, looked over the meat, and made their purchases.

Barak stopped to examine some fresh fowl. The young merchant was quick to point out the bargain price, but Barak inspected the small, limp dove and scowled. He dropped the bird and stepped back. Marcus leaned near. "Jerusalem is doing much business," he said. "We should have a good night."

Barak looked back at the lean birds, then stepped up and shooed the flies away. The merchant eyed him as he picked up the best of the lot and rubbed its flesh. Barak responded to Marcus with a wry smile. "Make no mistake, we shall have ours," he said, and placed the bird back on the small pile.

The pair moved on into the widest part of the street, where the vendors haggled over the most conspicuous space to set up a display of their goods. The thieves stopped several times, Barak nodding first toward one man, then another. He explained that these belonged to the band of Barabbas. Marcus frowned. "Barabbas is the father of thieves," Barak explained.

"I know his reputation as a zealot and rioter," Marcus countered, "but I didn't think he was one of us . . ."

"Yes, it is true. He is noted for attempts to overthrow the Roman pigs, but he is a thief just the same." He looked into Marcus' eyes. "You will be better off if you keep your mouth shut and listen to *me*," the older man said. "*I* shall instruct you." He was annoyed that Marcus should think for himself. "Barabbas incites a disturbance in a mob, then in the confusion he takes what he can and disappears into the hills of Judea, just north of our camp."

Barak's irritation vanished speedily. He was well pleased with the progress of his young protege. Marcus was tougher and more cunning; and he was learning the harsh realities of life and death, take or be taken. The boyish softness was giving way to a new boldness. Lost forever, Barak sincerely hoped, were the goodness and gentleness that could prove to be the undoing of a thief.

Marcus, too, was pleased with himself. He had learned much from Barak. His mentor was hard and at times too pessimistic, yet he was nothing like the surly Amalek. Marcus kept his distance from that one and his companion, the filthy Jehiel. He had some real friends in

Rhoda and Timaeus and learned from them also. As he strolled alongside Barak, he felt a sense of well-being, unknown since his boyhood days. This life of thievery wasn't so bad after all.

Barak grabbed his sleeve as he stopped to look at another stand of raw meat suspended from a pole.

Barak waved the eager merchant away and turned to Marcus. "Look over my right shoulder," Barak said in an undertone.

Marcus obeyed, oblivious to the bustle of people all around him.

"Do you see the fat pig in the striped robe?" Barak asked, his voice still low.

With his gaze moving past Barak to the far side of the street, Marcus nodded. He saw the fat man—obviously a Greek of education and wealth—fingering the fruit on display. The little Jewish vendor was darting around his portable stand, waiting on several customers at once.

"Look to your right, very slowly," Barak said.

Marcus looked past a woman dealing in purple and an old man selling water pots.

Barak watched the movement of Marcus' eyes and calculated their position. "Do you see the big man leaning against the cart?" he questioned. When Marcus frowned, Barak raised his voice impatiently. "Down by the tentmaker!" he snorted under his breath.

"Oh, oh yes," Marcus whispered.

"Is he still leaning on the cart?"

"Yes," Marcus nodded. Then, "No!" Puzzled, he looked at Barak. "He just moved away."

Barak smiled easily and tugged at the young Jew's arm, pulling him into the shadow of the meat vendor's awning. He turned to look across the street. "We will stay here and be witnesses," he said. "You shall see a very old profession as it unfolds."

With an almost undetectable motion of the hand, Barak waved toward another man. "He is the one to watch—the little one without headcovering."

Marcus observed the short man as he sauntered toward the fruit stand where the fat Greek was pinching grapes. The paunchy old man appeared interested in making a purchase. He pulled a leather pouch from within his robes. Marcus continued to watch as the big man who had been leaning against the cart also approached the fruit stand, withdrawing his money pouch. Then, in a motion so swift Marcus nearly missed it, the short, bareheaded man stepped up between the Greek and the other man, snatched both pouches and darted away. He quickly vanished into the mass of buyers and sellers.

The Greek screeched in protest. He whirled around, but the little man was already swallowed up in the press of bodies. His heavy jowls quivered and he looked as though he would take pursuit, when the other man grabbed his arm.

"What is happening now?" Marcus asked.

"You shall soon see," Barak nodded.

The theft victims were engaged in heated discussion. Then, obviously yielding, the Greek sent the other man after the thief.

In helpless frustration, the Greek leaned against a pole and allowed his large frame to slide down until he sat in the dust of the busy street.

The commotion had caused little distraction by the very fact that theft of the pompous Greeks somewhat delighted the local Jews.

Barak took Marcus by the sleeve. "Come," he motioned. "We will see if we can find the pair of swine," he chuckled, then amended, "I mean the *good fellows* who have just given instruction to my young friend." With that, he slipped his arm around Marcus' neck and led him in the general direction the two thieves had taken.

They melted into the crowds, leaving the Greek sitting in the street, throwing dust into the air and cursing loudly. By now, he had discerned what had taken place, and it angered him that he had played the fool.

Marcus followed Barak until there was opportunity to stand on his toes and look back. He stopped near a basket dealer's tent and craned his neck trying to see over the heads of the throng to catch a glimpse of the fat Greek. There he was, still flailing his arms and chattering furiously. Marcus chuckled and dropped back to his flat-footed stance. He turned to speak to Barak, but the older Jew had moved on. Marcus quickly pushed his way through the crowd.

After several minutes of searching and calling out over the drone of the bargainers, Marcus came to the steps leading to the upper city. He stepped up to get an unobstructed view of the bazaar area. Barak was not to be found.

From this vantage point, Marcus retraced their route, carefully observing every vending booth, but failing to find his companion. He squinted to focus more clearly. The man standing near the merchant of purple resembled Barak, but it couldn't be he, for the man was actually making a purchase. Marcus smiled at the thought.

The crowd grew as people continued to filter down from the upper city. Marcus forced his way up the stairs.

Struggling out of the main flow, he turned into a side street. It was narrow and lined with old store fronts. Many were vacant. Their owners had purchased tents and moved down into the heavy traffic area. Nowadays the greatest numbers of the populace shopped for bargains. The price-fixing of the Greeks and Romans forced the Jews to search out inexpensive goods sold by other Jews. The extortionate taxing of the people combined with military needs and outright thievery by Caesar's troops had reduced the standard of living of many Jews to a subsistence level. As a counter-action, they had formed little groups and did cooperative buying.

Eventually this practice had found its way into their religious customs. The farspread tribes who annually made the long journey to Jerusalem for sacrifice found it necessary to purchase the sacrificial animal in the city. It must be unspotted and without blemish according to law. The greedy sellers of doves, cattle, and sheep took every advantage of the situation. Even the money-changers doubled their rates during these high and holy days. The priests decreed the use of "Temple money" only, so many cooperative ventures were brought into being of necessity.

As Marcus surveyed the bazaar area, he could easily spot those merchants who were responsible for the inflated prices, and he vowed that he would someday do something about it. He turned away, beginning a slow trek down the narrow street in front of him.

Here, there were relatively few people going about their business. Some women carried water pots on their heads. One elderly lady was bent low with a load of sticks and twigs she was hoping to sell for a few coins. An old man sat in a doorway asking alms of those who passed by. As Marcus approached him, the man looked up through filmy, brown eyes. He stretched forth a frail hand. "Alms," he begged, almost apologetically.

"Why are you not down there," Marcus motioned with his head, "where all the people are?" He frowned anxiously. "You would have a good chance to make a living there."

The man withdrew his bony hand. "I am too old," he rasped. "They step on me. They push and shove until I am trampled almost to the point of death." He looked down at his wrinkled frame and touched his stained lioncloth. "Maybe death would be better," he muttered.

"But you could find a place to sit on a crate or among the high places one finds along the road," Marcus suggested. "You could make a living—a good living."

"I did find a place one time," the man choked. He coughed. "I had a lot of money too . . ." he hesitated. "Thieves took it."

Marcus bowed his head, for the words bit deeply. He wished for a coin to give the pitiful man, but he had nothing. Turning slowly he shuffled his feet and moved away. He swallowed hard and blinked back a tear.

It wasn't long before he emerged from the narrow side street onto the main thoroughfare. It was a large spacious area extending from one end of the city to the Fortress of Antonia at the other. He looked up toward the fortress, its wall towering in the distance. He planned to look for Barak down by the north gate where the wall separated Jerusalem's main city from the fortress and the outlying countryside.

As he walked along, he came to the Temple of the high priest. Several holy men and teachers, as they called themselves, were walking up and down the street praying loudly. Listening to them reminded Marcus of his mother's prayers. Yet she did not pray as these men. They preened with pride that they were not as other vile men, and rattled endlessly of their virtues. If *he* were God, Marcus speculated, he would turn a deaf ear to *those* prayers.

Marcus shook his head and moved on. He was so outraged by the hypocrisy of the priests, he forgot to look for Barak. Farther down the street, near the north

wall, he stopped. People moved swiftly past him, preoccupied with the business that had lured them into the
city.

Several soldiers stood to the left of the huge gate
leading into the area of the Fortress of Antonia. Two
others leaned against the wall on the right. Marcus
could see they were officers. He glanced toward the big
gate. An old Jew emerged, leading two white stallions
arrayed in studded leather. They were fine animals,
belonging to Caesar's chosen. The two officers pushed
away from the wall and took the reins.

Marcus watched the elderly man bow in deference. As
the centurions mounted, he stepped up to say something to the one nearest. The old man appeared to have
a serious matter to discuss; but the Roman, near Marcus' age, grinned in disdain. He wore his superiority as
brashly as he did his richly embellished uniform. Marcus scowled. The young Jew moved closer hoping to
overhear the conversation. He stopped before he should
be observed, still unable to understand their words.

The two soldiers were eager to move their mounts, but
the old man stepped closer, still speaking. The young
Romans looked at each other. The one on the far side
made a comment, and they bellowed with laughter. The
old man reached out, touched the Roman's leg, and
looked up at him pleadingly. The arrogant young
soldier sneered and kicked the wrinkled hand away, but
the old man continued his pleading. He reached for the
Roman's boot, as though to kiss it. With one powerful
kick, the heavy boot smashed into the bony face. The
sound of it was sickening, and blood spurted from the
man's nose as he fell backward. His head hit the stone
pavement with a thud. He lay motionless. The soldier
looked briefly at the man—then turned to his companion.

Marcus' body jerked involuntarily, and he ground his teeth to suppress the scream of rage that welled up within. Waves of nausea threatened to engulf him. He swallowed the bitter bile that rose in his throat.

His eyes remained fixed on the old man heaped in a pile on the ground. He raised his head as the centurions rode aimlessly past him, still smirking. The desire to pull them down from their lofty perches nearly overcame him. He stood his ground and narrowly missed being brushed aside by a booted stirrup.

Marcus stood in the middle of the street for a few moments, staring after the two proud conquerors. Then, his hatred frustrated, he turned to see the old man struggling to his feet. No one hurried to his side. No one cared. They glanced indifferently as he groaned, but all of them turned away—Roman, Greek, and Jew.

The young thief looked around. He moved a few steps toward the slumped figure, but hesitated as two men came out of Xystus, the gymnasium, and stopped. They looked down at the old heap of bones, shook their heads, and moved on.

Seething inside, Marcus cursed all of mankind. All caution aside, he moved quickly toward the old man. He knelt and took the frail, bearded face in his hands. A tear trickled down his cheek as the rage within forced an outlet. It mattered not that Barak might find him here, weeping with compassion. He reacted instinctively from his own gentle breeding, however deeply buried.

The blood was now flowing freely from the old man's nose and mouth. Marcus sat on the stone pavement and lifted the fragile head into his lap. His young hands stroked the matted hair, pushing limp, silver strands from the thin face. A large knot had formed on the back of the man's skull, and his lips were puffed from contact with the big boot heel. Marcus was unaware of the blood staining his own clothing. He looked up in search of help.

Then the old man winced and twitched. His eyelids fluttered. His milkish tongue pushed through parched lips, spreading the blood into his white mustache and beard. The veined eyelids quivered once more, then opened. Dull brown eyes sought to focus on the man who cradled him so tenderly. He attempted to speak, but could not.

Marcus choked with emotion. *Barak is right*, he pondered. *There is no justice, no humaneness left in the world. Is this thin bag of broken flesh really a man or merely a shell that once housed a spirit? Is he among the living dead whose existence waits on the whims of the conquerors? If so, then does death occur only when the heart stops beating and the final breath is drawn? Or is it possible that death is the end of all meaning, the cessation of the spirit and the will?* Perhaps the ultimate kindness would be to allow this body to seek its spirit which had long since departed.

Ah, Barak is right on two counts, Marcus chided himself. *I should leave the philosophizing to him.* He shook the disturbing thoughts from his mind, then turned to attend the feeble man, letting go the tears that welled up to blur his vision.

Swallowing, he choked, "Sir?" Marcus felt for a pulsebeat. It was thin and thready, like the flutter of a butterfly's wing. "Sir!" Marcus' voice rose. He shook the old man frantically.

The old man groaned and opened his eyes again.

"I want to help you, sir."

The old Jew heard tenderness in the young voice, a nostalgic sound which had escaped him years ago. His vision cleared. The sunken eyes rolled to one side, peering toward the gate, then back up into the face of Marcus. He stared for a moment, appraising the kind, dark eyes and smooth, young face. He attempted a smile, then took on a serious look. "Don't let them see you." He coughed, spattering blood on Marcus. "Don't help me. Don't stay here. It will go hard for you."

Marcus patted his shoulder. "They are gone," he said reassuringly. The man's color had improved. "Can you sit up?" The old man nodded slightly, trying to pull himself upright. "Here," Marcus said, "let me do the straining. Just relax in my arms." The man responded willingly. He rubbed his mouth with his sleeve, blood staining the garment.

Once the man was sitting up, Marcus stood. "Let me go for water," he said.

The man touched Marcus' sleeve. "No."

The young Jew's eyes clouded as he looked down at the torn face. The blood was clotting. "Why?" he asked.

"T-take me outside." With a feeble gesture, he pointed to the gate.

Marcus looked up at the north gate. It was wide and arched, heavily etched with carvings. He knew that the Fortress of Antionia was only a few hundred feet beyond the gate. Barak had warned him to keep his distance when the Romans were near. Yet this old man was asking him to go within a few paces of the very place the occupying soldiers were housed.

The man noticed his hesitation. "I am sorry," he said. "Just help me stand, and I will be on my way." His voice was very weak. "My simple dwelling is too near the fort. To be seen with me could bring you harm." He looked into Marcus' eyes. "Truly, I *am* feeling better. Please, just help me up." He reached for the strong arm.

Marcus felt apprehensive as he helped the old Jew to his feet. When he saw the man weaving as he tried to stand alone, Marcus spoke decisively, "You cannot go alone." He gripped the old man's arm firmly. "It's against my good judgment to go near the dogs, but you are in need. I cannot refuse to help." He smiled, "My name is Marcus."

The old man's legs were weak and shaking, and he held tight. "Marcus," he muttered. A grateful smile parted his swollen lips. "I am Oshea, the physician," he said, coughing.

Marcus caught a good hold on the doctor's robe and held him close. "Don't talk now," he instructed. "We will move very slowly. Come," he urged.

The two moved through the big gate; the strong, young arms guiding the frail, old man.

At that same moment, still among the ever-thickening masses, Barak had become enraged. "Marcus!" he called again. He had shouted the name periodically for over an hour now.

Barak stopped at one vendor's stall and grabbed a rough wooden crate containing two sickly chickens. He moved it to the street, pushing the vendor aside. The burly thief stood on the box and looked over the crowd. The wood cracked beneath his weight, but he didn't notice. "Marcus! You filthy son of a wretch! Marcus!" he yelled. Few people noticed the unkempt man. Most of them figured him for another fanatic summoning his followers.

Barak searched the crowd with increasing frustration. He shook his head. He had been especially watchful lately for signs of changes in Marcus' attitude and had found only loyalty. The boy was not unhappy. Surely the two of them had their differences on occasion, but not so much as to cause the boy to leave the company of the band. As the wooden crate began to crack again, Barak stepped down and moved on into the crowd. He was oblivious to the shrieks of the little man whose "fine hens" were now running about the street for anyone to pluck.

Barak wandered through the thick mass of people, deep in thought. *Perhaps Marcus is trying to get back on his own.* Aloud, he muttered, "If that stupid jackal thinks he now knows enough to go into the streets alone . . ." He shook his head again and spat, cursing under his breath.

Marcus looked uneasily at the towering turrets guarding Antonia. He was glad there was no need to go any closer. The old doctor had stopped at a door a couple hundred paces short of the gate of Samaria and the fortress which loomed menacingly nearby.

"Come inside, Marcus," the doctor whispered.

The young Jew looked into the room. "Are these your lodgings?"

The old man nodded. "Caesar has been most generous."

Marcus frowned when he saw the meager furnishings. A pallet of camel hair filled with straw lay in one corner. A small wooden table and bench filled the center of the small room. He closed the door and latched it as the old man opened the window.

Marcus noticed an earthen water pot, a large bowl, and a pitcher next to the door. He stooped down and picked them up. "Let me pour water to clean your wounds," he said. He placed the bowl on the table and dipped from the large pot. As he prepared the water, he seated the old man on the bench and asked about the incident he had witnessed.

"My son," the old doctor began, "it is a very long story—a story of failure." He leaned wearily against the table.

Marcus began cleansing the wounds. He soaked the cloth thoroughly and dabbed at the parched, broken lip. As he lifted the bony chin, he noticed a large jagged scar on the doctor's neck. He said nothing, but listened as the old man continued.

"I was a man of medicine. Six years ago, after a skirmish, a Roman soldier was brought to me for treatment. No Roman doctor could be found, so the captain of the guard sought me out for the task of saving the young soldier's life. He was cut high inside the thigh. By the time they brought him to me, he had lost a lot of blood and was near death." The old man sighed. "I worked all through the night." He stopped talking momentarily while Marcus applied the cloth to his lips again. "I had put pressure on the deep wound until my arms were weak, but to no avail. The soldier died at dawn."

"Why should they hold *you* responsible and in what way could it have resulted in the treatment I witnessed today?" Marcus asked. He dabbed at the abrasion on the old man's nose.

"The Proconsul said I could not be blamed," the old man smiled. "Unfortunately, the Proconsul is easily swayed by the loud cries of others, and . . ." He winced again. The cool water and linen cloth stung the raw opening in his lower lip.

"I am sorry," Marcus said as the doctor flinched.

"No matter. It cannot be helped," the old man reassured. "I should know." He smiled at the young Jew, but quickly grew sober as the swelling lip threatened to split wider. "As I was saying, two of the dead soldier's friends talked to the Proconsul and persuaded him to follow our Levitical teachings." He paused, bent his head sorrowfully, then looked at Marcus. " 'An eye for an eye,' " he quoted. " 'A tooth for a tooth.' " He choked with emotion. "A life for a life." The old man's last words were barely audible. To disguise his grief, he pretended concern for his wounds and motioned to a box near the head of his straw bed. "There is ointment in that chest."

Marcus withdrew a small jar from the box. He applied a little of the soothing mixture to the cuts on the lips and nose.

The balm felt good and restored some strength to the aged man. He began again. "In the final outcome, I would rather have been thrown to the lions than have . . ." His voice broke. "Yes," he shook his head. "I would rather have died and they knew it. So they talked the authorities into a worse fate."

The old man slowly untied the thin, leather string holding his tunic. Then he shrugged off all his upper garments, baring his frail trunk. His arms were pathetically thin, and the bones of his shoulders stuck out. Anyone who saw him like this could be sure of the number of his ribs, for each was visible beneath the taut skin. He turned so Marcus could see his back.

The young Jew stared at the sight, his mind refusing to comprehend the horror of it. His stomach turned. He couldn't tear his eyes from the mutilated mass of scar tissue. Stripe upon stripe criss-crossed, forming a ghastly geometric design over the old man's entire back. One scar ran to the side of Oshea's neck. Marcus had seen only a small portion of it earlier.

The old man turned to look at the shocked face. Then he said, "This is not the worst part. The great and mighty Proconsul of all Judea listened to the voice of another of the dead Roman's friends, one Gaius. You know," the old man said, "I think the two of them were lovers—the dead one and Gaius." He chuckled uncontrollably. Marcus was visibly shocked.

The doctor went on, "This Gaius kept insisting that the Proconsul do something. He wanted *me* to suffer the loss of a loved one." The old man looked down. His voice weakened. "I had a son and a little granddaughter, twelve years of age." The old Jew choked up and struggled for composure before continuing his grim tale. "Gaius had the Proconsul decree that, 'any Roman who had died while being attended by a Jewish physician would be allowed retribution to the same degree...'" Tears filled the already cloudy eyes. "The scum," the doctor cried out, "had my son taken apart at the groin, then left him for me to attend." The old man began to sob, his shoulders shaking violently.

Marcus, too, wept openly. He wiped his nose with his sleeve and tried to gain control of himself. He must try to remain calm for the sake of the old man. Then, reaching out, he gently pulled the old man's robes around the thin shoulders while tears streamed down his cheeks.

Several minutes went by without a word. The small, sobbing sounds of both men periodically broke the silence.

Finally, the old physician's heaving body quieted. He took the cloth from the bowl and squeezed it out. With shaking hands he placed it flat against his face. The cool wetness was soothing. He took a deep breath and let the cloth slide slowly down his face. Now, looking directly into Marcus' eyes, he read there compassion such as he had not seen in many years. The smooth face was stained with unashamed tears.

Marcus wiped his eyes, smiled, and grasped the pale hand, but could not speak.

"I have not finished my story." The old man swallowed. "The Consul, Gaius, the Proconsul, and a captain of one of Caesar's boats also decreed I was too old to care for my now orphaned granddaughter, so they sent her to Rome."

"What about her mother?" Marcus questioned.

"She had died at Priscilla's birth," the doctor said. "Priscilla—that is my granddaughter's name. It is pretty, isn't it?"

Marcus nodded, smiling.

"They said she should stay in Rome until she reaches the age of eighteen. The dogs have tutored her in the infidel customs. I can discern it in her letters." The old man scowled.

"Then you have not seen her in these six years?"

"That is right, my son," the doctor said, struggling with his tunic. "I receive a message from Rome every three or four months. They allow her no more than that." His countenance brightened. "The last one . . ." He eased himself to a standing position. Then, swaying dizzily, he sat back down. "Under my bed," he said excitedly, motioning to the pallet. "Get the scrolls!"

Marcus jumped at the command, catching the excitement in the old man's voice. He brought the little packet quickly.

The knotted fingers fumbled with the cloth binding the separate pieces together. "This is the cause of the stir you witnessed today," the old man said, waving one of the scrolls. "Since the unfortunate incident six years ago, I have been prevented from performing my duties as a physician. In fact, I am an outcast of my own people.

"You see, they will not allow me to work nor live with them. I am worse than a tax collector. They think the Romans will judge *them* with me. So I am sustaining myself by caring for the soldiers' needs. I polish boots, groom stallions, and the like. In return, I receive food and these poor lodgings."

"And treatment such as I witnessed today," Marcus added.

The old man pretended not to hear him. "I know I am worse than an infidel, but I must go on for Priscilla's sake." The doctor looked down at the scroll in his hand, then at Marcus, his face brightening. With a quick move, he unrolled the papyrus. "It says," he turned the letter to Marcus, "that she will be arriving in Joppa the middle of next week!" He grabbed Marcus' shoulders. "You!" he shouted. "You have been sent by the Lord God!"

"What do you mean?"

"You saw!" His voice was high-pitched, and he was stuttering in his excitement. "I-I was trying to talk the regiment captain into allowing me three days in which to journey to Joppa and accompany my Priscilla back to Jerusalem." The old man touched his cracked lip. It was bleeding again. "You saw his answer." He looked down. "I asked only for one donkey and a few provisions." Suddenly the old man raised his head, a broad smile spread across his face. His eyes brightened until they were nearly clear. "*You* will go!" he shouted. "Yes, that is it! You *have* been sent by the God of our father Jacob!"

Marcus frowned. He thought of Barak and the others. "I cannot," he said. "I-I . . ."

The physician realized he had read too much into this young man's helpfulness. His face fell in disappointment. He shook his head, disgusted with himself. "Forgive this old fool," he said. "I am sorry. It was a spark of hope for an old man's dream." He looked up into Marcus' young face. "In my excitement, I overlooked the fact that you have responsibilities too. Your family, your master—they are to be seen about, not the needs of a mere stranger. I am very sorry. Forgive an old dreamer."

Marcus looked into the sunken eyes. "I-I have no family," he confessed. "Well, not in Jerusalem anyway." He dropped his eyes and shuffled his feet a little. "And I can get away . . ." he stopped. "I mean, my master will allow me time off, I am sure."

"Marcus," the old doctor gasped, reaching out. "You would not fool an old man, would you?" He turned the smooth chin toward him. "Are you telling me you will go to Joppa to meet the boat?"

Marcus nodded. At this moment, he had no plan—only a determination to bring some joy to one who had been so cruelly abused.

The physician leaped up with renewed strength and grabbed the young man, shouting, "The God of Israel has heard this humble servant!" He latched a strangling armlock around the boy's neck and squeezed him close. "You are as my own flesh," he cried. "I shall offer a burnt offering while you travel, my son. I will pray the Lord God to make your journey safe from the thieves of the hills."

Marcus breathed deeply, not sure of what he had done. What would he tell Barak? How could he get away for three days? He looked at the excited old face. It seemed different now. Marcus felt a warm glow. "Will you be all right?" he asked gently.

The old man nodded. "I will be fine," he said. "Oh, yes," he added, securing all the scrolls except the lone one on the table. "You must take this, and I will write upon it. Priscilla would not trust you without my letter of introduction." He looked into Marcus' eyes. "Then again," he said, "anyone can see you are an honest young man."

With the precious scroll safely tucked away and the good physician's blessing upon him, Marcus set out for the thieves' hideout in the hills. His mind was reeling from the events of the day. He seemed to float through Jerusalem, through the crowds, through the east gate, and up into the far reaches of the Judean hillsides. *What story would he give Barak and the others?* he wondered.

CHAPTER IV

The road to Jericho was dry and dusty. The four men ambled along with easy strides, two in front and two behind. Their sandals flipped dirt into the air, forming small clouds at their feet.

Marcus pulled on Timaeus' sleeve, motioning him to slow his pace. He wanted to be sure that Amalek and Barak were out of hearing range.

The two older thieves spiced their conversation with curses and tales of robbings, beatings, and loose women. They didn't notice the younger pair dropping back.

Timaeus looked at his friend. "Now will you tell me what is going on?" He spoke in a throaty whisper.

Marcus grinned. "I told you most of it the other night when I returned to camp."

"That was two nights ago. I have been waiting for you to tell me the rest," he said eagerly.

Marcus smiled at his friend and suddenly realized that in this brief span of days and happenings he had become the older and wiser of the two. *Maturity is not measured in years*, he thought. Marcus leaned closer as they walked. "Do you remember how Barak exploded when he got back that night and found me already asleep?"

Timaeus nodded. "Yes, but he calmed down right away." He glanced up ahead. "What did you tell him?"

"Well," Marcus laughed, "I told him I was picked up by two soldiers and taken to the Fortress of Antonia. I was able to give him details of the area, so he believed me." Marcus grinned. "And he calls *me* stupid." He laughed aloud. "I told him I escaped from the old guard and fled on foot into the lower city and made my way to the hideout."

"You didn't tell him about the doctor or the promise you made?" Timaeus questioned.

"Quiet!" Marcus warned, watching the two men ahead of them.

Timaeus shook his head in disbelief. "You were so naive when you first joined us, Marcus. You've become a cunning fox." Timaeus hesitated, looking into his friend's eyes. "The difference is written on your countenance." He smiled. "But you're a likeable fox."

"You have been party to my change of view, too, my friend." He laughed and slapped a hand on Timaeus' shoulder.

"According to the letter, you should be in Joppa to meet the boat from Rome in just three days," Timaeus said. "What are you going to tell Barak and Amalek?" He pursed his lips. "You will need a good story."

"And I have one," Marcus smiled.

"From the look on your face, I would suspect this plot involves me," Timaeus stated. "Am I right?"

Marcus chuckled. "Most certainly," he said.

"Well?"

"It occurred to me since your home is in Joppa and your parents still live there . . ."

"Ho! Wait up, my friend. I don't have parents living in Joppa. Indeed, I don't have parents at all—at least none that I can locate."

"That is still better," Marcus nodded. He glanced at the two men walking ahead, engrossed in their own conversation. "In Jericho, you will meet someone who will tell you of an old couple living in Joppa who claim to have a son named Timaeus, whom they have not seen since birth. The couple is rich and ailing and desperate to find their son."

Timaeus was frowning. "All right," he said, "I see the reaction it could bring, but why would *you* be going?"

"Rhoda will be with you of course, but you will need *two* witnesses qualifying you as the son of this couple."

"A bit complicated perhaps."

"All the better," Marcus agreed. "Those two would never suspect two *stupid children* of creating such a story."

"You mentioned Rhoda," Timaeus said.

"Certainly. Is she not always with you?"

"I will go," Timaeus assured, "but I question the wisdom of taking Rhoda."

"What! Rhoda would love an excuse to be with you away from the others. And the adventure would appeal to her."

"Oh, there is no doubt of that. But I was concerned about the distance and the danger of traveling these hills."

"Oh, I see," Marcus threw his hands into the air. "The trip will be safe for the granddaughter of the physician but . . ."

"All right," Timaeus acquiesced. "You have made your point."

The young men talked on, not noticing that Barak and Amalek had stopped in the road and stood waiting for the younger men.

"It would be a day and a half to Jericho the way you two drag," Amalek barked.

Marcus looked up and elbowed Timaeus. They picked up their pace.

"They are young and stupid," Barak chimed in. "We are probably better off without them."

Amalek cast a sidelong glance at Barak. "If you will remember, I *warned you* in the beginning."

Barak looked full into Amalek's face. "They are mine to instruct or mine to . . ." He glanced back toward the two. He spat at their feet, turned on one heel, and continued toward their destination, motioning the others on. Amalek stomped after him and the two young thieves followed.

Tempers cooled and conversation resumed. Amalek turned his head so all could hear what he had to say. "I have been talking to Barak about a mutual friend. You wouldn't know him," he waved a hand. "His name is Zacchaeus. He is very rich—as it should be with thieves of his caliber. He is a big tax collector."

"Not *too* big," Barak laughed, stretching out his hand about waist-high.

Amalek grinned. "*Very* short, but *very* rich." He cleared the dust from his throat and continued. "Our friend has agreed to help us in several ventures. The two of you will be allowed to participate in a portion of our plans." He looked at Barak. "Barak talked me into this foolishness," he grumbled.

The two young men stared at each other.

Amalek continued. "If you follow Zacchaeus' teachings faithfully, I may change my mind about you." He sneered, as though the mere thought was distasteful.

The four walked over a small rise and down into a shallow valley toward the next knoll. The travelers on the Jericho road were sparse, and they were glad for the privacy.

"Ah, yes," Amalek broke the silence again. "I failed to mention that Barak and I have some *other business* in Jericho first. Do you think you can stay out of trouble for one hour?" The pair nodded.

Marcus looked down to see the dust caking between his toes. A cooling breeze swept gently over the crest of each hill and the cloudless sky lay a brilliant blue background for the little band. The road curved and wound around until it widened just outside Jericho. Here, the movement of strangers along the road increased noticeably.

"Look!" Timaeus pointed up the road to the city's entrance. A large crowd had gathered. Others rushed to join the throng.

Barak looked at Amalek. "That must be the one we seek."

Amalek nodded in agreement, then raised his hand, bringing the group to a halt. "This is where we must part company. We have business with a man in the gathering up ahead. Marcus, you and Timaeus go into the city. We will meet you later at the southeast corner of the synagogue." He waved them around to the right of the crowd as he and Barak turned to the left.

The younger men, stopped at the edge of the milling crowd. Marcus pulled at Timaeus' clothing. "I don't like all this secrecy," he said.

"I can see it written all over your face. You're up to something," Timaeus smiled.

Marcus motioned his friend into the growing mob. The people were yelling and calling each other until the noise was deafening. The young thieves locked arms. As they forced their way into the thick of the crowd, it parted. There, just a few feet from Marcus, stood the Nazarene. The young Jew's breath caught in his throat as he stared directly into the man's face. For an instant, their eyes met and held in a steady gaze.

The clamor gradually subsided, and a blind man was led from the side of the road to stand before the one called Jesus of Nazareth. Marcus was amazed that the Nazarene was able to control the great gathering without a word. That in itself was something of a miracle. He had been present many times when an entire legion of troops from Antonia could not quell the inevitable riot that arose over a controversial figure.

A voice from the back of the crowd inquired if Jesus were going to heal the blind man. There was no answer. A hush fell over the crowd. To Marcus, it seemed as though the entire countryside waited in anticipation.

The Nazarene looked at the old man who was totally blind. He had cast aside his outer garment which had signified his condition, obviously feeling he would need it no more. The old man's hair was matted and his clothes were soiled, but the Nazarene took no notice. He put forth his hand to touch the blind man. "What do you want me to do for you?" Jesus asked. His voice was low and gentle; yet it carried resonantly through the crowd.

The old man's voice trembled in anticipation. "Lord," he hesitated, "that I may receive my sight." The old man knelt on one knee and lowered his head.

Jesus lifted him up, saying, "Receive your sight." Then turning so all could hear, he said, "Your faith has saved you." The crowd murmured, then hushed expectantly. The silence was heavy, and every eye was fixed on the blind man.

The old man's lip began to quiver and tears formed in his clouded eyes. Slowly, his blank, unseeing stare changed. The eyes began to move in complete unison. Tears now streamed down his wrinkled cheeks.

The crowd pressed in on the central figures, hoping to see a miracle.

Suddenly, a shout of joy went up. "I see!" the old man shouted. Tears poured out of his eyes, washing away the years of darkness. "Master!" he shouted again. "I can see!" He grabbed the hand of Jesus and kissed it, then turned to a man who was weeping openly. The old man shook him, laughing and crying at the same time. "I see your tears of joy for me!" he said. Then looking at the crowd, he whirled around and touched several people, "You and you," he laughed. "I see you all!"

The crowd was stirred. Several people sobbed heavily. Others laughed and slapped the backs of those standing nearby. Some even fell to their knees and worshipped God.

Marcus stood stunned. He wiped away the quick tears that welled up in his eyes, not wanting Timaeus to see them. He swallowed the lump in his throat.

Suddenly, he pulled at Timaeus' arm and pointed to a rise in the landscape, some fifty yards away. Three men were engaged in serious conversation, unaware of the healing and the excited crowd around them. "What business are they up to, do you suppose?" Timaeus wondered.

"I don't know, but I should like to find out," Marcus said. He watched Amalek and Barak as they talked with a dark, little man who reminded Marcus of that filthy scoundrel, Jehiel.

"The man with them is part of the Nazarene's band," Timaeus observed. "I have seen this Jesus in Jerusalem many times, and that mousey one is always with him." He frowned. "Actually, he never really seems to be *with* Jesus, but makes his way through the crowds that gather. Once he asked me for a shekel or two—'for the poor'," he mimicked. "As if that scum ever cared for the poor."

Jesus had begun moving toward Jericho now, and the

people followed noisily, the two young thieves with them. As they moved in on the city of Joshua, others joined the crowd and the anticipation mounted. Everyone stretched to get a glimpse of the Nazarene. Although they pressed in, no one touched him.

Marcus leaned on Timaeus' shoulder and shouted above the noise of the crowd. "What do you think of him?" he asked.

"The Nazarene?" Timaeus shouted back.

Marcus nodded.

Timaeus shrugged his shoulders. "I don't know," he admitted. "If he is a charlatan as some say, then he is the best in all Judea."

The crowd had moved within the city now, and numbered upwards of a thousand. Men, both rich and poor, Jew and Greek, and an occasional Roman, followed close to the man of Galilee. Women stayed to the outskirts and children darted in and out among the milling adults. A few dogs ran alongside.

Marcus stood as tall as possible, peering up and down the street. His companion was curious to know what he was looking for, but Marcus didn't answer and kept a vigilant eye.

The main street was wide, even by Jerusalem's standards. The city fathers pushed for growth, yet the small shops were already hard against one another. Bazaars lined a narrow byway.

The crowd flowed with the Nazarene as he approached the end of the street and stopped near a tree. As he looked up into the tree, a hush fell. Everyone waited.

Marcus watched closely as Jesus called to the man sitting in the tree. As the small man descended, Marcus grabbed Timaeus' arm. "This is the man Amalek told us about!" he whispered loudly.

Zacchaeus was walking ahead, leading the way to his home. He continued turning toward Jesus and bowing as he walked.

Most of the people stood back, but a few followed at a distance. The people around Marcus and Timaeus murmured. Surely the healer would not consent to be the guest of a notorious sinner—a Jew who had become a tax collector on Caesar's payroll. "Zacchaeus is worse than a dog," yelled the man next to Marcus. The dissension grew.

Timaeus leaned close to Marcus. "Look," he said. With his arm outstretched, he pointed across the street where Amalek and Barak stood watching Zacchaeus and Jesus leave the crowd. "Amalek looks angry."

The two young men watched closely as the dark little man returned to speak with the older thieves. At his words, Amalek threw his hands into the air. His eyes burned with fire and his jaw chopped the air as he spoke. Marcus was sure Amalek was cursing because Jesus had interfered in his plan for Zacchaeus. Perhaps the little tax collector would be of no value now.

Marcus felt a sense of relief, though the reason escaped him. He was puzzled by the strange emotion he was experiencing, but there would be time later for sorting his feelings.

Shrugging them aside, he watched the trio as they entered a small shop just around the corner on a side street. He turned to Timaeus. "Shall we go see what they are up to?"

"Do you think it wise?"

"Probably not, but I will always wonder if we don't try."

"Wondering won't kill you, but by the look on Amalek's face, *he* might," Timaeus laughed.

The pair quickly made their way across the street and

around the corner. The street was heavily shadowed by the buildings knit closely together. They stepped to the door. Marcus knocked uncertainly.

A bolt slid easily to one side and the door opened narrowly. An eye peered through the split. "Whom do you seek?" the man's voice droned.

Marcus was sure it was the same dark, little man Timaeus had called the "mousey one." Even that one eye seemed to pierce his very soul. His instincts told him to flee, but it was too late to turn back. "We are with Amalek," he choked.

From within the dark room, Amalek's voice resounded. "It is a pair of frail girls!" he growled. "Is it not so, Judas?" The door swung open wide as Amalek pushed the dark man aside. "Come in," he said disgustedly, then turned to address the others in the small room. "What shall I do with these who will not follow simple instructions?" he asked.

The light from one flickering candle played grisly games with the rugged features of several faces. After the pair entered the room, Amalek closed the door and bolted it.

Marcus could hear his heart beating within his chest. His ears pounded with the sound. He wasn't so sure of himself now.

Amalek looked to the big man sitting at the end of the table in the center of the room. "Barabbas, how can we build a future with such youth?" He shook his head.

The big man leaned back in his chair and scratched his heavy beard. His bushy eyebrows merged over a large, bulbous nose. "In my band," he growled, "a good scourging would bring them into line." He pushed his chair back and rose to his full height. His massive shoulders were larger even than those of Ben-Elah. The sheer proportions of the man made Marcus cringe.

"If they were mine . . ." Barabbas snarled, leaning across the table toward the young Jews. "If they were mine . . ." he repeated. His eyes were fixed on Marcus and he slammed a huge fist on the table, jarring the wine cups so hard that some tipped over. "I would teach them a lesson they would never forget," he growled. He leaned back slowly and sat down again. "That weak one you call a leader," he spat to one side, "will see for himself the consequences of coddling our young men." He looked to his left to signal that he was through with the conversation.

In the temporary silence that followed, Marcus took a deep breath and let his eyes roam the faces in the room. There was the dark one called Judas, nervously biting his nails. Amalek stood next to the table now, with Barak just behind him. Marcus paused a moment to look directly into a dark corner. Someone was well back in the shadows. He squinted to see if he could recognize the face, but couldn't. Another man, unknown to him, sat next to Barak.

Barak broke the silence. "Let Judas tell of what he heard."

"Yes," Barabbas said. "What of Zacchaeus?"

Judas fidgeted nervously as he spoke. "The Master is breaking bread with Zacchaeus," he said. "I am afraid this man will be of little service to any of you." He shook his head. "When the Master spoke to him today, I could see in his eyes," he hesitated, "that he would never be the same." He looked around the room, suddenly gaining self-confidence. "You may laugh at me, but I tell you I have seen it many times. Matthew is living proof." He dropped his head and wrung his hands, suddenly nervous again. "Never mind," he sighed. "Just believe me. Zacchaeus is a man you cannot depend on."

"Forget about the little worm," Barabbas growled. "What about this other business?"

"Wait," Amalek said. "I am not sure if these two need to be a part of this." He gestured toward Barak. "*He* talked me into bringing them to Jericho with us, but the business we now undertake to discuss, well . . ."

Barabbas agreed. "You are right," he said. "What is said here is only for those *men* who are faithful. Let the children return to their weak leader."

Barak interrupted. "Marcus, you will see that Ben-Elah gets this message. Tell him we have been delayed, and it may take several days to complete our business."

The two young men left the shop and started for their retreat just outside Jerusalem. As they wandered down the main street, back toward the dusty road, they noticed a group had gathered in front of a stately dwelling at the edge of the city. Most of the people stood outside the gates of the estate, but thirty or forty had ventured inside the grounds.

"This must be the home of Zacchaeus," Timaeus said. "Look, there are some who follow the Nazarene."

As they passed close by, they overheard those who were still grumbling about Jesus entering the home of a notorious sinner. Marcus had to agree; it did cast doubt on the man's sincerity. He thought about it as they left the city.

The road was scattered with travelers now. Some led donkeys, heavily loaded with goods, while others seemed to be out for a leisurely stroll. Farther on, a family herding a small flock of sheep ran roughshod down the path, nearly knocking Timaeus to the ground.

They had gone several miles without a word when Marcus spoke of a matter that had been plaguing him. "You know the one they called Judas?"

"The mousey one," Timaeus nodded.

"He scares me," Marcus admitted.

"He is not so bad," Timaeus said. "Did you notice

Maath, Barabbas' right-hand man?" He looked into Marcus' face for a reaction to his next statement. "He was silent because he has no tongue. It was cut out." Marcus turned pale. "Barabbas killed the two dogs who did it, and Maath became his self-proclaimed servant."

Marcus took a deep breath, "And who was the man hiding in the shadows of the far corner?"

Timaeus frowned. "I didn't notice anyone," he said.

Marcus kicked a stone out of the road. "This may mark me as the stupid child Barak thinks I am, but I swear to you, he *was* hiding, and he was robed as a priest."

Timaeus' frown changed to a grin, then to laughter. He slapped a hand on his friend's back. His laughing continued as he dropped down to the side of the road.

Marcus sat down next to him. "I should kick the hide off you for laughing at me, but I swear by all I am, the man was in priest's robes."

Timaeus was immediately sober. "Oh, my friend," he said, "you have so much to learn." He shook his head. "The priests are the biggest thieves of all. Of course, the man could have . . ." The sentence dangled in midair. "That's it!" He looked back in the direction of Jericho. "How stupid of me not to have guessed," he said. "So that was their business in Jericho."

Marcus sat with his mouth agape, wondering at the outburst.

Timaeus whirled to look at his friend. "It was Rosh you saw!" he exclaimed. "Listen, Rosh is a priest of some repute in Jerusalem and cannot afford to be seen with men like these. I wonder what they are up to now. The last time Amalek, Barabbas, and that devil priest met, a riot broke out in Jerusalem within a few days," Timaeus continued. "Now I can see a stir coming. You see, Marcus," he turned his body around and crossed his legs under him, "Barabbas wants to overthrow the Roman dogs. Amalek and Barak are agreeable, but Ben-Elah feels it would be an unwise move. Now this Judas—I can't figure where he fits in—only that Rosh wants to get rid of the one Judas refers to as his Master, Jesus the Nazarene," Timaeus sighed. "This will be a big stir indeed."

Marcus got to his feet and put out a hand to help his comrade. "We need to be moving," he said.

The pair walked along silently. So deep in thought were they that they failed to notice the day was well spent and the sun was angling toward the rolling horizon at a swift pace. Shadows grew thick, covering the shallow valleys and extending to the base of the next rise.

"I have it!" Timaeus shouted.

Marcus reeled with the sound. "What is it?"

Timaeus cuffed his friend's shoulder affectionately. "I know what the meeting is about. I know why those sons of Satan met today. They plan to rob Jesus!" He hesitated, wrinkling his forehead and dropping his gaze to the dusty road. "Yet that is stupid," he muttered to himself. "The man does not even carry an extra coat, much less a pouch of any value." He shook his head, wishing he hadn't voiced his thoughts. He didn't speak again.

Marcus was preoccupied with thoughts of getting to Joppa before the boat from Rome arrived. He felt a compelling urgency to keep his word to the old physician.

As darkness fell more heavily, they hurried on toward their shelter in the hills.

CHAPTER V

The Roman grain ship arrived in Joppa's busy port on schedule. Timaeus and Rhoda waited ashore while Marcus boarded the vessel in search of Priscilla.

Timaeus, leading two donkeys, was agitated. "Why in the name of all that is sacred, did we have to bring *two* of these worthless animals?" he muttered. Then, looping their leads around a tree, he found a place to seat himself. He pulled off his robe and spread it for his lovely woman to sit beside him. He looked at the animals again. "One of those stupid asses is bad enough, but dragging two of them around is impossible." A vein bulged in his neck.

Rhoda spoke appeasingly, "You know we needed one to carry our provisions." She shrugged her shoulders. "And Marcus was right. The girl will doubtless have some things to be carried back to Jerusalem." She kissed his cheek. "Or would *you* rather be her beast of burden, my love?" She giggled girlishly and moved closer to rest her head on his shoulder.

Timaeus shook his head apologetically. "As always, you are right." He tilted her chin to look deeply into her dark eyes.

She smiled, suddenly shy. "My love," she whispered. Her eyes searched his. In a glance, he read the message of her heart, spoken without words. It was the way of women—a mystery that never ceased to fill him with wonder and delight.

Her eyes had captured all the sparkle of the sunlit sea. She felt his strong arm slide around her waist, his fingers gently caressing the slim curve of it. Their lips touched lightly. The donkeys, contentedly munching the sparse tufts of grass, were forgotten for the moment.

In the meantime, Marcus had been accosted by an old sailor who ordered him to wait while he brought the captain to the deck. The ship's master was a barnacled, old seaman, but Marcus approached him in what he hoped was his most official manner. "Captain," he said. "I am to escort to Jerusalem one Priscilla, granddaughter of the physician, Oshea." Withdrawing the scroll the physician had sent, he presented it for inspection.

The grizzled seaman pretended to read the message. He cleared his throat and spat over the side, wiping his mouth with his sleeve. Then, looking Marcus over, he observed, "You're hardly a year or two older than the wench herself. Not no decent bodyguard for somethin' pretty as she is." He laughed, showing several rotten teeth. "I'd like to had her for my own." He leered at the thought. "But Tiberius sent word he'd have me quartered if she didn't get to Joppa safe." He shook his head. "And she kept reminding me that she is a Roman citizen now."

He cleared his throat and spat once again, but this time it landed on the rail. He stepped over and slid his palm over it, then wiped the collection on his coat. He turned back to Marcus. "You go ashore," the captain said. "I'll have one of my men get her for you."

"I would like to take her ashore myself," Marcus insisted.

The captain glared at the young Jew. "If I were not a Greek and this mission of yours was not touched by the house of Caesar himself, I'd have you scourged and thrown overboard," he growled. Then pushing past Marcus, he grumbled, "Wait here."

The minutes stretched out interminably. Two sailors shoved Marcus aside roughly, cursing him. He leaned back against the rail out of the way, then remembered the captain's spittle and quickly pulled back. A huge rat scampered over the deck from a stack of crates to a hole in one of the bulkheads. The ugly creature stopped, fixed a beady stare on Marcus, then wriggled into the hold. The young Jew felt sick to his stomach at the thought of the physician's granddaughter confined for months at sea with both the dirty old seamen and the other forms of lower life aboard.

He checked fore and aft. Both ends of the ship were worked by foul men, their upper bodies bare and soaked with perspiration. All, he noticed, bore the markings of the whip. Marcus examined the ship; it reeked of rot and filth. His ears burned from the lusty obscenities of the crew, and the stench of sweat mingled with wine made him ill.

He turned abruptly—into the clear gaze of the most beautiful woman he had ever seen. The hood of her cape fell away to reveal a flawless face, framed with lustrous, black hair. Tiny ringlets, moist from the heat, curled about her temples. Her full, naturally red lips curved upward in a welcoming smile. Marcus envied the sun that had stroked her cheeks with its rays, for her skin shone bronze and rose.

The garment she wore, in the manner of the Romans, embraced a dainty waist. One shoulder was bare and a golden bracelet encircled her upper arm. The fabric floated in graceful swirls about her slender ankles.

Marcus gasped, able only to stare into liquid, brown eyes that teased gently but spoke of a chasteness and intelligence that excelled even the beauty of her face and form. This girl/woman was beyond his experience—a creature from another world.

One of the crewmen yelled an obscenity, bringing Marcus sharply back to his senses—or what was left of them. The captain overlooked the crew on the deck below, cursed, and called out a name. A swarthy man with shaven head stepped from behind a large crate and laid his hands on one of the sailors. Pulling a whip from his belt, he led the man somewhere below, out of sight. The poor man's fate was undeniable. The captain turned to follow the girl, and the crew resumed its work.

A sailor followed the captain, carrying a large wooden box. "Well," the old captain bellowed, "here is her trunk, boy!" The sailor slammed it to the deck. "Take it," he yelled again, "and get off my ship! I want nothing more than to be done with this wench and you."

Marcus, still in a trance, was oblivious to the captain's harsh words. He merely presented the scroll the physician had given him and stammered miserably, "I-I am Marcus. This message you sent your grandfather and the note I gave the captain should be credentials enough."

"Why is Grandpapa not here to meet me?" Her clear voice was edged with concern.

"No need for alarm," Marcus said. "The good doctor could not get away from Jerusalem, so we . . ." Marcus turned to glance ashore in the direction he had last seen Timaeus and Rhoda. "I brought two friends."

Priscilla frowned. "Am I to travel with three men? No proper lady would consent to such an arrangement."

Marcus hastened to reassure her. "Ah . . . oh, no!" he blushed. "Rhoda is a woman like you." He winced, knowing his words were those of a little boy.

The captain was decidedly disgusted with the whole business. "Take this crate," he said as he kicked the trunk. "Ouch!" He cursed loudly. "Now get off my ship!"

Marcus struggled with the heavy trunk, sliding it most of the way down the rotting gangplank. He beckoned to the young woman to follow close behind him. Hoisting the trunk to his shoulder, he led the way to shore.

Priscilla, "Priscilla—it is a beautiful name." The young lady didn't respond. Once he heard her stumble behind him, then felt the touch of her hand on his back as she tried to steady herself. He tightened his muscles to impress her. She would learn that he was more than a tongue-tied boy.

As they came ashore, Marcus looked back up at the old seaman leering after them. He had been watching Priscilla's every move. Marcus smiled and waved. The old man snapped upright, spun on one heel, and disappeared below deck.

Marcus grinned, then turned to see Timaeus and Rhoda approaching. He greeted them warmly; then introduced them to Priscilla.

She took a deep breath. "Everything is happening so quickly, and I'm so confused. Without Grandpapa here as I had expected, I . . . I . . . ."

Marcus looked at Rhoda imploringly. Instantly aware of his plight, Rhoda placed a hand on Priscilla's shoulder, leading her toward the spot where Timaeus had tied the donkeys. "You must be exhausted from your voyage, and we have a long trip yet ahead," Rhoda said gently. "Come and rest while Timaeus and Marcus prepare the donkeys for the return to Jerusalem." Rhoda suddenly seemed older than her nineteen years—almost motherly as she led the grateful Priscilla to the comfortable resting place beneath the tree.

Timaeus grabbed one end of the heavy trunk, helping Marcus strap it to one of the donkeys. He watched Marcus, who worked effortlessly, buoyed by a soaring spirit.

"Now I'm not a wise man like our father Solomon, but I am able to see the light of love as it shines upon a young man's face," Timaeus teased. He looked at the women chatting up ahead. "She *is* beautiful," he said.

Marcus and Timaeus walked behind, leading the donkeys which bore their heavy burdens. Marcus' eyes followed Priscilla's movements. "She glides," he noted.

Timaeus agreed. "Our father, Isaac, could not have found Rebecca as fair," he said, then noticed Marcus was not amused at his gibes. He lowered his voice in a businesslike tone. "I am happy we thought to bring two donkeys. The trunk would have been too much for one donkey to carry with the other provisions." He continued mumbling, more to himself, since his friend was obviously preoccupied with his own thoughts.

Marcus soon caught up with the women, allowing Rhoda to drop back, leaving him alone with Priscilla. Their conversation was strained, but the girl soon relaxed and listened eagerly as Marcus described his meeting with her grandfather and the incident with the Roman soldiers.

The seaport city of Joppa was extremely busy, with a cross section of humanity gathered for trade. The slave market was teeming, and the little group made a point of skirting it. As a result, they took the long way to reach the main artery out to the east. In so doing, they had to make their way around a herd of swine running through the narrow streets. It was indeed a strange sight for Marcus, since swine were not allowed to enter the walls of the City of David. Joppa, with its many sects, was a liberal city.

Another noticeable difference was the number of Roman soldiers in the port city. There seemed to be two uniformed soldiers to every civilian. At one point, Marcus had to pull the little group into a doorway as a squad of soldiers marched by, a lieutenant calling cadence. Each man wore full combat dress. Helmets gleamed in the bright sun, and breastplates shone from hours of polishing. The Romans often marched like this, proudly displaying their strength and discipline. As they passed by, their mail gave off an almost melodious chime, and their marching pounded out the beat.

As soon as they had passed, Marcus urged the group on through the city. Once, the trunk slipped and almost laid the donkey on its side. The two young men righted the heavy box and tightened the straps.

They continued on, through the east gate, out past the tent-people who camped there, into the hillsides of Judea. The road was wide and well traveled. They made simple conversation as they walked, Priscilla asking mostly of her grandfather's welfare.

The April sun warmed the arid land and the little party moved along smoothly. The donkeys were led, one behind the other, through the sloping landscape. Chatting congenially, the four young people covered several miles, stopping occasionally to rest or to drink from the waterskins.

About four hours after they had left Joppa, Marcus spotted a small patch of green with several trees prospering in the gentle, sloping hillside. "Lydda is just beyond the next rise," he said. "We can stop and eat in the shade of these trees and then travel straight through the town without hesitation."

Timaeus nodded. "Well spoken! I could eat *two* meals!"

Rhoda smiled at Priscilla. "The two of them eat as much as the rest of us, Ben-Elah inclu . . ." Her words trailed off as Marcus glared at her.

Priscilla pretended not to notice his irritation and helped Rhoda spread a cloth under the trees.

Timaeus and Marcus unloaded a basket containing fish and small, fragrant loaves of bread wrapped in individual cloths. Marcus reached deep into the pack on the donkey's back and brought forth a bulging skin. He held it high. "Wine," he announced. He reached in again, producing a small package. "And . . . a surprise!" He laughed a little as he handed the package to Rhoda, Marcus placed the wine next to the basket and took his seat across from the women.

Rhoda struggled to untie the package. Priscilla sat down beside her, curious as to its contents.

Thus occupied, the women failed to notice Marcus as he studied the pure young profile. Priscilla's nose was perfectly formed and her lips—he kept noticing her full lips—were parted now in anticipation. Her chin jutted out slightly as she leaned toward Rhoda, and the line of it was smooth and straight, rising from the slender column of her neck. *Indeed*, Marcus thought for the hundredth time, *she is beautiful!*

Rhoda squealed in delight. "Oh, Marcus!" She pulled the wrapper back so everyone could see. The dark gold block of cheese wore beads of moisture, and a greenish-blue fuzz had begun to form on one edge. Rhoda inhaled deeply the pungent aroma. "Oh, how delicious! Goat cheese is my weakness," she sighed. She closed her eyes and took another heady breath. "Where did you get it?" Her eyes opened wide as she stared at Marcus.

He was removing the dried fish from the basket. At her question he glanced up, shifting his eyes from Rhoda to Priscilla. "I picked it up in Jerusalem," he smiled. "Uh, from a Greek merchant." He waved a hand. "We had best eat," he said, passing out the fish and bread. "Timaeus, will you pour some wine for our honored guest?" With that, the meal began and an easy flow of conversation continued.

Priscilla ate very slowly. She watched the others, noticing something different about Marcus. His manner seemed polished in spite of the plebeian clothing he wore. She wondered about his position, but dared not ask—not yet, anyway. She sensed he had been educated under Greek tutelage. As he looked up at her, she quickly turned her eyes away.

"Now that we have a little time," Marcus said, "we must hear about your life in Rome."

Timaeus swallowed a large piece of bread. "Yes," he agreed. "Please tell us about Rome. Is it as magnificent as they say?"

Priscilla felt at ease for the first time since leaving her home. The warmth of the little group gave her a peace and security she had not found in all of Rome. They were waiting eagerly for her words.

"Rome," she began, "is cold. Rome is bitter. Tiberius is hated." She stopped and looked into Marcus' tender face. "Rome is not you, and you are not Rome." She leaned over and touched Marcus' hand. It was a spontaneous act, arising from the influence of the liberal city which had been her home.

"The city is full of bitterness, fighting, hatred, and murder. The lust for wealth and position exceeds your wildest dreams." She looked down. "I was fortunate to have had a father to teach me during the early years of my life. Without him and Grandpapa, I . . ." she hesitated, wiping away the mist in her dark eyes. "I don't know what would have become of me."

She gestured toward the trunk, and spoke of more pleasant matters. "I have papers granting me Roman citizenship. There is also a document directly from the hand of Tiberius' scribe and sealed with the seal of Caesar awarding Grandpapa a position as aide to the quaestors. He is to assist in tax collection and auditing. Also, my Roman parents have provided a home in Jerusalem for the two of us."

She looked at Marcus again. "Six years ago, when I was dragged from my dead father's side and forbidden ever to see my beloved grandfather, I thought I would never again know happiness. Yet, the Lord has been good. I have a new home. I have found new friends. Though I have known you only a short time, you are not strangers to me."

Rhoda wiped moisture from her eyes. "You mentioned your Roman parents," she said. "Who were they?"

"I lived in the home of a senator and his wife during my last eighteen months in Rome," Priscilla replied. "I don't know how much Grandpapa told you about me, so I will assume you know very little." She sipped at her wine.

"My mother's father was a Roman general, posted over the legions of Spain. He took leave to come to Judea. I was told that my grandmother was drawing water one afternoon when the general came by to drink from the well. Although it violated every code of that day, they talked often after that and soon found themselves deeply in love.

"By law and tradition, they were bound to stay apart; yet they found the time for love's expression, and after the general was called back to Spain, my grandmother was found with child—my mother. She was expelled by all factions of religion and society.

"As my mother grew into womanhood, she too was rejected. But my father fell in love with her, and I was conceived. My mother died at my birth."

She breathed deeply. "I guess all that has happened has been for my good fortune. Had we lived on in Jerusalem, the people would still consider us outcasts of the Temple. Now I come from a nobleman's household and will receive respect and honor. It will, in small measure, compensate my grandfather and me for our years of separation and suffering." She paused, expecting a response. "None of you seem shocked by my callous attitude."

Marcus smiled. "You will find it difficult to shock us. We . . ." He stopped, realizing he was in treacherous territory and quickly changed the subject. "Look," he laughed and waved a hand, "we want to hear more about you, and I was ready to begin *my* life's story." Everyone laughed. "Tell us, did you travel the city itself?"

"Yes," Priscilla said. "Always I was escorted by a handmaiden and a servant."

"How grand!" Timaeus teased.

Priscilla smiled at his boyish ways. "Not as grand as it may sound. But you asked about Rome, so I shall tell you of the fair city." She sipped the wine again.

"The Forum is the central marketplace where merchants buy and sell. Recently, though, the many buildings being erected are crowding out the small businessman." She looked into space a moment, while the others continued their eating.

"I pray that I will never allow my heart to harden like the leaders of Rome. They have no respect for the underdog. All they care about is adding to their already fat purses." Her voice trailed away as her mind drifted out across the sea, back to the conquering nation's capital city.

"If only someone could bring a loving, giving spirit to those hardened hearts . . ." Priscilla pleaded with her new friends. "The Romans are good people." Her forehead wrinkled with concern. "They have just been carried away with the lusts of life. Wealth and position are the devils that have pierced the heart of Rome with their filthy talons. I hate Rome and all she stands for on the one hand; yet on the other, I love the people themselves." The beautiful face contorted and a tear slid down one cheek. "I know all of you must want to stone me for defending them, but it is only because you do not know these people. It is because you have never seen the good in them."

"Like the centurion who kicked your grandfather when he asked for leave to come for you?" Marcus sparred.

Priscilla looked into his eyes. "Oh, Marcus, when you told me of the incident, I wept. Remember?"

Marcus nodded.

"Don't you realize how very hurt I was? Not just because of Grandpapa, but to hear of one human treating another in that way. There is where the real hurt lies."

Marcus was touched by her compassion. He closed his eyes a moment, not knowing how to respond.

Timaeus pulled his woman close to him. "You sound like my Rhoda here," he said as he hugged her. "She says she wants me to get a job like the other men in Jerusalem and quit . . ." He stopped abruptly, catching Marcus' gesture of warning. Swallowing, he took his arm from around Rhoda and began to fidget.

Priscilla turned to Rhoda. "Maybe *you* will tell me what great mystery you are concealing from me," she said.

Rhoda looked at Marcus. He smiled nervously. "Later," he said. "We will discuss it later." He leaned to one side and searched the sand at the edge of the cloth. Finding a small twig, he began tracing a line, following an ant darting over the little mounds.

Priscilla got to her feet. "Well, if you will not let me in on your little secret," she said, "we can continue our journey."

"Sit down!" Marcus ordered.

She looked into his face to read this sudden change of mood. His dark eyes were stern and his jaw was set. Though he seemed deadly serious, she didn't move.

"Sit . . . down!" he said more sharply.

Priscilla sat, astonished at his ability to command the situation. The young Greeks and Romans she had met were sniveling youths, easily manipulated by feminine wiles. But this Jew was different. He was a man after the cut of her father. She found herself responding favorably.

"We have a home in the hillsides outside Jerusalem," Marcus began. He continued on for an hour, telling her, as discreetly as possible, of his station in life. Timaeus and Rhoda helped from time to time, interjecting an anecdote or other interesting detail.

The conversation continued until the sun was far spent on the horizon. They decided to stretch a large cover among the grove of trees and stay the night. If they arose at dawn, they could easily make the gates of Jerusalem by noon. The women slept under the covering, while Marcus and Timaeus pulled cloaks over themselves and drifted into dreamless sleep.

CHAPTER
VI

The next afternoon found Phoebe, the mother of Marcus, in the village of Bethany. She had entered the little town on the outskirts of Jerusalem in search of meat and other staples. With only a few coins left from the goodly sum Marcus had brought a few months before, it would not take her long.

As the afternoon sunlight danced off the pinnacle of the Mount of Olives, the small woman made her way down the main street. As was her custom, she crossed over to avoid the merchants of costly spices and ointments. She disliked being yelled at by the aggressive dealers. The thought of one of these dirty, little sellers of alabaster breathing his nasty breath in her face was enough to make the extra steps worthwhile.

At least it wasn't as bad as the bazaar in Jerusalem, where there was no escape. No matter where you walked in the Temple city, the merchants got right up in your face and hawked their wares. It was an experience she always dreaded.

As she moved around the stands, with their rancid meat and half-rotten fruit, Phoebe sensed a strangeness in the air. She looked down the street. Several stalls, set up for business, had been vacated by their owners. Even some who faithfully tended their shops from sunup to sundown each working day were not in their usual places.

The little woman squinted into the sun. By her calculations it was only mid-afternoon or just a bit later. There was plenty of time for Bethany's merchants to make several sales before closing for the evening. She pulled at her lower lip, absorbed in thought. She noticed, too, that few shoppers moved about the streets in search of bargains.

She stopped to examine a copper pot. As she admired the hammered metal, she failed to notice a long-time friend approaching from behind. Phoebe's voice was soft as she spoke to the merchant who sat leaning against a post. "What price do you ask?"

The corpulent merchant pushed his stool forward and rocked with it, kicking dust with his bare feet. He pinched his chin, considering the amount he might persuade this modestly dressed woman to spend. He contemplated the striped cloth above his stall, then pursed his lips, pausing to reflect a moment longer. "My good woman," he began, but his words were cut short by the large woman standing behind Phoebe.

"Don't give her the same mumble-jumble you give everyone, Sala," the woman bellowed. Her big body heaved in tempo with her strident voice. Indeed, the two characteristics blended harmoniously. She waddled in closer to the bargaining area.

Without another word, she pulled the utensil from Phoebe's hand. She furrowed her brow, checking the rough edges of the pot with practiced fingers. Stepping out into the street, she held the pot so the late sun could light its insides, then snorted in disapproval and returned to the stand. Dropping the pot into the vendor's hands, she turned to Phoebe. "You would do well to buy in Jerusalem. Sala deals in merchandise which has been rejected by the merchants of the big city."

She smiled broadly and slipped her arm around Phoebe's shoulders. "Come with me and we shall find an *honest* dealer," she gibed.

The enraged merchant stood and shook his fist after the two women. He picked up the pot and looked it over, then slammed it down with a curse.

Phoebe glanced back over the big woman's arm. "Merab, you are shameful," she said to the woman laughing hilariously beside her. "Do you realize how angry you made that poor man? And you know I couldn't afford to buy. I was just admiring the craftsmanship and . . ."

Merab interrupted, "And you were thinking how nice it would be to own such a utensil." She withdrew her arm.

"Phoebe," she said with a serious note in her voice. "I know I was unkind to that merchant, but it would be different if . . ." She paused. "You are small and dainty, as a woman should be." She looked down at her own cumbersome frame and chuckled sorrowfully. "While I," she said, "I am like a great ox."

They walked on in silence, while Merab pondered how best to express her shame.

"Humiliating the greedy merchants is one way for me to strike back at all men for not . . ." She stopped and sighed in frustration. "Making Sala angry," she confided, "made me feel superior, I guess. Oh, no matter! I don't know how to explain it!"

Phoebe smiled sweetly. "Dear Merab, you do not have to explain anything to me. I am your friend."

The two women walked along, stopping occasionally to pick over the fruit. Merab scorned the bruised melons, the unripe figs, and the withered grapes already turning into raisins. Phoebe merely smiled at each scowling merchant before moving on to the next.

After a particularly difficult time with the merchant of textile, Merab looked troubled.

Looking down into her sweet countenance, Merab pleaded, "Phoebe, what can I do? I mean, how can I be different?" She shook her head and turned to continue their walk.

"I want to change. But do you know how hard that is to do? I have been this way for so long. It is not just my awkward body that shames me, but my spiteful tongue. I cannot ever remember talking any other way. My bitter words have left many wounds, I am sure." A tear trickled down Merab's cheek. She brushed it away, annoyed by her display of emotion.

Quickly she applied a false smile. "What have you heard from your restless son?" she asked, throwing her head back and gulping in deep breaths of air.

Phoebe's tender heart ached for her friend. Yet there seemed to be no words of comfort she could offer. Reluctantly, she answered the question, "He has not been home since the last Passover."

Merab turned to look at Phoebe's face. "You really miss that boy. I have seen you take long walks across the Kidron into the big city in the hope of seeing him. Am I speaking the truth?"

Phoebe nodded and looked down.

Merab slapped her palms together. "Now there is a fact I cannot understand!" she exclaimed. "A godly woman like you. A woman who has never done anything but good. A woman who prays and gives and never thinks of herself." She looked up and waved a hand toward heaven. "Why should such a woman suffer? The God of our fathers should shake some sense into that boy of yours so he will stop hurting you."

"Marcus is as you said—he is restless. Surely you, of all people, can understand. He, too, is in need of change. He will settle down. I know he will. The Messiah will soon reign in Jerusalem, and everything will be all right," Phoebe assured her.

The big woman frowned. "Do you still believe that nonsense?" She grimaced and sighed. "Phoebe, listen to me. Our own spiritual leaders say this Nazarene you call the Chosen One of Israel is really a fraud. Many know him as a carpenter out of Nazareth. They can call his mother and brothers by name." She stopped. Her voice was strained. "The Messiah will come in great power and glory. Surely the one who comes to liberate Jerusalem and all Judea will not be a lowly carpenter!"

Phoebe smiled through misty eyes, remembering the two instances when she had seen Jesus. "Merab, you have never seen him. He heals the sick. He makes blind eyes see. Someday you and my son will know he is the Chosen One. I feel it. I have asked the Lord to show you."

Her voice grew husky as she recalled vivid scenes. "I have seen a man covered with dreaded leprous sores come to Jesus. Instead of turning him away as the Pharisees do, Jesus called the man to him."

A tear ran down Phoebe's cheek and dripped off her chin. She let it run as others followed. "*With the power of his words . . .*" she whispered wonderingly. "Yes, Merab, with only his *words*, words of love and hope and compassion, he cleansed the leper!"

Now tears ran freely down her cheeks. "They say he teaches in the synagogues with wisdom like that of Solomon. I have heard men say the Holy Scriptures pour from his lips as though he himself wrote them." Phoebe stopped to wipe the tears.

Without realizing it, the two women had reached the edge of town, near the base of the Mount of Olives. Merab looked up toward the crest of the mount. A large crowd was gathering. Several people passed the two women. Merab stopped three young boys. "What's going on?" she demanded.

"The Nazarene, the teacher called Jesus, has come to the mount," one boy answered.

"We're going to see him!" another added excitedly, then darted off with his friends.

As an aged man passed the women, he turned and shouted to them. "Everyone who so desires may come up to the Mount of Olives. He turns no one away."

Phoebe's eyes glowed. "Did you hear?" she asked. "The Master is close at hand!" Her face flushed with excitement.

"I know you are going. I suppose this is as good a time as any for me to see him for myself," Merab sighed in resignation.

Already, several people had joined the old man. Others hurried to catch up.

"Come, Merab, we will not be able to see him if we delay." The two women scurried along, catching up with the gathering crowd.

Ascending the gentle slope was not easy for the heavy woman, and Phoebe had to stop several times to wait for her. "Merab," she said, "he is there." Her voice trembled with excitement. A similar current ran through the milling throng, as the two women approached the crest of the hill.

Phoebe attempted to push into the crowd, but made no headway. Without a word, she clasped Merab's hand and led her around the restless people until they reached a break in the crowd.

Merab pulled Phoebe close and shouted above the din. "I can see him! I think he is coming toward us." She stood up on tiptoe. "He is talking to many, and he is touching some," she reported.

As the Nazarene moved closer, she was startled to see the love and compassion on his face. *He really cares*, she marveled. A spark deep within slowly ignited, wrapping her in its warmth. She was aware of the strange sensation, but if one had asked what was happening to her, she could not have answered. It was the divine alchemy—an act of inner transformation that cannot be explained in human terms. Something so individually experienced defies description.

A tear trickled down her face. She let it go this time. "I saw him heal a woman," she shouted to Phoebe. "Phoebe, I saw it happen!" Before Phoebe could ask what she had seen, Merab was back up on her toes, craning her neck to see more.

Someone helped a lame man to the center of the crowd and seated him at the feet of Jesus. The Nazarene directed the man to rise to his feet and walk. Instantly the twisted ankles straightened and the withered leg regained its form and length. There was no longer any doubt. Tears ran down Merab's cheeks. She turned to Phoebe, with the light of understanding and acceptance illuminating her face. Words were not necessary. In that moment, radiating her newfound happiness, she was beautiful. Phoebe embraced her joyously.

Just then the crowd parted and Phoebe could see too. She blinked away her tears. The now familiar presence filled her with a peace and serenity that would linger long after she had ceased to see his face.

Merab, enraptured by her own encounter with Jesus, took up the crowd's chants of praise. Bending down, Phoebe gathered a few thin branches, and entwined them into a small wreath. Without a word, she pressed it into Merab's hands.

The big woman looked at the garland and a tear dropped, splashing on one of the leaves. The Nazarene was standing in the center of the crowd, speaking to some who had gathered to hear his words. She pushed forward, parting the crowd. Timidly, Merab reached out and placed the crown of olive branches on his head, then quietly withdrew.

Merab's eyes were fixed on the man. It was as though she had become a separate entity within the excited mass. She was aware of people around her. She could feel the tug of Phoebe's hand on her arm. She knew she was moving along behind the Nazarene as he walked among the crowd; yet in all that, she sensed a new and exhilarating dimension. The multitude moved forward shouting praises as they followed Jesus.

Several Pharisees pushed their way into the crowd. The leader called to Jesus above the throng, "Sir, rebuke these followers of yours, for they may riot." Jesus remained silent. The time had not come for rioting.

Phoebe pulled Merah aside. "I feel we should go to the Temple and worship," she said. "Many will come to pray and there will be no place for us. Let us hasten."

Merab was reluctant to leave, but she, too, sensed that Jesus was about to send the crowds away into the city.

As the two women started their crisp pace down the road, Merab spoke in hushed tones, "You were right. He is the Messiah. He has filled the emptiness I have known for so long."

Phoebe reached up to the taller woman and hugged her. "Oh, Merab," she cried. "You have come to believe in him as I have!"

They passed through the Kidron valley and came to

the large double gate of the east wall. As they entered the city, they looked back. The crowd had begun to disperse. Phoebe observed the distant look in Merab's brown eyes. "Come," she said, "let us go to the Temple."

The crowd was getting louder, calling cheerful farewells as they parted to go their separate ways. Down in the city, people milled about the gate, questioning one another as to the nature of the commotion on the mount.

The women stopped short on Solomon's porch and surveyed the activity of the Temple. The court was bustling. Phoebe drew closer to Merab.

"I am sorry to say this, my sister," Phoebe whispered, "but I feel I have entered the bazaar again."

Indeed, the scene reeked of financial gain. Moneychangers lined one side of the Temple area, while dealers of fatted calves, sheep, and doves lined the other. Men hustled among the people passing through the court of the Temple selling tickets of claim to a ram or calf. The purchaser merely handed his ticket to the priest in charge, and the selected calf was slain on the altar and offered as a burnt sacrifice for the sins of the purchaser.

The next day Amalek and Barak entered the gates of the city. Their journey from Jericho had been long and tiring. The preceding days had been spent in plotting how best to investigate the validity of the information given them by Rosh.

As they approached the Temple, a large crowd pushed its way in at the Gate Beautiful. "What do you figure brought all these lowly dogs to the Temple at this hour?" Barak asked.

Amalek scanned the seething throngs of people. Beggers and those of wealth, Sadducees and Pharisees, young and old—all appeared to be trying to enter the Temple at once. Amalek motioned to Barak, and the two men moved around the crowd and headed for the north gate. As they rounded the northeast corner of the Temple's outer wall, they noticed the singers had ceased their chanting.

Suddenly a commotion started, and Amalek broke into a run with Barak close behind. They turned into the north Temple gate, past the guard, and into the north portico, stopping only because of the press of people blocking their way. The two darted up the stairs to the balcony overlooking the court of Israel. As they took the steps, two at a time, they heard men screaming and cursing.

When they reached the top, they looked down to find the court in chaos. Tables were overturned and moneychangers groveled over the stone floor. Cattle had broken loose from their tethers and kicked nervously. Sellers of animals and fowl shook their fists and cursed, yet no one moved to stop the one responsible.

Suddenly the man who had created the disturbance stepped to the center of the courtyard. Silence fell thick. Even the animals and birds ceased their sounds as the Nazarene stretched out his hands, extending them upward toward heaven. His eyes blazed with anger. With a mighty voice he rebuked them, "It is written, 'My house is the house of prayer, but you have made it a den of thieves.' "

Without another word, he turned and left. The crowd parted, and he walked through, untouched. Even the priests plotting his overthrow stood transfixed until he was out of sight.

The spell broken, buyers and sellers, along with the moneychangers, scurried around the court floor in search of coins. As if on cue, the crowd surged forward, gathering up the scattered money to stuff their own purses.

Amalek grinned as priest and peasant rooted like the swine that were forbidden to enter the Temple area by sacred law. Putting an arm around Barak's shoulder, he pointed to the center of the room. "Look," he said, "there is the slithering snake himself."

Barak frowned, searching in the general direction of Amalek's pointed finger. "Judas," he mumbled. "Look at that little rooster scramble. I wager he collects twice as much as anyone else!" He shook his head. "A few coins mean so much to that fool."

With that, the two men turned to descend the long stairway. "The Nazarene was right about one thing," Amalek said. "This place *is* a den of thieves."

Barak threw back his head and roared with laughter. Still laughing, they left through the north gate and turned eastward toward the hideout.

CHAPTER
VII

After their arrival in Jerusalem, Marcus and his friends spent several days putting things in order. They helped Priscilla settle into a spacious dwelling in Jerusalem with her grandfather. Fully recovered now from the brutal assault, Oshea had assumed his new position. The weeks passed quickly as he flourished in Priscilla's tender care.

On one of her many trips to the Temple city, Phoebe had chanced to run across the little group. In her delight at the unexpected reunion with her son, she hadn't failed to see the glow in his eyes nor to guess the reason for its presence. One glance at the lovely girl at his side told her much about the source of his new contentment and explained his long absence.

Indeed, Phoebe perceived, *this child's beauty issues from some deep wellspring within. She will be good for my Marcus.*

Her step was light as she hurried back to Bethany to

share her joyful news with Merab and to put away for safekeeping the money pouch that Marcus had pressed into her hands as they parted.

On the first day of the new week, Marcus was rudely snatched from his sleep before the sun had beamed its rays over the rugged hillsides. The alarm that sounded was Amalek's gruff voice announcing that on this day all would know how well the two young thieves had learned their craft. Both Marcus and Timaeus had been given an assigned duty, and each was dependent on the other to complete his task.

Amalek and Barak, along with the two young men, arrived in Jerusalem by early sunlight. Barak turned to his companion. "Judas says his teacher is preparing to leave Jerusalem," he said. "He may have started out already."

"Not likely," Amalek countered testily. It gave him little pleasure to concede a point. Barak glanced at him inquisitively, but didn't argue.

The merchants were already setting up shop along the city streets, eager to take advantage of every daylight hour. As the four approached a small stall near the north end leading to the Temple, a large man, bent low with age, greeted them.

Marcus looked over his display of pottery. The merchandise was extremely inferior. Broken bowls and cracked waterpots lined the stand. Marcus thought it a wonder this man could sell anything. He shook his head and elbowed Timaeus, nodding toward the shabby rag used as an awning to shade the display. In the forefront were crude, poorly constructed items, while the better pieces were hidden in the far corner of the tent-stall.

Amalek picked up a small bowl. "Is your business thriving?" he inquired of the cripple.

The man leaned heavily on his crutch. His clothing was torn and reeked of filth. A thick gray beard covered his face, while the mantle draped low over his head further served to disguise his features. "Our plans have been altered," the man whispered huskily.

Marcus listened closely. Timaeus nudged him. There was no mistaking the voice. "Barabbas!" they murmured in unison.

The big man bent low, keeping up the pretense of selling. Two soldiers strolled by the little stand, glanced at the bargainers, then turned to climb the steps to the upper city.

"Judas has already been here," Barabbas said as he watched the soldiers mount the steps a hundred paces away. "He says the Nazarene is still teaching in the Temple area. He arrives in the early hours and gathers large crowds."

Amalek cursed and slapped the bowl he held against his open hand. "This Nazarene is becoming a nuisance," he snarled. "With him right there in the Temple, Barak and I will not be able to move for the crowds." He sighed in disgust.

Barabbas set the pot down and looked at the four thieves. "When most of my men were jailed or killed during our last riot, you agreed to cast your lot with me if I should need you. I trusted you to do the job, no matter what the obstacles. I still believe that." He looked directly at Marcus. "We will carry out the original plan, with one exception. The crowd in the courtyard calls for a change in strategy. Marcus and Timaeus, it is you who will seize the gold. It will take fleet-footedness and agility to outmaneuver the guards."

He leaned forward on his crutch. "Just remember, the guards will be posted near the Gate Beautiful; so when you make your escape, break for Huldah and the cattle gate. No one except old Hergon, the cattle prodder, is ever there. The Romans hate the smell of it. Their womanish nostrils have delivered our prize to us!" He laughed scornfully. "Now listen closely, all of you. Here is the plan."

As Barabbas outlined his scheme, another confrontation was taking place in the Temple. Rosh had cornered Judas. "I have kept my part of the bargain; now what about your promise, wretched one?"

Judas choked. "Barabbas. . ." he whimpered. "Barabbas swore to deliver him—not I." He squirmed under the pressure.

"Well, tell me," Rosh sneered, "just how does Barabbas suggest we take him?"

Judas looked past Rosh, toward his Master. Jesus sat near the north court wall, teaching a group of disciples. So eager were they to hear his words that no sound distracted them. The only interruption was an occasional question from a member of the group.

"I . . . I shall think of a way," Judas promised. "In the meantime . . . yes, I have it! Several of the learned men might sit at his feet and listen, asking questions about . . ." he thought a moment, "about where he gets the authority to make himself equal with God!" Judas smiled, definitely pleased with his answer.

Rosh, however, frowned and pursed his lips. He shook his head thoughtfully and turned away from the little man. Without a word, he slipped through the early morning crowd and out of the courtyard.

When the priest had disappeared through the Temple gate, Judas sighed and strode cockily to sit at Jesus' feet with the others.

Out on the street, Marcus and Timaeus walked together, discussing the day's activities. Having received their instructions, they had been sent forth to perform. The plan must be executed perfectly. There would be no second chance.

"Well," Marcus said, "This is the first time I have been tempted to quit." He dropped his head and kicked a stone. "We will never escape. We are no match for the Romans." He flipped a hand in the direction of the Fortress of Antonia. "This man we are to rob . . ."

"Sosthenes," Timaeus injected.

"This Sosthenes will have at least two men guarding him. The Roman soldiers will be everywhere—maybe even as far as the court of the Gentiles."

"Hold on, my friend," Timaeus said. "You heard Rosh. He assured us this man never allows anyone to accompany him when he brings his offerings to the Temple treasury. The priests praise him publicly for his large gifts. He would share that moment of glory with no man." Timaeus smiled. "As Rosh said, 'A sack in each hand and a loud voice by which to draw attention to himself'."

The pair strolled up to the outer walls of the great place of worship. A lame man sat just outside the Gate Beautiful. As they passed by he asked for alms in a quavering voice. Marcus stopped. Then reaching into the folds of his cloak, he withdrew a cloth knotted around a single coin. He loosened the knot and dropped the coin into the man's hand.

Timaeus urged him on. The majority of the crowd inside the gates had drifted to one side of the courtyard. Looking about, the two young thieves noticed only one moneychanger. He sat quietly, doing little business. The people seemed intent on nothing but hearing the Nazarene.

Marcus led the way through the court to the south side. He stopped to check the cattle gate—very little activity there. As he turned to speak to Timaeus, he noticed Rosh leading a group of men to join the crowd gathered around Jesus. "Look," Marcus whispered. "Rosh intends trouble. He is lower than a snake," he added. "My mother vows the Nazarene does only good, yet Rosh and all his ungodly friends seek to destroy the man."

A shiver ran unexpectedly up his spine. For what reason had he made such a statement? He shook his head, his thoughts muddled. This Nazarene was of no concern to him. Perhaps it was only the simple matter of injustice that had always prompted a response. Still, he could not shake an unsettling feeling for which he had no name. There was something about the man's eyes. . .

"Come," he said brusquely, masking his emotion. "We had better stand over by the east portico where we can observe Sosthenes the moment he arrives." He forced his mind to the task at hand.

It was good that Marcus didn't know exactly what Rosh was up to. The priest had forced his way into the inner circle surrounding Jesus and had adroitly redirected the line of questioning with the intent of trapping him in a blasphemous statement.

Meanwhile, Marcus and Timaeus took their positions and waited. "Did I tell you that Priscilla said there is talk of the Nazarene even in Rome?"

"No," Timaeus said distractedly.

"You seem little interested." Marcus was slightly annoyed with his friend's preoccupation.

"Huh? Oh, yes, Marcus," the other said. "I was trying to hear what was going on over there." He waved a hand in the direction of the moneychanger. "What did Priscilla say about him?"

"She said there were believers in Rome. Among them is a *soldier*—a centurion from the regiment at Capernaum. He was brought back to Rome and proceeded to spread the word that Jesus healed his servant. It goes without saying—he was severely punished and reduced to the status of a foot soldier. Caesar will have no gods but himself," Marcus sneered.

"And what do *you* think of this man?" Timaeus asked, smirking.

Marcus hesitated and glanced over at the crowd surrounding the man. He caught a glimpse of him as the crowd parted slightly, then closed again around Jesus. Marcus poked out his lower lip and pulled at his chin, deep in thought. Finally, he turned to look directly into his friend's eyes. "Barak once asked me that very same question," he said. "I cannot really tell you what I think of him. He is a good man, but it is hard to believe he could be the Messiah."

The expression on Timaeus' face changed abruptly. Marcus turned to look at the man who was entering the courtyard. "Sosthenes," he whispered.

Timaeus stood frozen, stone-like. His gaze was fastened on the figure carrying the two heavy sacks.

The man was a full head and shoulders above every other present and his great girth was robed in purple and satin. A large stone sparkled in the the forecrest of his headdress. His skin was dark olive and his beard, long and parted, looked somewhat like two inverted horns growing out of his chin. The whites of his eyes bore a striking contrast to their dark, baggy surroundings. Though he appeared to be in his late forties, he was surprisingly strong and agile. He looked around, pausing to assess the crowd surrounding the Nazarene. Then, with disdain still etched on his countenance, he glanced at the lone moneychanger.

Timaeus leaned closer to Marcus. "Look at the size of him!" His hand began to shake. "We won't be able to get close to him."

Marcus, equally shaken, tried to speak confidently. "All we need is a chance," he assured his friend. "Just one brief moment."

Just then Sosthenes turned to look at Marcus and Timaeus. "You!" he called, then quickly stepped over to stand beside the youths. "What's going on over there?" He waved one of the large moneybags in the direction of the crowd.

"J-Jesus," Marcus stuttered, awed by the mammoth proportions of his intended victim.

Sosthenes looked across the courtyard. Marcus nudged Timaeus and nodded toward the moneybags dangling just inches away.

"Now!" Marcus said. With smooth, well-rehearsed movements, each grabbed a bag, tearing it from the unsuspecting grip.

Sosthenes whirled his head around to see the young men darting past the moneychanger's table, past the chanting old man, and through the cattle gate. Indignation replaced the sudden shock of the theft. He broke into a run. "Stop! Stop those two! Thieves!"

The moneychanger quickly rose when he heard the yelling. He stepped out from behind his table to see what was happening, moving into the path of Sosthenes, who was dodging old men and priests milling around in the courtyard. He couldn't move quickly enough to avoid the man in his path. Sosthenes merely dropped a shoulder, and with a thud, sent him sprawling, overturning the table. Coins flew and rolled in all directions.

Out on the street, Marcus and Timaeus fled. Marcus led the way along the narrow streets of the upper city. The young Jew cradled the moneybag as though it were a babe. The size of it slowed his pace. He looked back. Timaeus was close on his heels.

Sosthenes burst out of the gate of Huldah, his face purple with exertion and rage. Someone pointed in the direction of the upper city. Without hesitation, he scaled the steps three at a time, his robe held high. He turned down the central street and spotted the pair far ahead. He fixed glazed eyes on them as he ran.

Marcus yelled to Timaeus, "This is it!" The pair stopped and looked back. The big man was bearing down. They turned into a side street, moving swiftly.

Sosthenes was tiring, but the thought of hanging the young snips by their thumbs drove him on. As he approached the corner where the pair had turned, a man, his garment stained and tattered, came out of the side street. He was barefoot and carried two water pots suspended from a yoke across his neck. Sosthenes stopped, exhausted. He put a hand up to stop the man, inhaling great gulps of air to ease his straining lungs. "Did you . . ." he gasped, "did you see two young hoodlums running down the street?"

The man only stared at him.

"Well," Sosthenes screamed. "Where did they go? I know you saw them," he shouted, grabbing the man. "Where did they go?"

The man made some guttural sounds, but was unable to utter a word.

Sosthenes held onto the tattered wretch and shook him, spilling water from the pots. Even in the busy city, the commotion attracted the attention of passersby— including a Roman captain and four foot soldiers.

The captain approached and ordered Sosthenes to release the victim of his rage, but the big man ignored his command. With a wave of his hand, the captain motioned two soldiers forward to restrain him. With some difficulty they pinned the huge man's arms, allowing the other to regain his balance. "What's going on here?" the captain demanded.

Sosthenes burst forth in a volley of words, liberally spiced with oaths. "Two youths have run off with my gold! They turned into this side street and passed this stupid oaf, but he will not tell me which way they went." He cursed loudly, "In fact, he will not speak a word." He lunged violently toward the beggar, requiring the assistance of the two other soldiers to hold him firm.

The captain looked closely at the silent man. "Come here," he commanded. As the man stepped forward, water splashed from the pots. "Your pots are quite full," the captain observed. He stepped closer to have a look. The man placed his hands over the mouths of the jars to indicate he wished to keep the water from ruining the captain's uniform.

The Roman sensed something was wrong. He looked into the man's eyes, then cupped his chin in his hand. "Open your mouth," he said. "Ah—it is as I thought." The captain pushed the man's face toward Sosthenes.

"There is your answer," the captain said. "He has had his tongue removed." With that, he shook his head in disgust. "You rich Jews are all alike," he muttered. He looked at the mute, anxious to impress these Jews with Roman clemency. "You may go now, my good man. And be careful not to fill your pots so full next time," he cautioned.

The dirty man smiled back and moved on down the street. He could hear Sosthenes as he began his high-pitched explanation again. As he looked back, water sloshed from the pots again, soaking his clothing. Maath didn't care; the gold was safe now. He grinned as he ambled along, reflecting on the fact that being tongueless is not without its advantages.

Down in the lower city, Marcus and Timaeus mingled with the bazaar crowd. They moved leisurely, stopping occasionally to inspect some fruit or to glance over their shoulders for signs of Sosthenes. Mostly, though, they moved along the middle of the street where the traffic flowed freely. Once they stopped to look over a collection of what the dealer called "rare jewelry from other lands."

Marcus moved in close while Timaeus inquired about a particular piece. The merchant displayed the ornament willingly, but Timaeus complained about the inferior workmanship. They moved on.

Along the streets of the upper city, Maath struggled with the yoke of water pots. He turned once to watch Sosthenes, still cursing and shouting, explaining to the Roman captain just what had taken place. Maath, however, merely turned back to his task, heading for the stairs that would take him down to the stand where Barabbas waited.

At that moment, Marcus and Timaeus approached the pottery stall. Barak and Amalek, maintaining their charade as bargainers, stood in front of Barabbas' booth. Barak looked up. He smiled at the approaching youth. "Smooth," he commended them. "Very smooth. You have learned well." He patted Marcus on the back.

The young Jews smiled at each other. "Did you expect less?" Timaeus boasted.

Barabbas roared with amusement. "He sounds like me when I was that age. A young snip. He has potential."

The grin on Marcus' face faded as he peered up the street. "Look!" he pointed. There, about fifty paces away, Maath weaved through the masses, water splashing on those unfortunate ones in his path.

The struggling mute looked up, past the people pushing around him, to see five pairs of eyes watching his every move. He grinned widely, showing several rotten teeth, and turned his thumbs up. His smile broadened as he watched the five turn to slap each other on the back and laugh with uninhibited glee. It reminded him of his boyhood, when one of his young friends would steal fruit from a merchant stand in the bazaar. All the others would watch. If the boy got away clean, the others would rejoice just as his cohorts were now. *We are still just boys*, he thought, *just bigger boys*.

As he approached the pottery tent, Barak and Marcus relieved him of the burdensome yoke and set it down gently.

Timaeus stepped over to the water pots with a small cup and dipped some water. "Is anyone thirsty here?" he asked. "This water is as precious as gold!" He laughed exuberantly, basking now in the pride of their accomplishment.

Amalek frowned darkly. He grabbed the young man's wrist, splashing the water over his clothing. "Will you ever cease your joking?" he snarled.

The atmosphere was suddenly charged with tension that ran like a current through the little band. Marcus looked down, embarrassed for his friend. Barak's smile disappeared, and Barabbas reached out and took the cup. "Let the boy go, Amalek," the big man said. "He is just a foolish youth, as we all were once."

Amalek released his grip, shoving the youth aside roughly, and spitting contemptuously at his feet.

Marcus frowned and cocked his head sideways, squinting and pursing his lips as his eyes met those of his friend. Marcus knew something of the savage streak in Amalek. Amalek was mean and filled with hate. This display might be a portent of things to come. Yes, Amalek was a man to be feared.

At this moment, Maath put a hand on Barabbas' shoulder and pointed down the street, grunting and making his guttural sounds. Barabbas looked up. Everyone turned to see.

There, walking slowly, was Justus, his cherubic face wreathed in smiles. Indeed, the entire scene was a portrait of innocence—the plump, old man clad in his priestly robes and the small figures of children flitting like butterflies beside him. As he walked he strummed his lute, singing little rhymes he made up. Tied to his sash was the lead to a donkey that followed reluctantly. The children darted here and there, laughing and calling out subjects with which to compose a new song.

Marcus smiled at the children and the two or three elderly women tagging along behind. Suddenly his eyes froze and his grin faded. There, dodging the hooves of the donkey, was a dog. Marcus' mouth opened slowly as he searched his memory. Then his face lit up as he recognized the little mutt. Although she was thin now, having long since dropped her puppies, he was sure she was the same.

As the little procession drew up to the pottery stall, Marcus squatted and called the dog to him. She turned at the sound of his voice and he put out his hand, hoping she would recognize the scent. The dog only looked at him. Marcus stood and took a step toward her. She tucked her tail and ran off into the crowded street.

The music had stopped, and a small voice cried out, "Why did you chase my dog away?"

Marcus looked at the child. He wanted to ask about the dog, but noticed all the small faces staring at him, and he couldn't speak.

Barabbas leaned forward. "Get out of here! The marketplace is no place for children!" he roared. "Go on!"

"We want to hear some more music," one boy whined.

With that, Barabbas started around a stack of pots toward the children. He was no longer playing the part of an aged merchant, but had risen to his full height. The children looked up at the big man towering over them. When he roared his disapproval again, they scattered. None looked back.

The big man turned to Justus. His eyes burned with rage. "You fool!" he shouted. Fearful that he had been overheard, he lowered his voice menacingly and spoke between clenched teeth, "You stupid, old fool! I told you to bring a donkey. A donkey! Is that a difficult assignment?" He turned, throwing his hands into the air. Glowering at Amalek, he pointed a finger. "You! You said this old idiot could follow orders!"

"I ask for a donkey, and what do I get? I get a donkey, a dozen children, a few old women, a dog, and a fat old fool with a lute, singing ditties to them all!"

He threw his hands up again, turning his face toward heaven. "My punishment," he muttered, as though sharing his displeasure with the Almighty. He sighed and dropped his hands in disgust.

Finally, he looked around at the silent group. "All right, let us get on with it," he said, waving to Barak. "There are leather hoods for the pots and strapping in that box. Cap those water pots and strap them to his animal." He turned to Maath. "You go on ahead with the youths," he commanded. "Barak and Amalek will accompany Justus. I will finish up here alone." No one uttered a sound. "We will meet in the camp of Ben-Elah by the last rays of the sun."

He bent to his task. Then his expression changed and he looked around at the somber group. "I am well pleased," he smiled.

CHAPTER VIII

Following the triumphant return of the thieves, Ben-Elah and Barabbas issued an order that all those involved in the latest foray were to remain close to the hideout. Marcus and Timaeus were especially vulnerable to arrest should Sosthenes ever lay eyes on them.

The balmy, carefree days gave Marcus and Priscilla the chance to deepen their growing relationship. First light often found them exploring the Judean countryside. Flowers that bloomed in riotous color became garlands for their hair. Birds sounded their mating songs and nested in the thick branches of the acacias and olive trees that covered the hillsides. Winding mountain paths invited long walks, and a few lush palms along the lower trails offered shade for picnics and conversation.

By night the young lovers returned to their separate lodgings, with another day of memories to store away and treasure as one would treasure precious jewels.

Priscilla spent the early evening hours tending to her grandfather's needs; then when work was done, she filled her thoughts with dreams of Marcus and their life ahead. A slight smile was always present on her soft lips.

Marcus, too, spent hours thinking of his only love. He would sit on the floor of the banquet hall in the mountain retreat and stare into space or walk the darkened pathway nearby, gazing at the stars.

Among the band of thieves, speculation arose as to the change in Marcus. When Justus learned of the blossoming love affair, he was delighted. "What every young man needs," he beamed. Amalek blistered the air with his curses condemning the "dreamy minds of stupid youth." Timaeus gibed his friend and tried to pry his thoughts from Priscilla. "She is not one of us," he warned solemnly. But Marcus was past heeding any of them.

On one tranquil evening, Marcus walked the pathway near the courtyard of the hideout. When Timaeus called to him, Marcus looked around and stared blankly. Rhoda stood at Timaeus' side, her face a portrait of concern. Marcus smiled slightly and blinked. As the smile faded, he pushed out his lower lip and began pulling at it. Feeling Marcus might want to be alone, Timaeus excused himself and Rhoda.

Marcus looked at his two close friends as they turned to go into the banquet hall where the others laughed and talked, ate and drank. "Wait!" he called, suddenly realizing his need for companionship. "Don't go." He motioned them toward some roughhewn logs which served as makeshift seats. The moon cast eerie shadows across the flat surface of the flagstone floor, and the reflections from the water in the pool shrouded the air with mystery. "Come," he urged, "we will sit and talk."

Timaeus and Rhoda exchanged puzzled looks, but

followed his lead. "I thought you wanted to be alone again and think," Timaeus said as they sat down.

Marcus smiled. "I have done all my thinking. Now it is time for action."

"Have you been at the wine again?" Timaeus laughed. "You have seen nothing but action since the day you joined this camp."

"It is true I have helped bring a few shekels to Ben-Elah's coffers," Marcus held a finger up in protest. "But no more."

Rhoda looked startled. "Marcus, you will not challenge Ben-Elah, will you?" she questioned. "Rumor has it that Barabbas will soon stand to be heard."

Marcus' smile broadened. "No," he laughed, "just the opposite."

Timaeus looked over his shoulder toward the rear entrance of the banquet room. "What have you planned?" he whispered. "If it is some stupid scheme to go out on your own or form another band . . ." his words trailed off as Marcus shook his head slowly.

Timaeus was becoming upset. "Well, what is going on? What *do* you want to talk about. Is it Priscilla?" He looked at Rhoda. "As though we haven't heard enough about her. For weeks now we have heard nothing but her name. Why not just marry her and get it over with!"

Marcus leaned close. "I have no proper job to enable me to take a wife," he confided.

Timaeus was still fuming. "Well, get one," he blurted. "Just go in there and tell Ben-Elah you want out and go . . . go make tents or something!"

Marcus smiled and stood to his feet. Timaeus looked up at him. "Where are you going?"

"To see Ben-Elah as you suggested."

Timaeus jerked Marcus back down. "What!" His mouth dropped open.

Marcus smiled. "It is just what I was considering anyway. You see, I have been praying to the God of our fathers—I told him . . ."

"Praying!" Timaeus interrupted.

Marcus ignored the outburst and continued. "I told him I wanted Priscilla, and if he was really a God who cares for his people, he would reveal to me what I should do next." He glanced at Rhoda. "He has done so."

The frown of concern distorting Timaeus' face added years to his countenance. Suddenly he felt old and weary. He looked at his woman. "He has been eating too many of those dates we acquired from the Arabian trader," he scoffed, rolling his eyes. "Tell me," Timaeus said. "Just how has the Lord appeared to you? In a dream? In a vision?" He chuckled. "Or perhaps in the flesh!"

Marcus' face grew solemn. "Timaeus," he said quietly, stretching out a hand and placing it on his friend's shoulder. "You alone have the power to wound me with your mocking words. As for the others," he waved toward the banquet room, "I can bear the scourging of their tongues by considering the source.

"Let me say this one thing more. I asked our God to give Priscilla to me. I asked for her total love. In return, I promised I would give up this life and work with my hands as other men. As you both know, he has filled her heart with love for me beyond my wildest dreams. I have been walking these hillsides in search of a way to be rid of this life—to begin anew." He paused and looked at Rhoda. Her eyes were moist.

"Tonight," he paused as Timaeus sought to interrupt. "You may not believe this," he added, "but please allow me to finish." Marcus cleared his throat. "Tonight I talked with our God and told him how difficult it would be to leave the band of Ben-Elah, to leave those who have been like family to me."

He stopped, looked down, and swallowed. His mouth felt dry, and he licked his lips. Timaeus and Rhoda waited silently. Marcus continued. "It . . . it was as though a voice exploded in my mind," he whispered, his speech betraying both excitement and apprehension. "I am sure it was the voice of God. I feel it was my answer!" He stopped a moment and gazed up into the starry sky. "I was not sure," he admitted to the heavens, then looked back at his two friends. "I was not really sure," he said again. "So I asked the Lord God to give me a sign, as Gideon of old. I made this pact: 'If Timaeus should speak the same command I have from within, then shall I know you have answered.'" A lone tear etched a tiny line down his cheek. "He has given Priscilla to me. Now I must follow through on my part of the bargain."

Timaeus laughed drily. Rhoda was visibly touched and wiped her eyes. Timaeus glanced at her, then at the brilliant canopy above. "You mean you actually believe the God of our fathers cares about a lowly, good-for-nothing thief?" He shook his head. "Marcus," he said, concerned for his only true friend. "If you want to go in there tonight and stand before Ben-Elah, then go." He stood. "According to you, the Lord God wants it this way!"

The young man walked to the far end of the court, deeply troubled. There seemed to be no way he could dissuade Marcus from action that would lead to certain death. He felt a quivering within his bowels and turned to look at Marcus through the gray haze of night. In desperation he shouted, his echo resounding in the trees of the hillsides, "You have heard the voice of death itself! If you insist on this insanity, you are walking into its very jaws!"

Rhoda jumped up quickly and moved to Timaeus' side. "Softly," she warned, leaning on his arm and placing a finger across his lips. "Do you want the others to hear?" She looked into his eyes, yet she spoke to Marcus. "My love means well," she pleaded. "He loves you as a brother, Marcus. Please realize he is only trying to spare you pain." She turned to look at Marcus. "Or even, as he says, *death.*"

Timaeus moved his mouth as if to speak, but no words would come. His insides heaved, and he wiped the moisture from his eyes. It was true. He loved Marcus as his own flesh.

"Go!" Timaeus insisted. "I see you are blind with love and this foolishness about God, so go quickly. I suppose if you were to live, you would only wander around after the Nazarene." He cursed loudly. "Go walk the last walk into death—I no longer know you." Then turning to face Marcus squarely, he grasped his hand and pulled him to his feet.

Marcus looked down at Rhoda's pained expression. He still held Timaeus' hand. Without a word, he gripped it in a farewell gesture, then turned to enter the mountain retreat.

The warmth of the banquet room was in sharp contrast to the cool breezes of the courtyard—a chill omen of the winter rains. The pungent odors of perfumes mingled with wine and roast lamb tingled in his nostrils. It seemed everyone had decided to remain inside. Not one of the members of the band was in Jerusalem. It was just his lot. All would be present to witness his humiliation when he confronted Ben-Elah.

Warmed by too much wine, the drunken thieves and their women reclined drowsily on pillows strewn haphazardly about the room. Occasionally, one of the revelers would snake his way to the table for another morsel, then crawl back to the comfort of the pillows.

At the head of the table sat Ben-Elah, his eyes glazed

with feasting. His head bent back, he was making futile attempts to pluck with his teeth the plump, ripe grapes Tamara held tantalizingly just beyond his reach.

"Marcus!"

At the sound of his name, Marcus jumped. He sighed with the realization that it was Justus who called. He looked at the fat old priest as he sat in his favorite place strumming his lute.

"Look at them," Justus sighed. "Ben-Elah and his noble band!"

Ben-Elah now lay back on several large pillows as Tamara playfully dropped the juicy grapes into his mouth, one by one.

Justus continued to play as he glanced about. "Ungodly lot," he observed. His voice carried with it no distaste, no contempt, and no hint of condonation or condemnation. He had merely stated the fact. With heavy, yet nimble fingers, he played a well-known tune. His soft eyes roamed the littered room as he spoke. "I see apprehension printed in large letters on your face, my son," he said, never looking in Marcus' direction. "What troubles you so?" He strummed more softly now, listening, although never appearing to hear.

Marcus studied the round profile. The double chin and pudgy cheeks made the old priest's eyes seem so small. Marcus sighed heavily. "I want to leave," he murmured. "I must get away from this life." His gesture swept the sad spectacle.

"Well, well," Justus said, strumming all the while. "Indeed, you have a legitimate reason for concern."

Across the room, Ben-Elah began to laugh. Tamara giggled. The big man's laughter grew louder, drawing the attention of all the others in the room. He reached up and pulled Tamara's robe. She laughed coyly and pushed his hand away.

By now the room was silent except for the boisterous couple at the table. Ben-Elah fell back, roaring with deep belly laughs. Pulling himself into a half-sitting position, he reached for the girl's clothing. A large finger caught in the seam near the neck. She laughed and struggled to free herself. Still laughing, she pushed at him solidly with both hands. In his drunken stupor, he toppled over, his full weight dragging at the fingertip hold he had on the garment. The gauzy fabric split to the waist, baring a breast. Enraged, she hastily pulled her robe together to cover herself. Ben-Elah howled with delight. Tamara pulled a sandal from her tiny foot and began flailing the great body. The leathery thong slapped against the big man's arms as he attempted to protect himself. He was weak with wine and laughter.

As the scuffle continued, Justus leaned over to Marcus. "The feline is furious, yet the great ox cares little. He feels only the mild prick of her claws. It is the wine that has made our leader carefree." He leaned even closer to Marcus. In a whisper he said, "Possibly tonight *is* your time." He winked.

Timaeus and Rhoda entered the room, drawn by the sound of Tamara's squeals and Ben-Elah's uproarious laughter. They stood and watched.

Now, however, Ben-Elah was sitting up. His expression had changed. Blood trickled from a small cut in his mouth. Tamara had aroused the hornet; she might still feel his sting.

Her eyes blazed, but as Ben-Elah stood to his feet, towering over her, she felt the first flicker of fear. He swayed drunkenly, attempting to focus bloodshot eyes on the small figure before him. He reached down and sank powerful fingers into her hair, slowly lifting her to her feet. She grabbed his large wrist to ease the pain. With his other hand, he got an iron grip on her throat.

There was no sound in the cavernous hall. Ben-Elah pulled her closer, aware that he was being observed. The silence of the room sobered him. He looked down into the beautiful young face and the petite figure that could be roused to fury. A slow grin spread across his mouth and with one quick jerk, he pulled her body up against his and bent down, kissing her full red lips. Nearly everyone stood and applauded, for all who knew Tamara loved her. Ben-Elah released the woman and turned to acknowledge the ovation with a bow.

Off to the side, Marcus sighed. The relief he felt was not only for the girl, but for the success of his own mission. He surveyed the room, searching out the reactions of the others. There was relieved laughter and spicy conversation. Amalek, however, was obviously upset with Ben-Elah's tolerant treatment of the young woman. Barak, too, wore a solemn expression.

Again Justus leaned close to his young friend. "Mark my words, there will come a day of uprising with those two in this camp," he predicted. "They are becoming too involved with Barabbas. He is looking for men like these to fill his own company. His lot is the worst. You would do well never to become involved with Barabbas again." Justus smiled. "I pray you will get out before the revolution of thieves begins." His fingers still danced across the strings of the lute. The melody was light and spritely, but his words were strangely out of tune.

Suddenly he stopped playing and touched Marcus' arm. "Look, he said. "Ben-Elah has sent the woman away—no doubt to change her robe. Now is your time, my son." There was an urgency in his voice.

Marcus looked at Ben-Elah as he assumed his place at the low table.

"Go!" Justus urged. "Do not hesitate. Do what you must."

With weakened legs, Marcus eased around to stand near Ben-Elah who looked up expectantly. "Marcus," he smiled, wiping the wine from his mouth. "Come sit with me." He reached over and shoved Vashni aside. "Remove your vile carcass," he boomed, sounding once more like the Ben-Elah everyone knew. "You have not brought so much as one shekel into this house in months. Make room for a thief-among-thieves." Vashni quickly moved to make room for the young Jew who sat hesitantly. "You have no wine," Ben-Elah said and filled a wooden cup to the brim.

Marcus swallowed hard and glanced over his shoulder at Justus. The priest continued playing, nodding for Marcus to get on with his business.

Ben-Elah lifted his cup. "A salute to you, Marcus," he said, looking deep into the young man's eyes. He put the cup to his lips and gulped half of it. Replacing the cup on the table, he wiped his mouth with the back of his hand.

"Although I feel the touch of the grape," he said, "I am not so drunk that I cannot detect your uneasiness." He took another swallow of the rich red juice, staring full into Marcus' face.

"Speak," Ben-Elah commanded. "What is it you have to say? Or perhaps you wish to ask a favor of Ben-Elah." He waved the cup. "Tonight the wine is good and I am in excellent spirits. Ask whatever you will, and it shall be yours," he declared.

Marcus cleared his throat and spoke hastily before his courage failed. "I wish to leave," he said weakly. "There is a girl. I must find work worthy of her trust."

Ben-Elah leaned forward, frowning. "My ears deceive me," he said incredulously.

Vashni patted Marcus on the head. "So this is the honored guest!" he mocked.

With one quick move, Ben-Elah reached past Marcus and grabbed Vashni's shoulder. His powerful fingers dug into his collar bone, causing the smaller man to writhe in pain. "You worm," Ben-Elah spat. "If you were half the man this one is, you could be proud. Now leave our presence before I feed you to the birds." He released the man violently. "If you breathe one word of this conversation to anyone . . ." He swiped his index finger across his neck ominously. "Now out of my sight," Ben-Elah snarled. Vashni scrambled away.

Marcus peered into his wine cup, embarrassed. "It was not my intent to cause division," he explained. "The girl I have chosen is far above my station, but for reasons I cannot understand, she has come to love me. I want to share my life with her. That is," he fingered his cup nervously, "I must seek a new way of life before I ask her to be my wife." He searched Ben-Elah's face, expecting the worst.

The big man's countenance was expressionless. The sounds of merrymaking offered strange accompaniment for the decision that would seal Marcus' fate. Ben-Elah's eyes were fixed as he thought. He tilted his wine cup. "Empty," he said. "As empty as life itself."

He looked at Marcus. "But you are young. There is still time for you." A pensive smile played on his lips. "At sunrise I shall kill you," he said quietly. "Until then, you are free to go." With that, he reached out the hand that had dealt the death blow to many and grasped Marcus' wrist in a final farewell.

CHAPTER IX

The brawny man, stripped to the waist, reached into a bed of burning coals, fired to a white heat. Removing the hot metal ring, he dipped it quickly into a large kettle. The water sputtered in protest, fighting to escape the dull, red glow of the ring and the tips of the tongs that held it. Wisps of steam vanished into the air as the metal cooled.

Working with speed and dexterity, Obeha withdrew the ring and hammered the remaining gap to a tight fit, joining the reins and cheekstraps of the bridle. He stepped back to appraise his workmanship, then nodded in approval. Gathering up the strands of leather and metal, he wound it into a neat bundle and turned to his apprentice.

The young Jew had paused in the repair of a broken harness, laying aside hammer and studs, to observe the skill with which his master forged the metal bit. His own biceps bulged with new tissue, still tender from unaccustomed use.

In the few weeks of his apprenticeship, Marcus had learned much about his new trade, but more about his master. Obeha, he had found, was a hard worker and a man of incredible strength, yet patient and kind in his instruction. Among the decent folk in and around Jerusalem, he was well respected. Many turned out of their way to walk past the entrance to the open shop in order to call or wave a greeting. In turn, Obeha always flashed a broad smile and shouted back. It was a rare Jew who stood in favor with the Roman officials as well, but all who knew Obeha liked him.

"Marcus," he interrupted the young Jew's thoughts, "I shall be making a delivery." He waved the package. "It will take only a short time. Do you think it possible to complete that harness while I am gone, or will I return to find you gazing into the loft?"

Marcus felt a flush of embarrassment. "I—I have only been admiring your way with the hammer and anvil," he stuttered. "I shall continue my work." He grabbed a small hammer and a handful of studs. It would not do for the man to take him for a dreamer.

Obeha broke into good-natured laughter at the look of humiliation on the young man's face. "You will do well, my boy," he waved a hand to dismiss the matter. "Just try to have the harness of Demetrius repaired by sundown!" He left, still chuckling.

Marcus shook his head. His master was so amiable that it sometimes amazed him. There was one thing which bothered Marcus though. Obeha was a follower of the Nazarene. Lately, Jesus had become the focal point of considerable dissension among the Pharisees. Marcus feared for Obeha and others who might be innocently involved in the controversy. The man from Nazareth seemed destined for trouble.

He sighed and continued his work. Placing the studs

on the leather strips, Marcus laid them on the anvil; then with a quick, chopping blow of his hammer, he set the metal firmly.

Thus busily engaged, he failed to notice the slender figure sidling up to the wide mouth of the shop. Unobserved, the youth stood there for several minutes and watched Marcus.

Pitching his voice low, he called, "I should like to purchase a harness, lad."

Marcus did not look up as he replied, "My master is not here at the moment." He struck another stud. "He should be back shortly."

"I expect service now—not shortly!" the customer shouted indignantly. Marcus looked up, momentarily stunned. It was Timaeus! A smile streaked across Marcus' face, revealing two rows of even, white teeth. He dropped his hammer and rushed to the doorway, flinging his arms around his friend's neck. Marcus' fullblown laughter drowned out that of Timaeus.

"Let me look at you, my friend," Marcus said, stepping back. "Except for that sparse population of hair attempting to forage a living on your chin," he reached out and pulled the thin whiskers, "you have not changed." He shook his head and smiled. "How long has it been now? Four, or is it five weeks?"

"Five weeks and one day," Timaeus grinned. "Rhoda has been keeping track for me." He tried to appear nonchalant. "She has been worried about you." He began to look around the shop, fingering several items. He strolled as he talked.

"So this is what you have come to." He picked up some finished work. "Very nice." With a glance at Marcus, he continued to amble. "You have changed, you know." He had measured the breadth of sinew that rippled rhythmically across Marcus' back and shoulders as he bent to strike the anvil. "You are . . ." he hesitated, searching for the right word. "You are filling out," he finished lamely.

"But there is something more. I read a new content-ment in your eyes." Timaeus frowned. "You have said little, but your bearing speaks for you. This life agrees with you," he admitted grudgingly.

Shaking off the note of seriousness, he poked a finger into Marcus' belly. "I can see you are also eating regular-ly," he laughed.

"Timaeus," Marcus said, his voice low. "You have changed also. There is a difference in your voice. You . . ."

"It was your leaving," Timaeus interrupted. "Your courage, the desire to live a normal life. I guess I was forced to reflect on my own useless existence.

"Rhoda deserves a *real* man who can give her security and protection. In that band of cutthroats, there is no guarantee that when she lies down at night she will live to see the dawn of another day," Timaeus sighed. Mar-cus sensed his hopelessness. "Are you trying to tell me something?"

Timaeus swallowed and drew a deep breath before he continued. "Last night I wanted out so badly." He sat down on a bench, his body limp. His arms hung between his knees. The palms of his hands were wet. "Ben-Elah was drunk with wine, as usual." He glanced up at Marcus' concerned face. "You knew about Barab-bas joining our band under the guise of being 'just another member'." He shook his head. "None of us were deceived. Barabbas would never rest until he had seized control. It was only a matter of time.

"Well," he continued, "last night Barabbas took ad-vantage of Ben-Elah's drunken state to challenge him. Rhoda and I were outside and didn't see all of it. By the time we were aware of the trouble, Ben-Elah had broken Maath's neck and Barabbas had run Ben-Elah through with his blade. Both men were dead. Barabbas defied any of us to avenge Ben-Elah's death."

"Barabbas has taken over the band?" Marcus asked in disbelief.

Timaeus stared into space. Then, without answering, he stood and moved deliberately across the stable-like shop. He stopped and fingered a finished bridle. His eyes narrowed and he turned to face Marcus. "I cannot leave now. Barabbas would kill me first." He listened to his own words. They seemed flat and lifeless. He raised his voice and pointed an accusing finger. Driven by fear and hopelessness, he sneered, "You were lucky! You got away when it was easy! Even you could not face Barabbas as you did Ben-Elah!"

Marcus' words were soothing. "I believe God was with me then, and I believe he will be with you now." He stepped to Timaeus' side. "Take my hand, my friend," he said. "We shall make a pact."

Timaeus looked suspicious, but tightened his grip on Marcus' roughened hand. "What kind of pact?"

Marcus placed his other hand over that of Timaeus and looked directly into his eyes. "I vow," he declared, "before the Lord God, to help you find a way to leave the band and begin a new life."

No sooner had Marcus completed the pledge than the solemn moment was violated by an outburst of profane laughter. "Ho, ho! It is better not to vow at all than to vow in the hallowed name of the Lord and break it," Justus roared. The priest pushed his way into the shop.

Marcus grinned. "This is one promise I plan to keep," he affirmed, quickly moving to greet his old friend.

"My boy," Justus smiled. He grabbed Marcus' hand and shook it vigorously, standing back to admire the young man's stalwart body. "Upon my oath, You are maturing," he laughed. Moments passed as the trio reviewed past escapades. Beneath the light banter lay a deep bond of affection and loyalty peculiar to men who have faced death together.

During a pause in the conversation, Justus nodded toward Timaeus, encompassing the shop in a sweep of his hand. "Marcus," he said gently, "your friend is not suited to this life. This is what love has done to you, my boy. But Timaeus has tasted of love within our lifestyle. You are expecting too much of him."

Rising, he began to stroll about the shop, measuring his words carefully before he spoke. "You have vowed to free him. Would you wish to forge the bars for another kind of prison?" He moved slowly around the shop, stopping occasionally to study a piece or two. "Your master does fine work. I have seen your woman and know of her grandfather. With her by your side, your future is assured."

The old priest turned to look directly at Marcus. "You have a rich life ahead," he said. He lowered his voice. "Are you willing to risk losing it to fulfill this impulsive vow—to fight to the death for your friend when perhaps it will not answer his heart's desire?

"This young man is *my* concern," he said, slipping an arm across the boy's shoulders. In a voice husky with emotion, he declared, "Leave Timaeus to me. I will help him. But you must keep away from us, Marcus. There is danger." Justus turned Timaeus toward the street, and the two moved quickly out of the shop.

"Please stay!" Marcus called, but the pair were swallowed up by the jostling crowd returning to their homes at the setting of the sun. Marcus stared after them, saddened at the thought that he might never again see his friends. As he turned to his work, he prayed silently that the Lord would find a way to deliver them from the evil influences which surrounded them.

With a well-directed blow of his hammer, another stud was set.

CHAPTER X

Early morning brought Marcus to Priscilla's dwelling just outside Jerusalem. The old physician opened the gate. "Marcus, my boy. Come in, come in!" His affection for the young man was undisguised.

Marcus passed through the courtyard into an airy room that spoke eloquently of Priscilla's touch. He sensed her presence even before she appeared in the doorway. He breathed in the sweet scent of her perfume and felt his pulse quicken.

Priscilla paused at the entrance to the room and her dark eyes misted as she watched the two who sat chatting companionably—the frail, old man and the sturdy, young one. Marcus. Their love was still so new, so wondrous. Yet it had deepened steadily into a relationship undisturbed by time or distance.

Marcus jumped up at the sight of her and his breath caught in his throat. She was so lovely! Always when he saw her, his delight was edged with apprehension. What they shared was not a fragile emotion. Yet they lived in uncertain times, aware that they could be cruelly separated at the whim of the Roman dictator. It was at such moments that they wept together and vowed that only death would part them. He recalled Priscilla's whispered words as he wiped her tears, "It is all right, Marcus. I feel a power of love which knows no bounds. My love for you is so strong, so sure that I am compelled to love all of mankind—yes, even those who would try to destroy us." Her goodness always humbled him and left him at a loss for words—as he was now!

Oshea interrupted their reverie. "Will the two of you stand there dreaming the day away?" he teased.

"If you are ready then," Marcus said to Priscilla, his face flushing a deep crimson, "we will be on our way to Bethany."

The doctor stepped over and took Priscilla's face in his hands. Their eyes met, and everything was communicated there. He brushed her forehead with his lips and sent the couple on their way.

Down in the streets of Jerusalem, the shops had opened. The babble of vendors hawking their wares and the noisy interchange of bargaining signaled the beginning of another day. The couple moved along slowly, oblivious to the shops, the street vendors, and the gathering crowds. They sidestepped children playing rough and tumble games along the walkways, beggars crying "Alms!", and animals lazing in the warm sun.

Marcus and Priscilla approached the main street which would take them to the gate leading out to Bethany, but instead of turning toward the gate, Priscilla pulled Marcus in the opposite direction. "What are you doing?" he asked. "Bethany is that way!" He waved toward the gate.

"Please, Marcus." She looked up into his face, her lovely, dark eyes pleading. "I want to go to the Temple first."

"Why must you go now?" As the surety of the answer dawned, he muttered, "It must be the Nazarene again."

He started to protest further, but she touched his taut lips with a soft index finger, stopping him cold. "Please?" she cooed. This time her lower lip protruded slightly in a charming pout. Marcus sighed deeply, disgusted with the weakness to which he was reduced by one delightful female.

As they walked toward the Temple, he looked straight ahead, walking a little more briskly than before. "The Nazarene," he mumbled. "You and my mother," he snorted contemptuously. "What power has this man over the two of you? And not just you women. It seems all of Jerusalem has lost its senses. Even Obeha closed the shop today to go and hear him!" Marcus shook his head. "I cannot understand any of you. Are you bewitched? Why this man blesses the Roman dogs along with the Israelites.

"I understand he was a carpenter before he began teaching and preaching. What is that? He is no different from me. At least I have finished the first phase of my apprenticeship and Obeha has increased my pay so that we should be able to marry soon."

His mind raced ahead; thus, he was completely unprepared for Priscilla's impulsive embrace. He stumbled, but regained his balance quickly, her arms still tightly wound about his neck.

"I love you!" she squealed. "Oh, Marcus, I love you!"

Such conduct by a woman in the streets of Jerusalem was unheard of. Marcus stopped in utter astonishment. His face flushed, and he gasped in disbelief. She was still holding on. Passersby frowned their disapproval.

"Stop!" Marcus objected through clenched teeth and tried to pry her loose. "Priscilla," he reproved her, "people are beginning to stare at us."

She released him reluctantly. Under the pretense of straightening the sash around his waist, Marcus kept his gaze low. Then slowly he turned to walk from the spot. Priscilla caught his hand, but he eased it away. She walked silently behind him. Marcus looked straight ahead, but spoke from the side of his mouth. "What in the world made you do that?" he demanded.

Priscilla moved up to walk beside him. "I-I," she cleared her throat. "I thought I heard you say we would *marry soon.*" She stopped and pulled him to a halt. He flinched. Looking up into his eyes, she whispered, "Forgive me for making a scene. But I love you, Marcus." She dropped her eyes submissively. "You do not understand my feeling of freedom, I know. But in Rome, women have rights too. I will try very hard to be an obedient wife, but it is so difficult when I feel as if I shall burst from loving you!"

Tenderly, Marcus took her face in his two hands and eased her chin up until their eyes met. "My love," he said, disregarding the stares of a few curious onlookers, "I want you just as you are." He shook his head. "Do not ever change." He slipped an arm around her, and they turned toward the Temple.

Small crowds milled around the gate of the Temple, while inside, Jesus sat and taught the people. "You hypocrites!" Jesus reprimanded. "Who are you trying to deceive with your trick questions? Give me a coin." Someone handed him a penny. "Whose picture is struck on this penny?" he asked the hecklers, holding the coin up for their inspection. "And whose name is imprinted there also?"

"Why Caesar's, of course," one of the Pharisees called out.

"Well, then," the teacher said, "give to Caesar those things which are his, and give to God that which belongs to him."

With that, the most vocal of his adversaries left the court.

At the same time, Marcus and Priscilla entered the Gate Beautiful. They stood on the portico and listened. If they entered the Temple court, Priscilla would be required to separate herself to the women's section. They elected to stay together and strain to hear the teachings. Marcus stood tall to look at the crowd. Priscilla glanced up at him, admiring his manly height and broad shoulders. *It was true,* she thought, *he has grown strong and fit in the shop of Obeha.* But it delighted her more that Marcus had revealed a new depth—a sensitivity to new ideas. Perhaps . . .

"Obeha is right in the middle of the action," Marcus observed. He craned his neck to see more.

"Can you see the Saviour?" she asked. She watched to see Marcus' reaction to her question, but his head was turned and there was no answer. Suddenly his shoulders sagged. "What is wrong?" Priscilla's voice was shrill with alarm. "What did you see?" She reached up and drew his gaze to her. Her dark eyes searched his. "Marcus?"

Marcus shook the frown from his face and smiled weakly. "Nothing at all," he whispered, then turned and stretched up over the crowd once more. This time he ducked his head and took Priscilla's hand. "Come," he urged, pulling the young woman along behind him. They headed toward the stairs. The crowd around the Temple had increased by now. Weaving and twisting, Marcus led Priscilla through the maze of worshippers, bumping into some in their haste.

A voice roared like thunder over the hum of the people. "Stop him! Stop that thief!" The thunder grew louder. "You!" the man shouted. "Stop that couple!"

Just then a hand belonging to someone in the crowd jerked Marcus to a halt. "What is this?" Marcus demanded in his most resolute manner.

"Sosthenes wants you."

Marcus, with Priscilla clinging to his arm, looked up to see the big man bulling his way though the crowd. He brushed against an old woman, knocking over her grain basket. She cursed his father loudly, but he pushed by her, bent on reaching Marcus before the young Jew could run.

Marcus' eyes darted from side to side. His mind whirled. He glanced at Priscilla and cursed himself for the fear and confusion written across her face. He realized now he should have fled the moment Sosthenes spotted him on the portico.

He struggled with the iron grip on his arm. "Let go," he demanded. The grip tightened. *The truth*, he thought. *I'll tell the truth. I'll be forgiven.* He looked at Priscilla, then glanced at the irate man looming nearer. He swallowed. *There will be no forgiveness*, he thought.

At that moment he felt the jerk of powerful hands on his shoulders, and his entire body was shaken until his teeth rattled.

"This young man is a thief!" Sosthenes screamed. "He is one of those who stole the money I brought to the Temple!" Priscilla watched in horror. Sosthenes spat in Marcus' face. "Thief!" He proceeded to shake him again. "Thief!"

Priscilla grabbed at the big man, pummeling him with her fists. "No!" she screamed. "No!"

Sosthenes held on. He looked at the gathering crowd. "I tell you," he shouted, "the boy is a thief and should be stoned!" Each word was punctuated with a powerful yank, his fingers biting deep into Marcus' arms.

"No!" Priscilla cried. "Won't someone help?" Tears streamed down her cheeks.

"Let go of the boy!" It was the commanding voice of a Roman. Marcus recognized the captain, but couldn't recall where he had last seen him.

Protesting loudly, Sosthenes released the young Jew.

"Silence!" the captain demanded.

Priscilla sobbed deeply as she reached out to hold tight to Marcus' arm. She buried her face in his chest.

Four more soldiers appeared, and the captain dismissed the crowd. He ordered the arrest of Marcus, and told Sosthenes he would have to make a formal accusation. Priscilla clung to Marcus, begging to be allowed to accompany him, but the captain refused her plea.

"Marcus," she called as they took him away. "I will get help." With tears streaming down her face, she turned toward the Temple, stopped, then reversed her path. Her thoughts collided in confusion. With only a skeletal sketch of Marcus' past, she was unsure where to turn. Her sandals clicked as she hurried toward home and the wisdom of her grandfather.

In Bethany, Phoebe had risen early to fetch water for the day's work. It was only when she lifted heavy objects that she felt the twinge of pain in her chest. If she rested a bit, it usually went away and she could breathe more easily. These spells had bothered her since the night when she had left Marcus and his lovely girl to return to Bethany—the night of the attack. A lone woman at dusk was easy prey for the thieves who lived in the hills and waited in ambush for just such an opportunity. The heavy pouch that Marcus had given her was taken and she had been severely beaten and left for dead. Merab had found her or likely she would have perished there. Of course, Phoebe had sworn her to secrecy. Marcus must never know lest he be concerned for her safety.

She would certainly not be so foolish again. It was just that in her joy at seeing him, the time had stolen away . . .

Merab was waiting for her at the well. The two friends talked of all the Messiah had said and done recently. The change in Merab was noticeable. She spoke only kind words. Even when a smelly old goat herder pushed his way through the cluster of women gathered at the well, Merab merely smiled and offered to dip the cool water for him.

When the other women left, Phoebe and Merab stood a while longer, talking of Marcus and Priscilla. "They will be here today!" Phoebe cried excitedly. Merab hoped Marcus would meet Jesus face to face someday. Phoebe blinked the mist from her eyes as she contemplated the joy of that day. "O Lord," she prayed silently. "May Marcus soon know the truth. He is confused and needs the wisdom that only you can give . . ."

Meanwhile, in Jerusalem, Marcus was brought before the council where Sosthenes made his complaint. The big man looked around the room, "I know most of you, and you know me. I am an honest man. You know how I've upheld the word of Caesar, knowing it is *the* law. I have stolen from no man and lied to none."

"We know you, Sosthenes," one said. "The time is late. Get on with your accusation."

"This boy is a thief!"

"From whom has he taken?"

"He and another youth stole two bags of coin, both gold and silver . . ." he straightened indignantly, "from me!"

The room hummed with murmuring that threatened to erupt into loud comments.

"Quiet!" the court judge ordered. "Guard!" he called.

A soldier stepped forward. "Arrest the first man who speaks without leave." He glared around the room. "Continue," he ordered.

Sosthenes felt confident. He adjusted his robes and lifted his chin arrogantly. As he began to speak, he paced impatiently. "This young snip stood in the Temple with the other, waiting a chance to take my coin." He stopped pacing and leered at Marcus. "Each bag contained the worth of ten thousand denari. Ten thousand denari!" he shouted to the crowd. "This boy," he pointed a rugged finger in Marcus' face, "and another took the bags I had brought for the Temple treasury! They took my offering!" In a fit of rage, Sosthenes grabbed Marcus' throat and raised him to his tiptoes.

From the back of the room a deep voice cracked like the leather whips he fashioned. "Sosthenes!" Obeha ordered. "Release the boy!"

Everyone looked up to see the big smith push past the crowd gathered near the entrance of the court.

"Guards!" the judge shouted. Immediately two soldiers moved in to take the intruder. "Bring him here!"

Marcus, eyes wide, sighed with relief as Sosthenes released his hold. He watched as they brought Obeha forward. The man looked even bigger within the confines of the courtroom. The robe he had hastily donned before leaving the shop was stained with perspiration and his brow was beaded with the droplets.

"Obeha," the judge acknowledged, "what have you to do with this lad?" Before Obeha could answer, the administrator spoke again. "Can't you Jews take care of your own troubles? That teacher of yours . . . what is his name?" he searched the faces of those sitting on the bench.

"Jesus," someone offered.

"Humph," the judge snorted. "Yes, yes, this Jesus. Does he not teach you to work out your own differences?" He looked around the court. "And, Obeha, I would have thought better of you. What have you to do with all this?"

"I have come as a defense for the boy."

"Speak then," the judge nodded, leaning back in his chair.

Sosthenes objected. "What could this man have to say in defense of a common thief?" he bellowed.

"Bring him to silence, your honor," Obeha said.

The judge only leaned back smiling. He was inclined to let the Jews tear at one another. It could only strengthen his case against the whole lot of them.

Obeha stepped over to Marcus and slipped an arm around his shoulders. "This young man is a trusted employee in my shop," he stated.

"Consorting with known thieves," Sosthenes scoffed.

Obeha looked around the room. His eyes moved from face to face. "Can anyone corroborate this man's story? Is there not one who saw this lad make off with such a large sum?" The crowd hummed again, but the judge kept smiling and let it pass. "Was everyone blind today?"

"Not today," Sosthenes protested. "The boy and his cohort were in the Temple some months back. They made off with two sacks of money I planned to give to the Temple treasury."

"So," Obeha interrupted, "you planned it for the Temple treasury." He smiled at Marcus confidently. "And after some youths snatched the money . . ." he paused, scratching his head and pursing his lips. He eyed the huge man, looking him up and down. "By the way, Sosthenes, just how did such frail youths take money from you?" The crowd snickered. Sosthenes glanced around. "No need to answer," Obeha said, holding up a hand. His voice was clear and distinct. "Did you return again to the Temple with a replacement offering?"

Sosthenes frowned. "Of course not!" he sputtered. "Do you think I am so rich? I give what I am able, but surely you could not expect . . ."

Obeha signaled silence once more. "So you *did not* replace the Temple offering," Obeha repeated. "You, then, lost nothing, as you were depositing the money in the treasury anyway." Sosthenes was about to protest further when Obeha added, "Are we not taught that God knows our hearts? You have lost naught, for God has seen your heart and will reward you accordingly. If your thoughts were pure, he will accept the intent, if not the gift."

Obeha turned to face the judge who was moved by the able argument of this ignorant Jew. "Sir," he said, "it is clearly the Temple's loss. Now if we can find two who can witness against this lad, I shall gladly cast the first stone." The people murmured. Obeha raised his hand, "Ah, I see one of our respected leaders among you—Rosh, a Temple priest. If he states that this boy has committed this profane act, then I shall cry, 'Stone him' along with the rest of you."

At a command from the judge, the priest approached the bench. Marcus watched anxiously.

The judge leaned forward, his smile gone for the moment. "Rosh, is it?" The priest nodded. "See if you can identify the boy as a thief." The judge waved a hand in Marcus' direction.

Rosh stepped over to make the identification. As he looked into Marcus' eyes, the young Jew felt his heart sink. He saw only blind hatred cloaked in religious garb and wondered if Rosh would take his vengeance. Marcus knew the ungodly priest used the band of thieves more now that Barabbas had proclaimed himself its leader. He dampened his lips with the tip of his tongue and swallowed. The two stood inches apart. Rosh's eyes narrowed, and he turned to face the judge. "I have not so much as seen the lad before," he lied.

With that pronouncement, shouts of approval filled the room. Sosthenes cursed loudly and hurriedly made his exit. Obeha grabbed the young man at the waist and lifted him high victoriously. With his massive arm resting across the boy's shoulder, Obeha and Marcus left the Hall of Justice.

Out on the steps, Priscilla caught a glimpse of the two men. She turned and whispered to her grandfather standing next to her. He smiled. "Go ahead, child," he urged. "I'll wait here." Priscilla kissed the old man and started up the long steps.

Walking behind one of the large pillars, Priscilla was hidden from Marcus' view. When she reached his side, they embraced with muffled cries. "Oh, Marcus, Marcus," Priscilla sighed. She leaned back, savoring the sight of him. "I was so afraid." She turned a grateful look toward Obeha. "Grandfather said Obeha would know what to do." She reached out to touch his hand. "How can we thank you?"

"Yes, what can I say?" Marcus mumbled.

In this moment of triumph, surrounded by friends and the woman he loved, his dark past hovered like a great, black specter. Marcus looked beyond Priscilla and Obeha to the old physician waiting patiently at the bottom of the steps, his trusting face upturned. *Whatever the outcome, it was the time for truth.*

"Come, let us join your grandfather, Priscilla," he said. "I must speak with you all before we go to my mother's home."

His tone was solemn. They followed him down the steps in silence.

CHAPTER XI

"What are we waiting for?" Amalek growled.

From the upstairs window, Barak could observe the people milling in the street below. The burly man pulled at his beard. Without a pause in his vigilant scrutiny of the Jerusalem thoroughfare, he mumbled a short reply, "Barabbas and Rosh."

"Bah!" Amalek snorted. "Barabbas! Barabbas! That's all I ever hear anymore!" He slammed his fist on the table where he was seated and leaped to his feet. "Look!" he yelled, his eyes scanning the others in the room. "We don't need this son of a sow's belly to lead us! Before *he* came, *I* was to succeed Ben-Elah." He waved a hand. "Garth, you old wretch, are you with me? And you, Phinehas?" He addressed the turncoat, "I know how you felt about Ben-Elah. You were in our camp more often than you were in your own. Will you allow the dog who put a knife in our master's ribs to lead you?" His voice trembled with rage. Phinehas was stone-faced. It was true he had no love for Barabbas.

Timaeus was sitting on the floor in the corner. Amalek only glared at the young thief with scorn. He breathed deeply, then looked at Barak, who kept watch at the window.

"The day is coming to a close and I smell rain," Barak announced, not turning from his post. "They should be here at any moment."

Amalek could contain himself no longer. He rushed to Barak's side, pulling wildly at his clothing. "Listen to me!" he shouted. "We must unite!" With mounting excitement, he began to jerk harder as he spoke. Barak attempted to turn back to the window, but Amalek held his grip.

"Pig!" he screamed, spitting at Barak's feet. "Don't you understand? Are you so stupid?" Barak looked into Amalek's eyes, contempt veiling his face. Amalek continued. "Follow me and we will build an army! We could overthrow Barabbas *and* the Roman dogs!" A white line of froth formed at the corners of his mouth. Amalek's curses grew louder and his agitation produced labored wheezing. "Barak!" he gasped. "We have been together a long time. We can take over if we kill Barabbas tonight!" His voice was hoarse and graveled. Nearly drained of strength from his outburst, he repeated, "I tell you, we *must* kill Barabbas." His words trailed off as he watched the expression on Barak's face change. Slowly Amalek turned.

The heavy wooden door to the upper room slammed shut. Silence hovered like death. The day was well spent, and the evening shadows cast eerie configurations. The two men, robed in hooded black garments, appeared as two spiders crouched at web's edge.

Amalek seemed frozen, still holding stupidly to Barak's robe. His eyes were wide and his mouth partly open. It was the first time Timaeus had ever seen stark fear written on the big Jew's face. Amalek swallowed hard and released his hold on Barak.

Slowly he stood erect, turning to face Barabbas and Rosh. "We were waiting for you," he said, in a futile attempt to mask his horror.

Barabbas stepped toward the center of the room.

Rain dropped lightly outside, and the darkness of the evening closed in. Phinehas lit the candle on the table. Its flickering light sent shadows dancing wildly around the walls. Amalek stepped forward to meet Barabbas, smiling faintly. With a practiced move, he drew a blade from the folds of his robe. He took another step, a knife concealed in the sweaty palm of his hand. His breathing was light and shallow. The knowledge of sure death if he failed in his objective slowed his pace. One last step. Barabbas was now within range.

The glint of forged steel flashed as Amalek thrust hard. Barabbas moved, then groaned in pain. Seizing the opportunity, Barak leaped to the center of the room. His knife, too, sliced the damp air, coming down forcibly into muscled flesh. The blow was right on target. Barabbas moaned once more, then slumped into a chair. Amalek dropped to the floor, the handle of Barak's blade protruding from his back.

Their violent struggle drove the candle's tiny flame to dance a bizarre performance on its pool of melted wax. On the walls the shadows jumped to the same tempo. The odor of blood and sweat filled the narrow room. Outside, the rain fell steadily and the air grew heavy with the dampness.

Timaeus, still squatting in a far corner, watched fearfully as Phinehas moved around the table to tend Barabbas. He pulled aside the big man's robe, baring the upper half of his body. The massive torso was covered with tangled hair. Blood ran freely from a wound in the left side of his chest.

"Looks deep," Phinehas said.

Barabbas looked at Amalek, lying on the floor. The unseeing eyes were open wide, fixed forever in a death mask of hopelessness and hatred. "Scum," Barabbas snarled. He glanced at Barak. Their eyes met in silent celebration.

"Aaagh!" Barabbas writhed suddenly in pain. He cursed loudly, then leaned forward. "Do what you must, but finish it quickly!"

"The wound must be cleansed," Phinehas said, as he continued wiping the torn flesh with a piece of his clothing.

No one noticed as Timaeus rose slowly and moved around behind Rosh. All eyes were riveted on their leader and his wound. Catching a glimpse of Amalek's knife lying near his body, Timaeus scooped it up, stuffing it into his sleeve, handle first. He secured the point of the blade under his leather wristband, then folded his arms across his chest and watched the others.

The rain was slackening now, but deep darkness had cast her blanket over all Jerusalem. Down in the streets, a few Roman foot soldiers walked through the city. The gates had been closed and guards posted. All was calm.

Upstairs, in the room overlooking the city, Barabbas' voice split the placid night. "Garth!" he shouted. "You alone loved him." Barabbas waved a hand at the lifeless form. "Take him to a decent place and leave him." He flinched as Phinehas bound the wound. Then, with another motion of his large hand, he commanded Timaeus, "Go with Garth into the streets to guarantee his safety."

Startled, Timaeus responded, "Y-Yes, my lord."

Barabbas looked the younger man in the eye. "And before you go, bring the knife to me," he said, his tone low and deliberate.

Timaeus frowned. "My lord?"

"The knife!" Barabbas demanded. His voice rose sharply. "Bring me the knife you took from Amalek."

Timaeus swallowed hard, looking around at the others. Slowly he withdrew the knife from his sleeve. Its long, slender blade gleamed in the light of the flickering candle. Timaeus swallowed again, then eased around the silent body toward the big man. He forced himself to look directly into the stony face. Barabbas looked stern and hard. There was no compassion.

A large scar was clearly visible beneath the dark hair of his chest. It ran from his collar bone across the right breast and made a jagged hook before disappearing under his arm. Timaeus couldn't keep his eyes from it as he handed the knife to Barabbas.

"Are you admiring my scar?" Barabbas asked, looking down at his disfigured chest. "Ha! It is a badge of honor," he laughed. "Just wait, boy! Wait until you have been at it as long as I, and you shall have a few of your own." With that, Barabbas shifted stiffly in his chair to give Timaeus a full view of his back. "The cat has licked my back more than once," he chuckled. Timaeus winced at the sight. The broad shoulders and back were laced with scar tissue, criss-crossing from one side to the other. The entire area bore jagged marks and misshapen lumps of flesh that had struggled to cover gaping wounds after many a fracas.

Barabbas turned, smiling at the stricken look on the young face. "You should be prepared to take as many licks from the biting tongue of the cat-of-nine-tails when I am finished with you. You shall be my prize creation. I shall forge in you a mind and body of steel which will stand you in good stead for just such times as these." He smiled and squeezed Timaeus' shoulder. "Go with Garth. You must be his eyes and ears, so watch carefully and listen well."

As Timaeus turned toward the door, Garth cursed under his breath. "I am no feeble old woman. I can do without this young calf," he muttered.

Barabbas pushed Phinehas aside and stood to his feet. Even in his weakened condition, the man towered several inches above Garth and he drew close to make the most of the contrast. "Did I decree it?" he asked, his voice low and foreboding. Garth nodded dumbly. Barabbas smiled. "Then so be it," he said and sank back in his chair.

Immediately, Garth motioned for Timaeus. The young Jew helped lift the limp body to the other's shoulders. Then, opening the wooden door, he stood back to allow Garth to carry Amalek's body through the small opening. He slipped out behind him and closed the door.

The night air was heavy with moisture, and the fragrance of rain lingered. A distant clatter of horses' hooves sounded on the street below. The two looked down the stairway leading into the darkness.

"Let's go," Garth said, motioning Timaeus to take the lead.

Back in the upper room, Barabbas turned to Rosh. The priest stood well back in the shadowy corner nearest the door. "Come, my friend," Barabbas beckoned. "Sit with us." He turned to Barak. "We have work to do."

Rosh moved slowly and deliberately. He remained standing until everyone else was seated. When all eyes were focused on him, he sat. From within his coat, tucked in a band of linen encircling his waist, he withdrew a papyrus document bearing the seal of Tiberias himself.

Rosh made no attempt to conceal his contempt for

the group gathered about the table. "Before I begin," he said with an air of superiority, "you must know that this meeting shall finish our business."

He looked straight into Barabbas' eyes. "You have bargained for silver and gold, while I have bargained for something of much greater significance. I have fulfilled my obligation to you. The information I have given has brought you the wealth you seek. On the other hand, you have not delivered the man into my hands as you promised." He leaned forward, his features contorting in fury. "This time," he snarled, slamming his fist on the table, "I want him dead! The Nazarene is poisoning the people against us. *He must be stopped!*"

In the midst of his venomous speech, the priest paused and searched the room. Puzzled, he turned to Barabbas. "Where is Judas?"

"I am not his keeper," Barabbas shrugged. "He follows the Nazarene, and comes and goes as he pleases."

Rosh pursed his lips thoughtfully. "I must see him," he muttered, then cleared his throat and resumed his discourse. "This time we are bargaining for *all!*" He turned a threatening look upon each of the men seated at the table. He shook the document so all could see the official seal. "This piece of papyrus will make you the richest men in all Jerusalem." Unexpectedly, the priest let his hand drop to the table. The scroll fell away and rolled off onto the floor. No one moved to pick it up.

Rosh sat stiffly. He allowed a heavy silence to descend. A full minute passed without a word. Barabbas, aware of Rosh's dramatic tactics, only smiled.

In a low, almost inaudible voice, Rosh spoke once again. "My price is death," he said. "Death!" His voice grew louder. "This Jesus *must* die!" He pounded his fist on the table emphatically. Rosh stood to his feet, tipping the chair over behind him. Reaching down, he snatched the document from the floor and waved it wildly. "The price for Caesar's treasury," he screamed, "is the life of the Nazarene!"

Down in the street, Timaeus eased around the corner of one building, darted across an opening, and crouched low on the other side. Checking to make sure all was clear, he motioned to Garth. With the weight of Amalek's body on his shoulders, Garth moved slowly.

The two men started around another building, when the sound of soldiers making idle conversation stopped them short. The voices carried through the damp night air, giving the impression that they were nearby. Timaeus pressed against the wall, tuning his ear to detect their position. The voices became more distinct. It seemed as though the two Romans were approaching rapidly.

Garth backed close to the wall, stepping into a small pothole filled with water. The weight of the dead body across his shoulders threw him off-balance. Timaeus, still attempting to locate the soldiers, was unaware of Garth's predicament. He heard a sharp grunt and turned to see the big man topple to the street, the body sprawling in abandon. The sound of it thundered like stampeding horses.

Garth struggled quickly to his feet. He moved to the side of the building next to Timaeus. He pressed close, careful of his footing. He froze there, leaning against the young man. The silence, like the damp air, hung heavy. The sound of footsteps and voices had ceased abruptly. There was an air of uneasiness that chilled Timaeus to the bone.

Adjusting his eyes to the thick darkness, Timaeus recognized the street where Obeha's shop was located. He tried to recall its exact location.

Suddenly there was a growl, followed by the deep, throaty bark of a stray dog that had moved into their path. Quickly the city came alive with sound. One of the soldiers called out. The sharp report of his voice echoing through the empty streets aroused every stray in the city. The night was filled with the din of barking, baying, and general commotion.

Garth leaped toward the big dog, thrusting a heavy foot into its side. The mongrel yipped, ran a few steps, and stopped to howl in protest. The Romans rounded the far corner of the building, while Garth darted around the near corner out of sight with Timaeus close behind. By the time the soldiers made it to the spot where Garth and Timaeus were last seen, the two had disappeared into the dark recesses of the city.

Back in the dimly lighted room, Barabbas questioned Rosh concening Timaeus. "What have you against the boy?" Barabbas asked. "He is swift and agile. He follows orders. I had planned to take him into my confidence and teach him all I know."

"I have a feeling about the boy," Rosh said. "He can no longer be trusted."

Barabbas looked into the priest's eyes. He pursed his lips and looked to the side. "And what is your opinion, Barak?"

Barak shook his head. "The boy could be hanging in the balance," he agreed. "I know he envies the other one, Marcus."

"Well," Barabbas said, "enough of this. We have no choice. We must use Timaeus as a runner." He put his hand up to signal the end of the discussion.

"Now, let's go over this once again." He unrolled the papyrus and laid it on the table. "We have official word stating the exact time the condensing station opposite

Herod's palace will contain maximum tax monies." He looked at Phinehas. "What is your duty, Phinehas?"

Straightening importantly, Phinehas recited: "I am to alert certain of the Sadducees of a stir in the Temple courtyard. I will blame it on the Nazarene."

"At what hour?"

"The sixth."

"Then what?"

"I wait until the seventh hour and go to the gate of Antonia to observe the timing of the new quaternion. Then, I meet Garth with the two donkeys he will be leading. We wait at the weaver's shop, picking out four baskets which will hold at least one ephah each, and substantial strapping. After acquiring the baskets, we lead the animals to the end of the street and secure them there. It should then be the ninth hour."

Barabbas smiled and ruffled his hair. "You have learned well," he said. "It is good to have one such as you in my camp." He looked at Rosh reassuringly.

"All right," he said, "this is where the swift feet of Timaeus will be a boon." He glanced back for Rosh's reaction, then continued. "While Phinehas and Garth are busy setting up the donkeys strapped with strong baskets, Timaeus will watch the proceedings at the condensing station." He grew very serious. "Now listen closely. As we have all observed in the past, when the last tax table has been accounted and the money deposited at the condensing station, a changing of the guard takes place." He checked the papyrus. "According to this timetable, that will be exactly the tenth hour." He looked up. "What happens then, Barak?"

"Phinehas shall approach the centurion in charge, and alert him to the rioting at the Temple area."

Barabbas nodded in approval. "I shall be disguised as before. My face is too well known in the city. I shall appear old and feeble, hobbling with a crutch." He looked back into Barak's eyes. "What else?"

"Phinehas will call out to the captain of the guard, 'Rioting! Murder! At the Temple!' and they will, without doubt, move out quickly. This will leave only one quaternion of tired men who have been standing guard all day.

"As soon as the others have disappeared, Timaeus is to attack you and steal your purse. You, in turn, will struggle with him, falling to the street. I shall run to your side. With four soldiers on duty, two should set out after Timaeus."

"If I do my job well," Barabbas injected, "two shall pursue Timaeus, and two shall come to my aid." He looked up. "Remember, we must do all this after the money is secured, but before the change of guard. The timing is of prime importance." Reaching into his garment, he withdrew a knife, laying it alongside the one taken from Amalek's body. "This should stop one of the remaining guards," Barabbas said.

"And this," Barak said, as he drove the blade into the table, "shall find rest in the ribs of another of the Roman pigs!"

"What if just one man chases the boy?" Rosh challenged. "Or none?"

"If I fall to the street screaming that he has taken my *tax money*, they may *all* set out to catch the little thief," Barabbas laughed heartily. Everyone joined in, enjoying a release of the tension that had charged the atmosphere all evening.

"Ho!" Barabbas exclaimed. "You mean those traitors to the faith? If you speak of the tax collector who attends the condensing station in the upper city," he choked with laughter, "I know the thief. His name is Tofer. He will fall to his knees begging for mercy at the sight of my blade." Barabbas feigned an act of cutting his finger. "Why, the rodent would faint at the sight of one drop of his own blood." He cursed loudly. "Of the man who assists him, I know nothing, save he is old."

"Listen!" Barak whispered, a frown furrowing his craggy brow.

There was silence in the room.

"What is it, Barak?" Barabbas questioned softly.

"Someone is moving up the stairs."

Everyone listened intently. "Garth and Timaeus," Phinehas suggested.

Barak shook his head. "Only *one* man," he said.

The creaking boards of the stairway allowed the thieves to follow the movement of the intruder as he climbed the steps and stood just outside the door. No one flexed a muscle or drew a breath.

Slowly the door opened. Every eye was trained on the entrance.

"Garth!" Phinehas shouted, splitting the silence.

The man slipped into the room and quickly closed the door. The men stood to make room for him at the table.

"Garth, you slimy pig," Barabbas said. "You had us on alert, for certain," he frowned. "Where have you left the boy?"

"Let me get my breath," he gasped. "Carried the body one way and ran for my life the other." He slumped down in a chair and leaned his head on the table. "I don't know where the stupid one is," he said.

"What about the body?" Rosh questioned. "What did you do with the body?"

Garth took a deep breath, relieving the tension tightening his chest. "We dumped the body . . . somewhere," he sighed wearily. "I don't know exactly. No matter. It is far from here. No one followed me."

"What about the boy?" Barabbas leaned across the table. "Where is the boy?"

"I don't know. We were edging along a building when that clumsy one fell against me, causing me to lose my balance, and I dropped the body," he lied. "The boy panicked. I tried to calm him, but he made a commotion that brought three quaternions down upon us. I urged the boy to run, but he froze, just as I allowed he would." Garth warmed to his tale, embellishing the lie as he went along. "I was barely able to escape with my life. When I looked back, the Roman dogs had him." He curled his lip. "The boy was useless." He thought a moment longer. "He was struggling when I last saw him—maybe he got away."

Barabbas reached out and grabbed Garth's cloak in a vise-like grip. He cursed him, then pushed the man away in disgust. Pacing the narrow room, he slammed his fist against the walls again and again. The heavy lines in his brow revealed his frustration. He looked at the men, all silent now. "We *must* have him! Our mission depends on him!" he moaned, flinging his hands in the air.

As a sudden burst of inspiration fired his memory, he cocked his head and eyed Barak. "I understand," he said, as he ambled back to the table, "that you also recruited the other lad—Marcus."

"No!" Rosh interjected, reading the big man's thoughts. "He is of no value. He was brought before the council only yesterday. No man bore witness against him. There was proof only of loyalty to his master. Also, he is near marriage and would not jeopardize his relationship with the girl." Rosh chided Barabbas. "You should know—the young pup has taken leave of his senses since he met that girl!"

"Yet there is no other. The boy has done well in the past," Barabbas mused. "You can persuade him. Threaten to expose him to his master and his woman."

He looked intently at Rosh. "You want this Jesus. I must have Marcus."

CHAPTER
XII

Jerusalem, scrubbed clean by the night rains, sparkled like a jewel in the early morning sun. Chilly breezes blew through the damp city streets. Yet the chilly dampness did not deter the progress of the greedy vendors, nor did it hinder the beggars in their pursuit of alms.

As the sun crested the hills on the distant horizon, Obeha walked briskly toward his shop. The big smith rounded the corner, nodded, and bade "Shalom" to several passing by. With a quick step, he hastened to greet his young apprentice.

"Good morning, Marcus," he called cheerfully.

Marcus was not his generally outgoing and happy self. It was as though he preferred to avoid any confrontation with his master. "Good morning, sir," he mumbled, giving the appearance of tending his chores. Idly he fingered a few pieces of leather stripping, thinking how best to break the news to Obeha.

Marcus' concentration was broken at the sound of

Obeha's heavy voice. "Have you prepared the cart load?" Obeha called out. When Marcus failed to answer, Obeha turned around. "Marcus," he repeated, "have you loaded the cart?" He waved toward the back of the shop. Marcus shook his head and lowered his eyes apologetically.

Obeha frowned. "Son, this is not at all like you. What is the trouble?" He stepped over to the boy. "You knew of the importance of departing for Emmaus early in order to make this delivery to my brother's shop before sundown. What have you to say for yourself?"

"I'll do it right away, sir." Marcus moved languidly toward the cart. Obeha watched him with concern. Marcus' motions were slow and mechanical, and his mind was obviously not on business. He was loading the wrong merchandise.

Obeha placed his hands on his hips, "Marcus!" he shouted.

Startled, Marcus dropped the load he had lifted and straightened. "Sir?"

Obeha shook his head in annoyance and walked toward the back of the shop. Marcus darted around the cart, then leaped a bench, stopping directly in front of Obeha. "I-I must speak with you, sir," he said. The older man looked down at him, waiting. Marcus swallowed hard.

Obeha's eyes narrowed, reflecting his puzzled thoughts. "I have an odd feeling that you are hiding something from me." He noticed that Marcus had positioned himself between the smith and his own sleeping quarters.

Obeha placed a hand on Marcus' shoulder. "My son," he began, "you need hide nothing from me. Have I not treated you as my firstborn always?" With that, the smith craned his neck to peer into Marcus' room. "We have a guest?" he inquired.

Marcus turned to stare into the room. A bare foot dangled off the straw-filled pallet, in full view of the big man's gaze. Obeha smiled and stepped closer. Timaeus was sleeping soundly. Marcus sighed in relief at the look on Obeha's face.

"Is this the lad you told me about—the one who was with you when . . ."

"Yes," Marcus interjected. "He, too, has forsaken the life of thievery. I couldn't turn him away," he added in a whisper.

Obeha placed a hand on Marcus' shoulder, directing him toward the front of the shop. "Come, we will sit down and you can tell me how this came about," he spoke reassuringly.

During Marcus' recital of the night's events, Timaeus awakened. He heard the murmur of voices and decided to lie quietly and listen. After the whole story had been told, Timaeus was elated to hear Obeha's response. The kindly smith offered to take Timaeus with him to Emmaus. "My brother will take him in and put him to work. He will be safe there."

Later, after the team was hitched and the cart loaded, Timaeus helped Marcus with the last-minute details. Though the young fugitive had consented readily to Obeha's plan, his expression revealed that he was still despondent.

"What about Rhoda?" Timaeus asked Marcus.

"What about her?"

"She was due to come into Jerusalem with Justus. She was to meet me."

"But how could she know you were going to come here? You said it was not planned in advance," Marcus reasoned.

"You don't understand," Timaeus explained. "We had planned to get together here in the city after my business with Barabbas and the others was completed. They were all going to go over the wall last night, but I had decided to stay in Jerusalem to meet Rhoda."

Obeha interrupted the earnest conversation. "Dismiss the matter from your mind. Marcus will close the shop at noon and look for her."

Marcus smiled gratefully, pleased with his master's acceptance of his friend and his willingness to help. "I can do better than that," Marcus said. "When Priscilla comes at noon, we will both go into the streets to search for Rhoda. Then she can stay at Priscilla's home until Timaeus can send for her."

When Obeha had checked the final order and secured the cart, he called to his new charge. "Come, Timaeus," he signaled. "We must be off. We face a long trip to Emmaus."

The two young men shook hands, looking into each other's eyes. Mirrored there was deep affection and respect. Timaeus felt a lump forming in his throat as he attempted to voice his gratitude. He bit his lower lip and climbed quickly into the cart. He didn't look back, but threw up a hand in farewell.

Marcus watched as the cart rolled noisily down the back street. He sighed, contented that Timaeus would soon be safe in the care of decent folk, far from the vengeance of the thieves. With all his strength, he pulled the big back doors shut and returned to his work.

In front of the open shop, a beggar asked alms of a priest robed in purple. The priest was obviously a Pharisee. He sneered at the beggar and pushed him aside. "Out of my way, dog," he snarled as he entered the shop. The beggar moved on.

Marcus was hard at work fastening some leather strips together. He looked up at the priest. The purple robe was hooded, concealing with its ample folds the face as well as the body. "May I help you?" Marcus asked. He was amazed that a man of the priestly order would enter a shop of this type. The priest looked up, pushing his hood back and revealing his face.

Marcus stared at him, his smile turning to an expression of disgust. "What are you doing here?"

Rosh moved closer, pulling his hood back over his forehead. "It is not my desire to walk in this swine's pen," he sputtered. He looked around the shop. His nose wrinkled and his lip curled as he eyed the trappings. "Barabbas has sent me," he said. "He has need of you."

Marcus laughed and continued his work. "I have no need of *him*," he said. He looked directly into Rosh's face. "Nor you!"

The priest's eyes narrowed and his mouth tightened. "There is money . . ."

"I'll hear no more," Marcus interrupted. "Get out of this shop!"

"More money than you could make in a lifetime of work in this filth," Rosh tempted. He looked distastefully at the pieces of leather hanging from the open rafters and the oddly shaped metal lying on the benches. "Come and hear the plan before you dismiss it so lightly," he countered.

"All of you are greater fools than I thought. Coming to *me* for help proves it," Marcus chuckled.

"Stupid one!" Rosh snarled. "I shall inform Obeha of your past activities—then where is your pride? Your arrogance shall leave you without means of livelihood. Then what will you say to helping Barabbas?"

Marcus continued placing the leather strips together. "My master knows about my past life," he said flatly, "and, unlike the Pharisee, he has forgiven me."

Rosh stared at the smiling face. He had a compulsion to grab the boy and shake him, but restrained himself. He drew a deep breath and sniffed. Marcus was the key to dealing with Barabbas, and Barabbas alone could deliver the Nazarene.

Rosh began to pace in front of the workbench where the boy continued his chore. "What of your woman?" he asked. "Surely her family would not allow her to see your face again if they knew of your unsavory associations."

"Are you trying to trick me?" he asked. "I would not have expected deception from a priest!" He feigned distress, shaking his head. "Priscilla and her grandfather know everything," he said, placing one piece of leather upon another. "They know also that you lied to the council the other day."

Rosh could contain himself no longer. He snatched the leather strips from Marcus' hands and swung them above his head, coming down with a stinging blow across the boy's shoulder. Turning on one heel, he stormed out of the open shop.

Marcus merely rubbed the smarting shoulder and stood watching the frustrated priest push his way through the busy street and disappear into the crowds.

By noontime, Marcus had completed all his work and Priscilla had arrived. As she helped him clean up and secure the lock on the back door, Marcus told her of the previous night's activities. The conversation continued as they closed up and headed down the street.

"If Rhoda is with Justus, we might find them at the Temple," Priscilla said. She smiled at the look on Marcus' face. "Please, Marcus," she begged. "Remember, you promised to keep an open mind about Jesus. If we go to the Temple, we can look for Rhoda and Justus, *and* we might hear him."

"All right," Marcus weakened, grinning. Although he regarded the Temple as a den for the lower elements of Jerusalem, including Rosh, he did like to hear the teachers sometimes. The thought of Rosh reminded him to tell Priscilla of the priest's visit.

"Marcus," she warned, "you must not mock or scorn this man. He is very powerful in Jerusalem. Grandpapa has told me many stories concerning the sect of the Pharisees, and this Rosh is said to be able to sway the masses against the Nazarene." She touched Marcus' hand. "Stay as far from him as you can," she begged. "And watch for Barabbas, please."

Marcus stopped and gazed into her beautiful eyes. He glanced around, then grabbed her hand impulsively, leading her around the back of a small canopied tent where a stack of boxes shielded them from the street crowds. Alone now, he kissed her tenderly. "What would I do without you?" he whispered. "If you should forsake me, I should surely die. You are my reason for existence. You are life itself for me."

She snuggled contentedly against his broad shoulder. "Your love has made me very happy. Only one thing more could make my happiness complete."

They kissed again. Marcus pulled her tight against him. His lips brushed her cheek and moved to touch her ear. "Let's not go to the Temple," he said.

Priscilla danced lightly out of his arms. As Marcus reached for her, she laughed merrily and quickened her step. "Hurry!" she called. "We must get to the Temple!" She started down the busy street. Marcus stood looking after her. She stopped, cocked her head, and placed her hands on her hips. "You promised," she said.

Marcus shook his head, grinned, and followed reluctantly.

By the time they arrived, Jesus had left the Temple

and an elder named Agabus was standing in the midst of the worshippers. He had chosen to read from the writings of Esaias. His resonant voice intoned the prophetic words.

Priscilla left Marcus at the entrance as she stopped to speak with some of the followers of the Nazarene. She urged Marcus to join the men who had gathered to hear the readings from the Scriptures.

Agabus was already reading when Marcus entered and seated himself. The old man glanced up briefly to acknowledge his presence, then resumed chanting:

" 'See, my Servant shall prosper; he shall be highly exalted.

" 'Yet many shall be amazed when they see him—yes, even far-off foreign nations and their kings; they shall . . . see and understand what they had not been told before. They shall see my Servant beaten and bloodied, so disfigured one would scarcely know it was a person standing there. So shall he cleanse many nations.

" 'But, oh, how few believe it! Who will listen? To whom will God reveal his saving power? In God's eyes he was like a tender green shoot, sprouting from a root in dry and sterile ground. But in our eyes there was no attractiveness at all, nothing to make us want him. We despised him and rejected him—a man of sorrows, acquainted with bitterest grief. We turned our backs on him and looked the other way when he went by. He was despised and we didn't care.

" 'Yet it was *our* grief he bore, *our* sorrows that weighed him down. And we thought his troubles were a punishment from God, for his *own* sins! But he was wounded and bruised for *our* sins. He was chastised that we might have peace; he was lashed—and *we* were healed! *We* are the ones who strayed away like sheep!

We, who left God's paths to follow our own. Yet God laid on *him* the guilt and sins of every one of us!

" 'He was oppressed and was afflicted, yet he never said a word. He was brought as a lamb to the slaughter; and, as a sheep before her shearers is dumb, so he stood silent before the ones condemning him. From prison and trial they led him away to his death. But who among the people of that day realized it was *their* sins that he was dying for—that he was suffering *their* punishment? He was buried like a criminal . . .' "

Marcus pulled at his lip, thinking. He wondered about these words. He blinked his eyes and shook his head, focusing his attention on the reader.

The elder continued. " 'But when his soul has been made an offering for sin, then he shall have a multitude of children, many heirs. He shall live again, and God's program shall prosper in his hands. And when he sees all that is accomplished by the anguish of his soul, he shall be satisfied; and because of what he has experienced, my righteous Servant shall make many to be counted righteous before God, for he shall bear all their sins. Therefore, I will give him the honors of one who is mighty and great, because he has poured out his soul unto death. He was counted as a sinner, and he bore the sins of many, and he pleaded with God for sinners.' " The elder stopped, rolled up the scroll, and handed it to another.

For a few moments Marcus sat in deep concentration. The man nearest him stood, disturbing his thoughts. He, too, rose and left the Temple, joining Priscilla in the outer court.

The pair spent the rest of the afternoon walking the streets of Jerusalem in search of Rhoda and Justus. Marcus and Priscilla **wandered through** the shops and checked the side streets. They talked of the future and the promise of happiness held there.

From time to time, Marcus withdrew into himself to consider the strange reading he had heard in the Temple. He wondered about the Servant that Esaias was speaking of.

Priscilla was acutely aware of his wandering thoughts. It was beginning to irritate her. Finally, when he didn't answer her questions—three in a row—she stopped in her tracks. Marcus absentmindedly slowed his pace, but he was so preoccupied he didn't really notice she was no longer at his side.

"Marcus!" she called sharply. She ran to his side and jerked his arm. "Marcus!"

"W-what?"

The position of hands on hips and the scowl on her face needed no interpretation. "What is wrong with you?" she questioned. "You're drifting along on a cloud or something. You have not heard a thing I have said!"

Marcus blinked. His mouth opened in wonder. He hadn't seen Priscilla like this before. Somehow it pleased him. "You're so pretty when you're angry," he smiled. "What have I done to anger you so?"

"What have you done?" she echoed. She dropped her hands in exasperation.

Just then Rhoda's shrill voice rang out and Priscilla and Marcus turned to see her running swiftly toward them. Behind her, Justus rolled along. Her irritation forgotten, Priscilla ran to greet her friend and embrace her warmly. Rhoda smiled at Marcus, appraising the happiness he radiated. She squeezed his hand, then turned to watch Justus still working his way toward them. "Come on, fat one," Rhoda called.

Justus was huffing and puffing by the time he reached them. "Age, my dear . . . has its . . . limitations," he gasped. He smiled and put out his hand to Marcus. "Well, Marcus . . . my boy . . ." he wheezed, shaking his hand vigorously. "Let me catch my breath." He looked around, spotted an old crate, and eased over to sit on it. The others followed. "Come closer," he said, motioning them into a tight circle.

The crowds in the street were thinning now. The morning rush for goods had ceased, and the hectic pace was slowing. Fewer people were milling around. Those who were out seemed to have precise goals in mind, and moved quickly from one place to another in order to reach their intended destinations without delay.

Justus reached out and took Rhoda's hand. He looked up at Marcus. "Tell us," he said gently, "have you heard from Timaeus?"

Rhoda searched Marcus' face intently. "Will he meet me here today?" she inquired.

Priscilla began to speak, but Marcus signaled her to wait. "Let me assure you that he is safe. He has left the city. He has escaped the band of Barabbas and will send for you soon." He turned to look at Priscilla. "I think it would be wise for you to take Rhoda to your home, and there you can explain with less danger of being overheard." He placed a hand on Justus' rounded shoulder. "I will walk with Justus and give him the details."

Rhoda was troubled. "Please, Marcus," she begged, "don't try to hide his fate from me!"

Marcus placed his hands on her shoulders. "I am telling you honestly. Timaeus is safe and you will soon be together." He smiled, brushing away a tear trickling down her cheek. "Now, go with Priscilla and she will tell you everything."

He glanced around at the people hurrying along on either side. "Remember, the streets of Jerusalem hear all and tell all. We must part now. You can hear the secret in the privacy of four walls." He shook her gently. "Go quietly."

Rhoda smiled at the fat man still seated on the crate. "Justus told me you would help us," she said softly, then turned to Priscilla and took her hand. "I am ready." The two women left hurriedly, disappearing around an old building.

Justus hoisted himself to a standing postion. "You wanted to talk with me?" he asked Marcus.

"Yes," Marcus eyed him quizzically. "I will tell you of the night's happenings. But first, tell me how you knew Timaeus would escape the band, when Timaeus himself did not know beforehand! Are you a prophet like Esaias?"

Justus smiled and began to move slowly into the street of vendors, patrons, and children playing. "When you are as old as I, my son, you shall foretell many things." He shook a finger. "You shall read a man's thoughts as I do. The eyes reveal all the secrets of the soul." He stopped and picked up a small mesh bag filled with almonds. He looked it over and returned it to the table. The merchant watched the pair guardedly. "Timaeus was looking, nay, searching diligently for his chance to loose himself from the hold of the band."

Marcus was amazed. "You *knew* his thoughts?"

"Yes."

"Then you realized he would not meet you today," Marcus said.

"No, I knew neither when nor how the opportunity would arise. I knew only that he would seize it when it came." He smiled broadly, the fat cheeks bulging with the tasty nuts he had just pilfered from the merchant of rare delicacies. "Tell me, how *did* he get free?" As an afterthought, he said, "But that can wait. You must talk with me about the other matter."

"Other matter?"

"Yes," the old priest said. "You want to talk to me about something else—something which deeply troubles you." Justus looked full into Marcus' eyes. He moved on ahead while the younger man stood transfixed.

"You are indeed a prophet or a soothsayer!" He laughed and scratched his head. "You have read my thoughts!"

Justus stopped at a covered stand, vending fruit. "Overripe," he said as he squeezed some, then moved on. "Marcus, my boy, you have much of life yet to learn." He stopped again to finger some linen. "You ask how I could know your inner feelings." He waved the merchant away, then dropped the cloth and moved on, Marcus following closely. "As Rhoda and I approached, you and Priscilla were arguing. Am I right?" He smiled at the astonished look on Marcus' face. "It wasn't difficult to spot. You had the look of a scolded puppy, while she, with her hands on her hips, appeared to be chastising you properly."

"You are right," Marcus flushed. "I . . ."

Justus stopped him. "Please," he cautioned. "Your personal affairs are none of my concern. I merely wanted you to know how I was able to 'foretell'." He began walking slowly again, sidestepping a lazy dog. "Now, of course, you want to know how I suspected there was more to be discussed than the fate of our dear friend, Timaeus. Well, for one thing, you had no valid reason for sending the women away. Your excuse was a feeble contrivance. Secondly, you have a troubled look in your eyes, as though you need the guidance of Solomon himself." He stopped to examine some carved statues. Marcus stood beside him, thinking where he might begin.

"Ten drachma!" the old merchant called, coming

from the rear of the small booth. "Ten drachma, and not a penny less!"

Justus inspected the carving closely. "Will you take six?" Justus said, using a skeptical eye.

"Ten!" the dealer chanted. "Ten! Ten!"

Justus turned the piece upside down. "Six," he muttered, without looking up. "And it's not worth that."

The old merchant waved a fist in the air. "This piece was brought in from Athens," he lied. "It is extremely valuable!"

"Bah!" Justus said, returning the piece to its rest. "Come," he said to Marcus, and the two moved on. They could hear the old dealer call to them. He began to lower the price of the carving. Justus stopped and turned back to look at the old man.

With that, the merchant smiled. "Seven?" he called. "Will you give seven?"

Justus grinned broadly and shook his head, waving the man down.

Cursing filled the air, and the dealer shook his fist at the two.

Justus turned back to Marcus. "I shouldn't tease them as I do, but they're all such thieves." Marcus laughed with him. They walked on. Marcus quickly told the old priest what had happened to Timaeus on the night before and of his trip to Emmaus.

"Now tell me, Marcus, just what is causing you such deep concern. One of your years should not have a forehead creased with wrinkles."

"When I went to the Temple today, Agabus was reading from the book of the prophet, Esaias."

"What portion?"

"It was that part which tells of someone who shall come and 'bear the sins of many'."

"Yes," Justus nodded. "I know the passage."

"Well, Esaias says this man shall die and yet live again. But the Sadducees teach there is no life after death."

Justus frowned. "The Sadducees, the Pharisees—bah! The Sanhedrin itself is at odds with both the law and the Prophets. Don't listen to any of them. They are as these merchants, out to get what they can from the common folk, and the rest of the world can burn in Gehenna, for all their concern!"

"But they are wise and have a large following. I promised Priscilla I would try to keep an open mind," Marcus admitted. "But I don't understand much. Everyone seems to have his own thoughts as to what is right, and no one seems to have an answer to the mysteries of the Prophets."

"First of all," Justus admonished, "don't go along with every whim of man. Follow the dictates of your *own* conscience, not those of others. If you will look to God and ask for his guidance, he will not forsake you."

"But who will explain the Prophets to me? Who will reveal the secrets hidden in their writings? I have come to you because you are wise and have studied the writings of our fathers. You can search the hearts of the Prophets and know the mystery of their words. Will you tell me one thing?" he asked.

"Surely," Justus replied.

"Who is this one who shall die for the sins of many, yet live again?"

Justus stared blankly at Marcus. The question hung heavily between them. The pair strolled through the Jerusalem streets, silent now. Each wore an expression of deep, puzzled thought.

CHAPTER XIII

In the weeks that passed, Marcus enjoyed a new contentment and security. He and Priscilla would marry soon. His knowledge of his craft had progressed to the point that he would soon be able to open his own shop. And his two young friends had been reunited at last. He was satisfied that they were well out of danger in Emmaus.

On the surface, everything appeared settled. Yet, there were sinister undercurrents of which Marcus was unaware. He had completely forgotten the visit Rosh had made to Obeha's shop. Should it have crossed his mind, he would have merely laughed at the way he had goaded the godless priest.

He had no idea that Rosh was even now plotting his revenge. It was fortunate for Marcus that he had not defamed the priest before witnesses. It was also to his advantage that Barabbas needed him. By now the thieves' leader could have recruited several young men to do the job he had outlined, but he was bent on having Marcus. None other would do.

As the colder months were upon them, the wearing of heavier garments aided the cause of thievery, affording more cover for the petty little items the members of the band stole from the merchants and street vendors. In spite of this, they had been unable to slow the swift depletion of the small fortune acquired from Sosthenes. Consequently, they now eked out a meager existence in contrast to the days immediately following that event. All of them yearned for a chance at the big money once again. Rosh knew their greed and continually dangled before them the great wealth waiting to be taken from Caesar's treasury.

Deep in the hillside east of the city, where the hideout melted into the surrounding landscape, Barabbas, Barak and Garth met privately in the little conference room. They sat around the wooden table. A candle flickered, giving off its eerie glow. Sounds of laughter and song drifted down the corridor from the banquet hall. Justus could be heard fingering the lute.

Phinehas appeared at the doorway of the little room. "Come in," Barabbas said, "and shut the door."

Barak moved over on the bench to allow room for Phinehas. "What did you learn?" Barak asked impatiently.

"His mother lives in Bethany, as you told me," Phinehas began. "But I fear we're on the wrong course." Acting the role of informant against Marcus rankled him. He had always liked the boy.

"I'm not asking for opinions!" Barabbas snapped. He leaned back in his chair. "Just tell us what you found out!"

Fearing the big man's displeasure, Phinehas quickly

spouted the discoveries he had made in Bethany. "His mother's name is Phoebe. She lives in a small house just outside the city. She is very ill, so I spoke with a friend, one Merab, who is staying with her." He stopped and looked down into the folds of his robe. "I brought this," he said, producing some cloth. "It is the old woman's shawl."

"What is that for?" Barabbas asked, his voice edged with contempt.

"I thought possibly we could trick Marcus. I figured you wouldn't want to become involved with an infirm old woman. This shawl is evidence enough that we have found her."

Barabbas rocked back and forth in his chair, pulling at his beard.

Garth, attempting to gain favor with his new leader, interjected, "You fool! That was a stupid thing to . . ."

Suddenly Barak reached across the table and slapped Garth across the mouth with an open hand. "Hold your tongue!" he barked. The sudden action stunned the man into complete silence. "Barabbas will determine the wisdom of our actions!"

Barabbas smiled. Barak's spontaneous outburst disclosed the depth of his commitment to the new regime. He had hoped to find the characteristics in the man that might parallel those of Maath, but until now he had not been sure they existed. He leaned forward and took the cloth from Phinehas. "The old one will be cold without a covering for her shoulders," he said, smiling wryly. "It is possible we can fool Marcus, but if not . . ." he said, wadding the cloth into his fist, "we shall be forced to send two men to Bethany to bring back the package."

"I thought it would be a simple solution," Phinehas said. "When I talked to this Merab, I found they are trying to keep the old lady's condition a secret from Marcus. The old woman herself requested it so as not to upset him."

"You are not expected to think. *I* can handle the boy," Barak put in.

"What do you have in mind?" Barabbas asked.

A stormy session followed. Barak proposed a plan of action, firing enthusiastic response from the other thieves. Their meeting continued far into the night.

On the following day, Marcus was surprised at his work by a visit from Justus. The old priest brought disturbing news. "Phinehas told me he was sent on a mission to Bethany." He paused. "They have found your mother's home. I fear she is in grave danger unless you follow Barabbas' instructions and help them rob Caesar's treasury," Justus warned.

Obeha sat at his bench, working on a new design for a team-hitch. He looked up at the plump intruder. "Are these scoundrels still bothering you, Marcus?" he asked.

Marcus didn't want to involve Obeha, but had to confess they were trying to pressure him into joining them. "I must go to Bethany at once," he said. Within the hour he was on the road, a dread premonition his only companion.

Justus made his way out of Jerusalem and back up the hillside to the hideout. It was late afternoon when he arrived, and Barabbas, Barak, and Garth were waiting in grim silence.

"Come in, old man," Barabbas called. "Where have you been?"

Justus glanced at the ominous gathering. "I went down to Jerusalem," he said.

"And what was your business?"

The old priest examined each stony face, but did not answer.

Barabbas looked past Justus to the doorway through which he had entered. Justus turned. There in the entrance stood Jehiel, his twisted smile displaying rotting teeth.

"Jehiel has been following you all day," Barabbas announced. He looked at the filthy man. "Pray tell," he smiled, "where *did* the fat one go?"

Jehiel's smile broadened. He eyed Justus scornfully, prolonging his answer in sadistic pleasure. Slowly he eased around the priest, until he stood next to Barabbas. "This one has always looked down on me," he sneered and stepped toward Justus. "He thought he was my better!" He stood inches from the man, then spat in his face. "The fat pig has sold us out!" he announced dramatically.

Justus didn't move to wipe his face. Instead, he allowed the thick spittle to slide down the edge of his bulbous nose and over a rounded cheek. Somehow, he knew this would be no ordinary reprimand.

I found him at the shop of the smith," Jehiel reported. "There he had a nice, long talk with the boy. The pig even sent him on his way," he waved a hand. "On his way toward Bethany!" Jehiel shoved Justus into the circle of thieves who advanced slowly and closed in around him.

The sun was fading into the hills when Marcus arrived at his mother's home. As he approached the house he felt a sudden chill. It was not the cold wind sweeping down from the Mount of Olives that penetrated his heavy robe. Rather, it was the sight of several women standing just outside the door of the little house. Marcus' eyes widened. Perspiration dampened his palms.

"Mother!" he screamed, then bolted through the cluster of mourners, past the rabbi, into the little room where Merab knelt beside the lifeless form. Marcus stopped, his mouth agape. He fell weakly against the doorway. "Oh, God," he sobbed. "Oh, my God, no!"

A comforting hand reached out to steady him. "Easy, my son." The man's voice was gentle. "Here, come and sit down. I have something that may ease the hurt." The man turned to one of the women consoling Merab. "Please get a cup of water," he said.

Marcus looked up into the bearded face and frowned. The woman brought the cup to him. He took it mechanically. The doctor added a vial of amber liquid and instructed Marcus to drink it all. The grief-stricken young Jew only stared into the cloudy contents.

"What is this?" he asked.

"A medicinal herb," the doctor said. "It will relax you."

Tears gathered in Marcus' eyes as he looked past the man to the bed where the lifeless body of his mother lay, her sweet face at rest. The tears ran down his cheeks in salty rivulets. The man bent down to help him lift the cup to his lips. Marcus pushed the cup away, causing it to slip from their hands and smash on the floor near his feet. He sobbed heavily, leaning forward to cover his face.

"My son," the man said. "Perhaps you are right. My medicine cannot cure a broken heart. Weeping is a more healing balm."

Marcus wiped his eyes with his sleeve. He looked up into the compassionate face. "Who are you?" he questioned.

"I am Luke, a physician."

"You are Greek?"

"Yes, Syrian."

"What have *you* to do with us? Why are you **here?**" Marcus asked contemptuously.

"I have come down from Antioch to observe **the** works of the Nazarene. I was here in Bethany to **talk** with one whom Jesus raised from the dead—a **man** named Lazarus," Luke said.

Marcus looked at his beloved mother. He slumped **in** his chair. "*She* followed your Nazarene," he mumbled. "She called him Lord!"

He raised his voice in rage. "Where is your Messiah now?" he demanded. "Where is this magician who raises the dead? Where is this teacher of love and kindness?" He stood and looked into Luke's eyes. His face was twisted with bitterness and grief. "Call your great healer to perform his miracles," he said, spitting out his vehemence.

"My mother told me of this Lazarus and of his miraculous resurrection. She was convinced that the Nazarene had raised him." He pointed at the lifeless frame. "Well," he screamed, tears streaming down his cheeks, "let him bring my mother back to me!"

After the outburst, he staggered slightly. Luke caught him before he fell and led him back to the chair.

"Another cup of water," the physician ordered. It was brought to him. Again he added an ingredient. He gave the potion to Marcus and encouraged him to drain the cup.

After a few moments Marcus felt the powerful medicine begin to take its soothing effect. He allowed the physician to help him to a pallet. The sound of mourners chanting and groaning their travail outside the little house seemed remote to him now. Someone placed a blanket over him, and he drifted off to dream of happier days.

The traditional **rites of burial were** performed under a

somber, gray sky that threatened to spill its tears on the sorrowful group. Marcus and Merab walked back up the small rise to the house.

"Why was I not told of her illness?" Marcus asked.

"Marcus," she began, "you know how Phoebe was. She never complained. She always gave to others, never asking in return." The big woman paused, considering whether to divulge the full story. "I don't want to upset you, Marcus, but I feel your mother would want me to speak. It's about the Nazarene." She glanced at his expressionless face. "Now don't close your mind before you hear what I have to say."

She cleared her throat, as though readying for a long speech. "Your mother and I followed him closely and learned from him. Whenever he was in the area, we were among the crowds. We . . . ." The word was difficult to utter. "We love him. In fact, I shall follow him as your mother did, until the day I die." She smiled as she recalled a recent experience. "We were near him when he healed several hundred in one day . . . ."

Marcus held up a hand in protest. "Then why was my mother not healed?"

Merab smiled and shook her head from side to side. "Others," she said. "Phoebe always thought of the others. I urged her to go forward and ask Jesus to heal her. She always put it off, telling me there were those who were in greater need than she.

"But Marcus, there is more. Too much has been left unspoken for too long. You must know the whole truth."

When Merab had finished her grim tale of the ambush which had left Phoebe's body weakened and frail, she glanced at Marcus. His eyes blazed with an unholy light. There was no hint of understanding or forgiveness. She saw only a hate-filled stranger bent on revenge.

"Marcus," she cried. "You must not feel this way. Your mother forgave them long ago. Her heart was filled with love for all people just as the Nazarene teaches . . ."

"Don't speak to me of the Nazarene." His voice was cold and brittle. "He healed others. My mother he could not heal."

Marcus departed for Jerusalem without further delay, leaving the disposition of his mother's meager belongings to Merab. Her pleas that he remain a while longer and collect his thoughts fell on deafened ears. He spoke only of "unfinished business" that could not wait.

The young Jew's jaw was set and his mind was fixed on only one objective as he approached Jerusalem. Just over a small rise, he could see a stream of smoke ascending. There was no breeze today, and the trail of vapor rose in a vertical column. He was glad the air was calm, for the stench from the ever-burning refuse of Jerusalem stung the nostrils. For an instant only, his morbid thoughts turned to a hill beyond the city—Golgotha, "the place of the skull"—a place of death.

Now that my mother is gone, Marcus brooded, *I wonder what they'll try next.*

CHAPTER XIV

The next day, a small cart drawn by a single donkey, pulled up in front of Obeha's shop. A young boy, having not yet attained his rites, jumped down from the rugged seat.

"Well," the lad called, "there she is." He waved toward the cart as he ambled up to Obeha. His bare feet were dirty and his unwashed clothing smelled. "You got my money?" he questioned, holding out a grubby hand.

Obeha frowned at the urchin, "We don't contribute to beggars in this shop. We give . . ."

"I'm *not* a beggar!" the boy objected. "I *work* for my pay! And when I do a job, I *get my money!*" He wrinkled his forehead, angered at the insinuation. Somehow he appeared much older than his years. "Now I delivered that broken-down cart, and I *want my pay!*"

"Wait," Obeha said, holding up his hands. "Wait just a minute. I know the problem," he smiled. "You have the wrong shop. You want the shop of . . ."

"Aren't you Obeha?" the boy interrupted.

The big man raised his eyebrows in surprise. "Yes," he said, "I am he."

"Well then, this is the right place. This is where the man said I should deliver it." He placed his hands on his hips. "Now don't tell me you're going to cheat a little kid!"

Obeha squatted down to meet the accuser face to face. "We're not in the habit of cheating anyone," he said. "By the way, what's your name?"

"Don't have one," the boy stated matter of factly. "Don't have no family—just the street lice." He looked straight into the smith's eyes. "Hey, you gonna pay me?"

The big man nodded. "I think we can come to an agreement. First, though, I'll need a little information."

"Yeah?" The boy cocked his head.

"Who was this man?" he asked. "The one who told you to make this delivery."

The boy made a face and shrugged his shoulders. "I don't know his name," he said. "He just stopped me at the east gate and told me to deliver that broken-down rig to the smith's shop. I asked him which shop, and he named the name of Obeha. The old thief told me you'd pay for the delivery," he smirked.

"He said I'd find a younger man here too." He looked at Marcus. "That's you," he stated bluntly. "I'm supposed to tell you, 'The music has faded' or something like that." He frowned. "And . . . beauty is gone . . . after the blade."

Marcus mimicked the words inaudibly. He stared at the boy, frowning. His lips moved slightly as he recited them mentally once more.

"How much do we owe you?" Obeha asked.

"Two shekels."

"And you call the other a thief?" Obeha grumbled. "Here, take this and be off with you!"

The boy looked at the coin, grinned smugly, and vanished as quickly as he had appeared.

Marcus and Obeha walked out into the street and eyed the small cart, piled high with twigs and branches. It was old and ready to fall apart. The metal bands encircling the wooden wheels were missing. Hitched to the cart was an ancient donkey with splotchy hide and swayed back. Neither the contraption nor the animal pulling it seemed able to travel much farther.

The two men walked around it speculatively. Obeha shook his head at the unsightly rig. "What do you make of it?"

Marcus glanced at the outsized load of withered weeds and twigs. As he did so, he spotted something shiny. He leaned closer. Working his hand into the heap, he clutched a familiar object. Carefully, he withdrew the lute, one broken string dangling from its peg.

"It belonged to Justus," Marcus explained, worriedly.

A look of horror passed between them as the truth took shape. They moved to the back of the cart and lifted the gate. "Oh, no!" Marcus murmured. Among the debris was the sandaled foot of Justus. Marcus reached out, but Obeha stopped him.

"Wait!" he cautioned, glancing around the busy street. "If he is dead, uncovering him here will do us no good. If he is still alive, a few moments more won't matter. I'll replace the gate. You drive the cart around back."

Obeha removed the crossbar and swung wide the big back doors while Marcus pulled the cart into the rear entrance. The two men moved quickly, removing the tailgate and carefully lifting the pile of weeds and twigs from the motionless body.

Marcus leaped up into the bed of the old cart and gently slipped his hand under the white head. Looking down into Justus' face, he nearly retched. Obviously, the man had been beaten to death. His nose was broken, and his eyes were puffed and yellowish, ringed with deep purple. His upper lip was swollen and the lower was torn at one corner. Splotches of dried blood stained the wooden bed of the cart. The man's large frame appeared weak and fragile. Quick tears sprang to Marcus' eyes. "I am the cause of his death. He came to warn me that my mother was in danger. They must have known." He got a blanket and tenderly covered the body. "He gave everything to me—everything!"

The young Jew picked up the lute lying next to Justus and sat down on the end of the cart. He could feel neither hatred nor grief—only a soul-deep numbness. With one finger, he strummed across the strings. The sound was discordant and flat. He took a deep breath. "Indeed," he murmured, "the music has faded—gone forever." His eyes misted once more.

Shaking his head to clear his thoughts, Marcus looked at Obeha. "What did the lad say about 'beauty and the blade'?"

"Don't dwell on it, son," Obeha advised. "The old man lived an unsavory life. His end was inevitable. The word of our fathers came down through Solomon: 'The man who pursues evil, pursues it to his own death.'

"Justus was wise enough to suspect his life might end violently. That he *gave* it for a friend was indeed the most noble act of all. But I must warn you, Marcus," he said sternly, lifting the young man's chin to gaze deep into his eyes, "if you continue to harbor bitterness and hatred, you will walk headlong into self-destruction. Barabbas and all his band cannot steal a man's soul.

"Enough of my admonitions," Obeha smiled warmly. "We must carry on our business as though all is well. Later, when it is dark, we can dispose of the cart and find a decent resting place for your friend. Come now, there is much to be done."

No sooner had Obeha pushed open the heavy front door than two Roman captains entered. They walked stiffly into the shop, eyeing the fine leather goods. The big man nodded and bent slightly at the waist, greeting them courteously.

Marcus looked up from his workbench to observe the transaction between Obeha and the Roman soldiers. The young Jew's eyes narrowed as he recognized the captain who had mistreated the old physician, Priscilla's grandfather. Priscilla. How he longed to take comfort in her sweet presence, but his visits only increased the danger of exposure to Barabbas' brutality. *How much more?* he thought. *How much more can I bear.* Then, mercifully, his mind blocked the events of recent days and he returned to his work. With adept fingers, he held a rivet in place and set it in the leather strip with a blow of his hammer.

The negotiations had drawn to a close. Marcus heard Obeha quote the price of the purchase. The men were about to pay him and leave, when one of them turned to look into the back of the shop. He stared at the cart, the donkey still in its traces. By the look on the captain's face, Marcus knew he sensed something strange.

Obeha tried to appear unconcerned. "Will there be anything else?"

"That old cart," the captain began, motioning toward the rig. "It fits the description of the one reported stolen from Simon's shop just yesterday."

"Yes," Obeha admitted. "That is the cart." His mind raced furiously in search of a reasonable explanation. His main concern was to keep the Romans from further investigation.

The captain's eyes narrowed. "Before we left Antonia this morning, the guard at the east gate reported that he had spotted a small boy bringing the cart into the city.

When he stopped the youngster, he was told by the boy that he was Simon's son and had failed to tell his father he was using it. Simon refuted the boy's story." He eyed Obeha skeptically. "Yes," he said, "this has to be the same one. There can't be two old heaps like this in all of Jerusalem."

Fear suddenly gripped Marcus, and he turned to look at Obeha. He could see his master was at a loss also. Perspiration formed little beads on his forehead. The breeze blowing through the open door didn't cool his feverish flush as the Romans examined the cart.

"Trash!" one soldier scoffed. He turned to Obeha. "What is a cart like this to you?" He shook his head again. "You Jews," he said. "You are all thieves. You steal from us. You steal from the Greeks. Now I see you even steal worthless trash from each other. What do you want with this heap?" he asked. The other soldier began poking around in the pile of weeds with his dagger.

"Well, sir," Obeha began, "to tell you the truth, the boy you spoke of *was* here." He watched anxiously as the captain continued prodding. He raised his voice, attempting to gain the man's full attention. "That is just a heap to be discarded," he said. The captain sheathed his dagger. "The boy left the cart out in front of my shop. It is quite an eyesore, as you can see," he added. "I do hope you will get it out of here and back to its proper owner."

"Why did you bring it into your shop?"

"As you can see, sir, the cart is old and near falling apart, and that animal is also near his death. I can't afford to have a thing like that sitting in front of my shop—it's bad for business."

"That's all you Jews think of—business!" the Roman snorted.

"Why haven't you reported it?" the other inquired.

"I no sooner got it out of the way of my door and around to the back than you appeared," Obeha hastened to explain.

The two captains looked at one another. One of them glanced at the purchases they had made. "The heap *was* reported stolen," he said menacingly. "We could have you locked up."

"Now wait," the first man said, stepping in. "I'm sure this shopkeeper is an honest man. He will see to it the cart finds its proper owner." He turned a questioning look toward Obeha. "You *will* see to it, won't you?"

"Of course!" Obeha agreed.

The Roman captain picked up his package. "And what is the price of these two parcels?" he asked, handing the other to his friend.

Obeha saw the glint in the Roman's eye and clearly read its intent. "You've already paid for them, tenfold. Would there be anything else?" He eased them toward the front of the shop.

"Just see that Simon receives his broken-down rig," the Roman answered.

Obeha nodded and bent at the waist once more. "Done!" he said.

The two soldiers were preparing to leave when one of them spied the lute. It was lying on the bench next to Marcus. The soldier walked over and picked it up. "Ah," he said to the younger man, "do you play?"

"N-no, sir," Marcus admitted.

The Roman looked it over and frowned. He turned to Obeha. "Play us a tune, merchant," he demanded.

Obeha saw the fear written across Marcus' face. Obeha took a deep breath. "Sir," he stated honestly, "I cannot play either."

"What!" The Roman looked around in mock surprise. "Where, then, is the musician who plays it?" he asked, smiling. "Are you telling me this fine instrument has fallen into your hands as a gift from the gods?"

The other soldier chimed in. "Possibly the owner of the lute is hiding here in the shop. I would wager he is a fugitive, and these two are protecting him."

"No!" Obeha insisted. "I swear to you there is not another living soul on these premises."

"Then who owns it?"

"I do," Marcus blurted.

"But you said you couldn't play."

"The lute is my inheritance from a dead friend." He hung his head. "It is the only memento I have."

The Roman cocked his head appraisingly. "The instrument is quite scarred, and I see one string is broken." He strummed a few times, running the fingers of his left hand up and down the neck. He placed his index finger across the frets, strummed, then moved the finger down and strummed again. It was obvious he understood the mechanics of the instrument and could make it sing once more. "Not bad," he admitted. "I'm sure I can work on it. Of course, it will need refurbishing." He looked up at Marcus. "How much do you ask?"

"It's not for sale," Marcus answered bluntly.

"It is yours," Obeha interrupted. He stepped over toward Marcus, looking meaningfully into his eyes. "That is, it is yours for, say, ten shekels. That is a fair price."

"Agreed," the Roman said. He picked up his package and nodded to his companion. "We must get back. Send a boy to Antonia to receive your money," he said, waving the lute high. Then, turning, he slapped his friend's shoulder and they left, laughing uproariously.

CHAPTER XV

Obeha could see Marcus was having difficulty recovering from the tragic events of the past week. In fact, he surmised, the boy wasn't coming out of it at all; rather to the contrary. Daily, Marcus' inner struggle was mirrored in his eyes and in the hardened lines of his face as hatred forged its inroads. Each time Obeha tried to talk with him, he shrugged it off as though nothing were wrong.

The big smith had become so concerned about Marcus, he had excused himself from the day's work, claiming he must keep an appointment. Marcus had barely acknowledged his leaving. He merely grunted and continued mechanically cutting leather strips with a large knife.

Obeha was scarcely out of sight when three men entered the open shop. One of them began closing the big front doors, while the other two strode back to Marcus' workbench.

Marcus was startled to see Barak approaching from one side of the bench, and Barabbas from the other. With one quick motion, he flashed his knife at the robber chief, the object of his blinding hatred. Barak quickly caught Marcus' arm. By now Jehiel had secured the door and had come to help.

Though Marcus unleashed all the pent-up fury and heartache of the days just past, he was no match for the three of them. As they subdued him, fire flashed from his reddened eyes. With death only a command away, he gave full vent to his emotions, cursing wildly, until tears of frustration streamed down his cheeks and he sagged to his knees, fully spent.

As Marcus sobbed uncontrollably, Barabbas looked down at him. "*Now* I think he has gotten our message. We just may have ourselves a runner for this job." He reached down and took a handful of Marcus' black hair, jerking his tearstained face upward. He scowled as he spoke. "The good doctor, the young girl, and the owner of this establishment are all vulnerable to the blade of Barabbas," he warned. "I shall take them, one at a time." He released Marcus' head and turned to walk around the shop, stopping to look at the figure slumped to the floor. He motioned to Barak and Jehiel, who promptly seized the young man under the arms and lifted him to a standing position.

Barabbas peered across the shop into the expressionless face. "I want to take Caesar's treasury just three days from now. Are you with us?" He stepped toward Marcus. "I must have your answer now! Wait a day and someone dies. Two days, and another life ends." He cursed and spat at Marcus' feet.

Barabbas moved within inches of the young Jew and scowled. "If you go with us this once, it will be the last you see of us," he declared. Marcus turned his face away. Barabbas motioned the burly thieves to release him.

Rubbing his aching arms, Marcus eased over to another bench. The three men watched him closely. Barabbas felt reassured by the thoughtful look on his face. The young Jew picked up a leather strap and moved it between his fingers. Absentmindedly he dipped his fingers into a container of dressing and rubbed it into the leather.

Barabbas could see he was on the brink of decision. Lifting a hand, the big man spoke arrogantly. It was a gesture he had seen used by the Roman orators. "You should feel honored," he emoted. "Not many are recruited by Barabbas himself."

He paced restlessly as he awaited Marcus' response. Annoyed by the delay, he seized the boy's cloak and jerked him around. With one quick move, he lifted Marcus off his feet and shook him soundly, then slammed him to the floor like a rag doll. Barabbas' chest heaved from the exertion. The container of dressing rolled off to one side, and Barabbas jerked the leather strap from Marcus' hand. He raised it high over the young man lying at his feet. "What shall it be?" he bellowed. "Give me your answer before I flog the skin from your bones!"

Marcus lay motionless, past caring for his own life. The image of Priscilla flashed before him. He pictured her beautiful face, and realized that the message the urchin had brought clearly concerned this beloved woman. "Beauty is gone—after the blade." He had no choice. His eyes met those of the giant towering above him. The other two stood ready to kick him to death at a word from Barabbas. Marcus closed his eyes and breathed deeply. He nodded his head. "I'll go," he muttered.

Barabbas smiled slowly. He clapped Barak on the shoulder. "We have your boy," he chuckled.

"Hhrrumph!" Barak grunted. "He's no boy of mine. I wouldn't claim the stupid one."

Marcus slowly pulled himself to his feet as Barabbas nodded, "Rosh will be pleased."

"I'll be a part of this on two conditions," Marcus said. He brushed the straw from his clothing.

"So!" the huge man snorted. "Now the young snip bargains with Barabbas." He glared at Marcus, his smile faded. "And what *are* your conditions?" he asked, intrigued by the boy's boldness.

"I want none of the money, and you must keep your word."

"None of the money?"

"None!"

"And what *word* do you speak of?"

"You promised that hereafter you would leave me alone. I want to live in peace. Upon these conditions only, I will do as you say."

Barabbas placed his hand on Marcus' shoulder in a fatherly gesture. "Why certainly I'll keep my word," he said hoarsely, winking at Barak. "But you must have your portion of the spoils, my boy. After all, this operation could not succeed without you, Marcus."

This was the first time Marcus could remember Barabbas calling him by name. It smelled of deceit and mockery. Besides, what weight was there in the word of a thief? Yet he had no alternative but to trust. "I can't take *any* of the money," he repeated. "Not one mite!"

Barabbas' grin broadened. He glanced at the boy and then back to the others. The three slapped each other's shoulders and roared in laughter. "He doesn't want any money!" Barak bellowed. "Can you beat that? The stupid one is true to his nickname!"

Meanwhile, on the other side of Jerusalem, Obeha

was keeping his appointment. Out of concern for Marcus he had confided his fears to the old doctor and his granddaughter, hoping that they could explain the young man's strange behavior.

"May I say something to strengthen your thoughts and give them substance?" Oshea asked politely. At a nod from the big smith, the physician continued. "I feel Priscilla has related enough to me that I can actually see the direction the boy is taking. Now, with your words, I am certain of it." He looked into his granddaughter's eyes. "I'm afraid if Marcus doesn't receive help soon, he is headed for destruction."

Priscilla nodded. "You are right, grandpapa," she admitted. "I have been very worried about him these last few days," she told Obeha. "Marcus has not been himself since his mother's death. He has spoken only a few words to me." She swallowed and dropped her head, struggling for composure. "H-he merely stares off into space. Even I cannot reach him."

Oshea shook his head. "Marcus has been as my own flesh from the first day we met," the old man recalled. "In these months, we have come to know his every mood. Never have I seen him like this." He studied his wrinkled hands and stifled a sob. He reached out to clasp the hand of his lovely granddaughter. "This girl is suffering too," he said. "The boy is allowing bitterness to rule his life. He is filled with hate. I fear he has become obsessed with the thought of avenging his mother's death and the murder of Justus."

"He can't prove anything!" Obeha injected.

"We all know that is truth, and I firmly believe Marcus knows it too, but that won't stop him from trying to find and punish those responsible," the old man said sadly.

Priscilla began to weep softly "He w-was coming so close, Grandpapa."

"I know my dear. I know."

"Coming close?" Obeha mused. "Close to what?"

Priscilla looked up. "The Master," she said. "He was so near seeing Jesus as he really is—the Messiah." Another tear trickled down her cheek. "He told me of a conversation he had with Justus concerning the teachings of the Pharisees and others. I know he was trying to justify a longing to follow Jesus. I had such hope of seeing him turn to the Master." She cried out in grief and buried her face in her hands.

Obeha drew one hand down across his face in a vain attempt to wipe away the wearying frustration. "I'm afraid, with his attitude, we will need a miracle from the Master himself." He shook his head in despair. "I feel he may do something foolish—very foolish." As an afterthought, he said, "He shouldn't be alone like this. I must get back."

Priscilla begged to go with him. Obeha consented, hoping that the sight of her would snap the boy from his withdrawn state. Between the two of them, possibly they could talk some sense into his head.

They left the house of Oshea and headed down the dusty street. A cold wind whipped the dust and fallen leaves into a frenzied swirl. Priscilla drew her shawl more tightly around her shoulders. The bleak backdrop of winter seemed to reflect their thoughts as the two walked on silently.

"The Passover will take place next week," Priscilla said brightly. "It will be a time of celebration. Surely Marcus will catch the spirit of rejoicing."

Her argument sounded feeble and foolish in her own ears. Obeha merely nodded. They both knew Marcus was so consumed with hatred for Barabbas and the others that he would not be distracted by a religious festival.

Suddenly Priscilla stopped and held up a finger. "We must take Marcus to my uncle Joseph. He is a mediator. He will plead our case to the Consul and have the band arrested. Don't you see? Marcus will be free of them and they will receive their just punishment." Her voice was strong and confident.

"Wait," Obeha warned. "We must consider every possibility." They walked on while he pondered her suggestion. "If we allow the Consul to become involved, then we must admit Marcus was part of the band. Now that we know he was party to the theft of Sosthenes' purse, we would also be called before the court. No, my dear. There is too much to lose, and nothing much to gain. No," he repeated, "we must find a way to settle the matter quietly among ourselves."

Priscilla felt Obeha was right, but she clung to her one bright hope. "I know we will find a way."

Obeha looked down at the frail young girl. She was spunky. He admired her attempt to cover the deep concern lining her pretty face. But he was definitely worried. Barabbas had spun an evil web around Marcus that was draining his very life from him.

As the couple approached the shop, they noticed some men gathered in front. "About time," one called to Obeha. "We need to make some purchases and your shop was closed."

Obeha stepped to the door and looked through the crack. There was no sign of life.

"Well, don't you want our business?" the man asked. "Or are there more pressing matters on your mind?" He leered suggestively at Priscilla. "Maybe you're going to be too busy to open the shop today." The others took up the chant, making lewd comments.

Obeha, grasping the man's ugly insinuation, grabbed a handful of clothing. The man gasped as Obeha lifted him fully off the ground, one-handed, and slammed his body against the building. The big smith's other hand was drawn back, ready to smash the man's face, when Priscilla reached out and caught his wrist with both hands. Had he wished, Obeha could have shaken her off as he would a pesky insect. Instead, he looked down at her face, flushed with fear and excitement. "Please," she begged. "Let him go!" A tear trickled down her cheek. "Marcus!" she said. "We must see about Marcus!"

Obeha released the man, allowing him to leave with his friends. "Scum," he muttered under his breath. He watched them stumbling down the road away from his shop. Priscilla was trying to peer through the crack, the unfortunate incident already forgotten.

Obeha touched her shoulder. "Let me try to open it," he said. She stepped aside. Obeha pulled at the doors, but they were bolted from the inside. He frowned.

Priscilla could not miss the puzzled look on his face. "Where could he be?" she asked, her voice shrill with excitement. "What has happened?"

"Come!" he directed. He took her hand and led her around the building to the large back doors. They had been pulled shut but were not bolted. Obeha gave a shove, and both of the big doors swung in. The two stood there momentarily.

Obeha's eyes narrowed as he stepped inside. He glanced to the left into Marcus' room. Nothing. He scanned the entire shop, alert to any signs of foul play. Again, nothing. The big man scratched his head. "Maybe he . . ." he hesitated. "No," he admitted, shaking his head. "The shop would have been completely secured if he had left voluntarily." He stepped toward the front of the shop where the front doors were bolted.

"You mean someone has . . . has . . ." She choked and clasped her hands. "What can we do?"

Obeha examined the front door. "The door has been bolted but not chained. Marcus did not lock this door. He *always* puts the chain on it."

"Then someone *was* here!" Priscilla cried.

Obeha placed a strong arm around her shoulder and led her gently to a bench. "Calm yourself," he said, "We must think clearly. It is a simple thing for the imagination to run wild like an unbridled horse."

He began to pace as he sought some logic in the strange affair. "First, there is no sign of a struggle. If someone had forced Marcus to leave, we know he would have put up a fight. Now this brings us to the conclusion that he left of his own accord."

Priscilla frowned. "Where?" she asked, "And with whom?"

"I don't know yet," Obeha answered. "But I can tell you one thing. Marcus wanted me to know he was all right. There should be some clues to his whereabouts." With that, he continued pacing and thinking.

"Oh, I wish we had gone to Emmaus with Timaeus and Rhoda," Priscilla groaned. "We would be able to live in peace."

Obeha stopped his pacing and looked at her. "That's it! I can see it all now!" he shouted. "Marcus is now doing the job Timaeus told us about."

Obeha pulled a stool from the nearest bench and straddled it. Looking into Priscilla's face, he noticed that the confusion etched across it didn't mar the youthful beauty. He smiled, trying to set her at ease. "Timaeus and I did some talking the day I took him to my brother's home in Emmaus. He told me much about Marcus' past life and about the band of thieves."

He stopped and cleared his throat. "Now bear with me, Priscilla," he said, "because I shall be doing more than just relating the facts to you. I shall be attempting to put all of it **together** for my own understanding too."

He eased himself off the seat and began pacing again. "Timaeus told me he was in that upper room the night Justus was killed. He said the men in that meeting were laying plans to rob Caesar's treasury."

"Caesar's treasury!"

"Yes," he continued, "Timaeus had been briefed by the same man Marcus told us about—the nasty one, Barak. According to Marcus, the man has sold his soul to Satan." He pulled at his ear. "Apparently, Timaeus was to play an important part in the robbery. Timaeus said the man kept wishing the 'stupid one' were with them." There was a look of perplexity on the pretty face. "Apparently, the scoundrels referred to Marcus as the 'stupid one'. Timaeus said it was Barak's nickname for him," Obeha explained.

"Now that Timaeus is gone, you think Marcus has joined them, don't you?" Priscilla began to cry. "He would *never* return to that life!"

Obeha patted her shoulder as she placed her head on his desk. Her sobs grew heavier and Obeha paced restlessly. He stopped at the bench where Marcus had last worked. There, among the leather strips, metal rings and tools, was the container of leather dressing that had been overturned. A large mass of the jelly-like substance was smeared on the bench. As the light from the open back doors struck the surface, he could see the unmistakable signs of a message scrawled in the soft dressing. Obeha moved to the side, trying to get another angle on the lightly tinted substance. There were definitely four letters.

"Priscilla!" he shouted.

At the sound in his voice she immediately ceased her crying and hurried to the bench. "What is it?"

"Look!" he said. "Look down here." He pushed her shoulder to help her find the angle. "Do you see it?"

"Wait," she said. She strained to make out the marks. "Yes!" she exclaimed excitedly. "There are four letters there." She began to call them out. "I . . . M . . . U . . . S, 'Imus?' " she questioned, wrinkling her nose. She looked up at Obeha.

He raised his eyebrows. "That is what I read, too," he admitted. "Don't ask me what it means. He eased his head down into another angle and studied the letters once more. "It's 'Imus', all right . . . Wait!" he gasped. "Look at that!" He pulled her head down next to his. "There is a wider space between the first letter and the others. It's as though he were writing two separate words. Yes," he said. "That's it!" He was delighted with himself. "The message, if it had been completed, is 'I must—go'."

Priscilla's face was strained and white. Obeha spoke reassuringly. "I'm certain Marcus has gone back to the thieves," he said. "Indeed, he must have been forced. If he said he had to go, it could only mean he was under great pressure. What pressure, we can only guess. But," he looked deep into her eyes, "I know he had no choice. I suspect he would go back for only one reason." Priscilla sighed, completely spent. He looked down at her. "*You*," he said. "They must have threatened him with *your* life."

Priscilla's head dropped. She wanted to cry, but the reservoirs of her eyes had dried up. "If only we had gone to Emmaus. If only . . ." She choked back the tears. "How will Marcus *ever* be rid of them?" she asked. "If I am around and he is forever haunted by the fear that harm will come to me, then they have won." She began to bite at her lip. "I am his downfall."

Obeha placed an arm around her again. "His downfall?" he laughed. "Never, my dear. Marcus has found the thrill of life in you. You are all he lives for now. In you he sees a better way. Don't worry, we will break the hold they have on him."

"How?" Priscilla asked. "What can we do?"

"Timaeus told me Barabbas was now the leader of the rogues. That rioter has been a barb in the foot of Roman rule for a long time. If I can find him and have him arrested, his followers will scatter like the vermin they are." He thought about it. Then, lifting her chin, he said, "We'll see."

CHAPTER
XVI

All was quiet along the ridge bordering the entrance to the thieves' hideout. The rich azure sky stretched a wide canvas from horizon to horizon. Here and there, small white puffs appeared, as though painted by the hand of God. On some of the puffs, he had dabbed wisps of light gray—just enough for contrast. The bright sunlight added splashes of gold and pomegranate.

Occasionally, a cooling breeze stirred the tops of the trees, and they rustled their new leaves in reply. The grass was unusually green for this early in spring, and the lush blades rippled like the tide flowing down the slope to the east gate of the city.

The spectacular beauty of the day escaped Marcus who sat on the edge of a small, cliff-like ledge, dangling his feet and pulling at the grass. He looked down the sloping hillside, following the path with his eyes. He recalled the first time he had scaled the rugged terrain, following Barak into a life that had promised everything, but had brought only pain.

215

In the distance he could see the men returning. Only two of them. He frowned. Distaste for them spilled an ugly slime over his mind, and darkened his mood. The sight of Barabbas and Barak intensified his determination—he *would* find a way to remove this evil threat. But for now, he would bide his time.

The young Jew sighed and gazed off into the sky toward Jerusalem. He saw the familiar trail of vaporous smoke from the city's dump, snaking its way upward. The pure sky seemed unaware of the danger and basked lazily in the sun, ignoring the poisonous serpent slowly injecting its gray venom into the blue.

Marcus could see a reflection of himself in the trail of smoke. He pictured himself stealthily moving through the darkness of Lucius' home to steal the Sacred Goat of Kahl. It seemed to him to have taken place in another time, to another person. Since Priscilla, all the ugly events of his life had been obscured by a light haze of love, happily clouding his mind.

Now his past rose ominously, poised like the serpent to destroy them both. There was no alternative but to obey Barabbas once more. Then, it appeared, he must take matters into his own hands if he and Priscilla were to live without fear.

He looked up into the blue sky again. The God who had painted the spring day with the colors of new life, the One who had led him out of the band of thieves into a better way, the One who had given him Priscilla— surely that God had forgotten him now.

A bird landed atop a small bush nearby, startling Marcus from his reverie. He estimated the creature to be about three full paces from his grasp. He smiled as it flitted over the small branches, choosing one near the top of the bush. Adeptly, the little bird cleaned its beak by scraping it sharply on either side of the branch on which it was perched. The action reminded Marcus of how Obeha had taught him to sharpen a knife on a block of sandstone. The bird scraped its beak a few times, then nervously cocked its head from side to side. Releasing its hold on the branch with one foot, it scratched at mites.

"We seem to have the same problem," Marcus observed, now leaning on one elbow as he watched the bird. "There is something biting at my head too," he said softly. "But it's on the inside where I cannot scratch." He waved a hand toward the two men, still winding their way up the hillside.

"There's *my* trouble," he said. The bird fluttered its wings at the movement of his hand, but didn't fly. The sound of the young man's voice was somehow soothing and it cocked its head, as if to listen.

"What would you do," Marcus continued, "if two hawks swooped down into your nest and threatened to destroy your loved ones? Would you fight to protect the nest to satisfy *your* grudge, or would you try to appease them and flee later?" He smiled as the bird cocked its head once again. "So, you'd appease them, would you? Then you think I've done the right thing?" The tiny bird fluttered again. "Good," Marcus said. "Thank you, sir." He took a second look at the bird. "Or madam," he smiled.

A sudden movement behind Marcus sent the bird soaring off into the blue sky. He looked up to find Phinehas standing nearby. The man grinned. "Ah, Marcus," he said jovially. "I didn't mean to frighten your little friend."

"It doesn't matter," he said.

Phinehas dropped to sit beside Marcus and looked down the pathway. "They should be coming along soon."

"Yes, they are on their way," Marcus said, then attempted to point out the men. "They were . . ." he frowned, looking at the place he had last seen the two men. "Look!" he said. "Farther down the path near the east wall. See them?" He pulled Phinehas' shoulder into the line of his extended arm. "There where the trail begins."

Phinehas squinted. "Ah, yes," he said.

"Who is it? What's going on?"

"Barabbas and Barak appear to be waiting for Rosh and Judas." Phinehas had spotted their leader and his companion sitting in the cover of a small cedar. "It looks like they're having trouble finding the path," he smiled. "I guess we can be thankful for that."

He leaned back and turned to Marcus. "Before they get here, I'd like to ask you a few questions."

Marcus knew this man was not hardened like the others, but was unsure of his intent. "What kind of questions?" he asked dubiously.

Phinehas looked down. "I'm considered nobody in this band," he began. "They trust me only with minor errands. I am told nothing, so I can do no harm. I found out about this plan of Barabbas through Tamara. Only then did they include me. I am fortunate. Tamara tells me everything." He peered down the hillside nervously. "I'm not mean enough, I guess. They all think I'm weak and harmless, so they tolerate me."

He looked back into Marcus' eyes. "But you—I hoped never to see you here again. You were not like the others."

Marcus looked at him skeptically. "What did you want to ask me?"

Phinehas glanced down the pathway again. "Tamara also doesn't understand why you are back. You don't belong here. I mean, since . . . since your mother died, we hoped they couldn't touch you."

Marcus looked deep into Phinehas' eyes. He continued staring for a few seconds, trying to fathom the man's thoughts. "You really don't know, do you?"

Phinehas shook his head.

Marcus took a deep breath and ran his fingers through his hair. "They threatened to kill Priscilla," he stated bluntly.

"Why didn't you leave the city with her?"

"How could I?" Marcus said dramatically, throwing his hands into the air. "They came barging into the shop where I worked and threatened to kick my head in. They forced my decision immediately, and when I agreed to this *one* job, Barabbas brought me here to wait."

"He knew what you would do," Phinehas said. "He knew you would leave the city with her."

"Never," Marcus said. "If I had left, they would have gotten to Oshea, her grandfather." He shook his head sorrowfully. "And if the three of us had fled, Barabbas assured me my master would die. He is like a father to me."

Phinehas shook his head. "Now I see." He rubbed his chin. "Barabbas and Barak are nasty and cunning in their separate ways, but together they are ten times worse. I hate them." He stopped abruptly and covered his mouth. A look of fear swept across his features. He looked over his shoulder at the entrance to the banquet room. With a quick glance down the hill, he wiped the perspiration from his brow. "I-I hope I was not overheard."

Marcus smiled and patted his shoulder. "Only you and I, my friend," Marcus assured him, then turned to look down the pathway. Indeed, the distant pair were still having problems finding the trail. He would have to admit—it was a blessing to know the path was well hidden. The band could rest easy, knowing their chances of being followed were minimal. Finally, the smaller man, obviously Judas, found the trail and the two started toward the hideout.

"They've never been up here before," Phinehas said. "There must be some money in it for Judas. He wouldn't come near this place for any other reason."

"Isn't he one of the close followers of the Nazarene?"

Phinehas nodded, watching the two.

"What is Rosh doing with him?"

"They are both thieves. Rosh thinks Judas has some information that will help destroy Jesus." He looked at Marcus. "They are playing a game of cat-and-mouse."

"I thought the followers of Jesus were . . ." he struggled for the right word, "honest people."

"You know little about the Nazarene and his disciples."

"True. But my mother followed his teachings. And Priscilla and Obeha are convinced he is the Messiah." He looked back into Phinehas' eyes. "I really wish he were."

"How do you know he isn't?" Phinehas murmured, returning his gaze to the pathway. "Look!" he said. "They've found Barabbas and Barak!" His tone changed, an indication he wanted to drop the subject of the Nazarene.

Marcus looked down at the four men standing under the cedar. He watched them move away from the spot and back onto the path, forming a single file. As they trudged upward, Marcus turned his mind back to the conversation. "You asked me how I know the Nazarene is *not* our Messiah."

Phinehas looked back at the younger man. He sighed and reluctantly picked up the conversation. "Yes," he said. "After all, he is **followed** by hundreds, and at times thousands."

"What are you trying to say?" Marcus frowned. "You sound as though *you* might believe he is going to over-throw Rome and set all Israel free. You couldn't believe the rumors of his claim to be God's Son. If you did, you would be following him openly—certainly not remaining here in this den of vipers!"

"Not necessarily," Phinehas said. "Look at Judas. The man follows Jesus everywhere, yet he obviously doesn't believe all the claims the man makes. If he did, he wouldn't be the thief he is." He raised his eyebrows and smiled at Marcus.

"Surely *you* can't think of him as the Chosen One of Israel," Marcus countered.

"As I run my errands for Barabbas, I have had the opportunity to see the man many times. To answer you bluntly—*yes*, I do believe he is the Messiah." He held up a finger. "But I also think he will be gathering men like us to take down the Roman dogs. When the time comes, I will be one of them."

"What?" Marcus was astonished. "That doesn't even approach the teachings of the prophets! It's absurd!"

"Certainly it does!" Phinehas didn't like the inference. His temper flared. "Look," he snapped, "I'm not the one they call the 'stupid one' around here."

Marcus' mouth dropped open. He had always viewed Phinehas as one who concealed his feelings or, perhaps, felt nothing; yet the man was visibly disturbed by the conversation.

Just as quickly as his temper had risen, it subsided. "Give me *your* ideas about the man, Marcus," he said, his voice again calm. "Surely you can't ignore the fact he has healed large numbers of men, and even women and children."

Without waiting for Marcus to reply, he continued, "I was on the hillside near the Sea of Galilee when he broke five loaves and parted two fish." He turned to look at Marcus, "There must have been five or six thousand people there that day." As he relived the scene, his voice betrayed his excitement.

"Listen," he said confidentially. "I've never told anyone about this." He glanced over his shoulder. "I ate my fill that day—that I swear on a sacred oath. With those fragments of food, every one of the five thousand was filled. I even saw some of the small children feeding a few stray dogs." He paused when he saw the look on Marcus' face. "You don't believe me, do you?"

"Y-yes," he answered. "Yes, I do. I have heard of such things. They say he . . ."

"Wait!" Phinehas interrupted. "There is more!" His eyes sparkled now. "After everyone was full, two of his closest followers went into town for a cart. They loaded twelve baskets full of leftovers with which they fed the poor!" He slapped Marcus' shoulder. "Explain that if you can!"

Marcus couldn't believe his ears. "If you're so strongly drawn to the man, then you should at least follow his teachings."

"I do," Phinehas said quietly.

"What?" Marcus gasped. "Why, you're a thief along with the rest of them. I'm here under threat of death. But you," he gestured with one hand, "you have no excuse."

Phinehas laughed. "I don't steal from my brother Jews. Haven't you been with us long enough to know we take only from the wealthy Greeks and Romans—never from the house of Israel?"

"What about the tax collector? He's a Jew—Tofer—isn't that the name?"

"He counts for nothing!" Phinehas scoffed. "Besides, Tofer is no longer there. They have a new man. In my opinion, he is a prostitute to Rome and can no longer be considered a Jew." Phinehas shook his head. He looked out into space, reflecting. "It is as Justus said when he referred to the sects of the Sadducees and the Pharisees. He said they were their own gods, and those who sold themselves to Rome are without a god at all."

As Marcus glanced down the hillside, he saw that the four men were nearing the summit. "Tell me quickly," he said, turning back to Phinehas, "who killed Justus?"

"I can't answer that," he said. "But Tamara will know."

"Please," Marcus pleaded. "I ask one more favor."

"Anything, Marcus."

"Go to Obeha, my master, and tell him I am safe. He will get word to Priscilla."

Phinehas nodded. "Before the sun rises," he promised.

Marcus looked relieved. "Thank you, my friend."

The six men seated themselves at the long low table. Rosh muttered about the inadequate facilities, and squirmed about in the large pillows like a dog arranging his bedding. Judas sat nearest him, yet kept a reasonable distance. The shifty little man didn't care for the sting of Rosh's sharp tongue. Marcus seated himself on the other side of the table next to Phinehas, who sat next to Barak. Barabbas sat erect at the head. He cleared his throat, calling the meeting to order.

The three men on his right seemed ready. Barak was tough and could take care of any trouble that came his way. Past experience had proven that he could handle three, possibly four Roman soldiers with his bare hands. Barabbas' eyes moved to Phinehas. The man had never been of much service before, but he would be able to follow orders and aid as a deterrent. He turned to Marcus. He looked the young man directly in the eyes. "Are you with us?" he asked.

Marcus returned a level gaze. "I am here," he stated flatly.

Barabbas' eyes narrowed. Marcus knew the big man distrusted him, yet Barabbas had all the leverage he needed, and Marcus was willing to follow instructions—for now. The young Jew flushed nervously as everyone looked at him. He was bothered most by Rosh's icy stare. The ungodly priest hated him. He wondered if his alliance with Obeha had any bearing on it. He knew Rosh kept a mental tally of those who adhered to the teachings of the Nazarene.

Barabbas was pointing to the map spread before him. The man seemed unusually congenial. He explained in detail what each man was expected to do and patiently entertained questions from the group. If one of the men stepped out of line, he reasoned, he could deal with the matter *after* Caesar's treasury became his.

Barabbas continued. "Garth is down in the city preparing everything we'll need." He turned the map so it faced them. They bent forward to get a better look. Barabbas pointed to the Temple. He looked up at Judas. "You're sure he will be there at midday?" he growled.

"I shall see to it," Judas responded. "I do get a portion of the treasury, don't I?" He rubbed his hands together greedily.

Barabbas didn't answer, but looked up at the little man, peering through gnarled, bushy eyebrows. Slowly his eyes returned to the map.

"I shall have my men there," Rosh assured them. "I have enlisted lawyers, gifted in the art of twisting his words. We shall cause quite a stir among the people." He sat erect and folded his arms pompously across his chest. "I can assure you, if this wretch," he glanced toward Judas, "will only make sure the Nazarene is there, I shall make sure he is responsible for creating a disturbance." His face contorted in a nasty sneer. "You shall have your treasury, and I shall have this Jesus."

Marcus studied Rosh's face. The granite gray eyes and the lips compressed tightly in a thin line made him appear as cold as stone. His inverted beard and the hatred written on his features reminded Marcus of one possessed by Satanic powers. Marcus wondered why he was sitting at the same table with such men. Suddenly he felt a wave of nausea and revulsion. He wished he were back in Obeha's shop with the clean smell of leather in his nostrils and the sting of honest sweat in his eyes. The young Jew thought of Priscilla. He pictured her shopping for the Passover lamb in preparation for the week-long ritual.

He forced his attention back to the present and glanced at Rosh once more. The man still sat frozen, his eyes stony and his lips pinched. Marcus wondered what Rosh had in mind for Jesus. Priscilla would never recover if anything happened to the Master.

He knew the Pharisees were unhappy with the fact that Jesus had been telling the people he had come to set them free. The Zealots were ready for his command, but he gave them none. The Pharisees, on the other hand, were ready to stone him for giving the people hope of freedom. He recalled how Priscilla had promised that if he would see Jesus as she did, nothing else would matter. She even intimated she would die for the man, and the death would be a victory. He frowned at the thought and made a guttural sound of protest.

"Is there something all of us should hear?" Barabbas snarled, looking at the startled young man.

"Ah, no . . . no," he sputtered.

The big man peered under his eyebrows at Marcus. "Then quit making those stupid sounds."

Marcus nodded, swallowing hard.

"Well," Barabbas said, placing both hands, palms down, on the table, "are there questions from any of you?" He looked around. No one spoke.

"Well then," he said again, clapping his hands loudly. "Tamara!" he shouted. "Wine!"

Chapter
XVII

The sea of excited pilgrims who filled Jerusalem were making their last-minute purchases prior to a shutdown of business honoring the anniversary of the Passover. Old men sat on crates or in alleyways, gathering children about them to rekindle the flame of a story grown cold through a year more commercialized than the last.

The numbers gathered in the bazaars and those mingling in the upper city pushed and shouted, creating exactly the atmosphere Barabbas had hoped for. The city appeared to be in mass confusion, with everyone grumbling about the exorbitant prices being charged for the sacrificial lambs and other animals. There were cries of protest over the high rate of interest being charged by the Temple moneychangers.

Marcus weaved his way through the crowds. Once in a while, he crossed an open area where he could breathe. The smell of the masses of people and animals hung heavy, and he welcomed a brief breath of fresh air.

His eyes scanned the scene, catching glimpses of faces both young and old, rich and poor. Absentmindedly, he looked for Priscilla. He hoped Obeha had gotten his message, but realized Priscilla would not rest until she had seen for herself that he was unharmed.

He reached another open space and stopped, surveying the area. He thought how much his life had changed since the last Passover. His relationship with Barak and the others had now spanned a full year.

The voice of an old man caught Marcus' ear. He was chattering animatedly as he passed the young thief. It seemed to Marcus that many of the Jews were merely caught up in the excitement of the holiday and cared little about the needs of others. He thought that to be a bit out of character with the meaning of the season. For surely every man, woman, and child celebrated the feast of the Passover with full knowledge of the gift of God to their forefathers.

To each of the faithful Jews, the celebration commemorated both the exodus of the Jews from Egypt led by Moses and the miracles which the Lord God of Israel performed to secure their freedom. The last miracle or plague was a visit from the angel of the Lord who slaughtered the firstborn male in every household not showing the designated sign. On the first Passover, each family was instructed to prepare an unblemished lamb. The blood of the lamb was to be be sprinkled on the doorposts and lintel so the death angel would pass over the homes of the faithful. Thus, all the homes displaying the blood of the lamb were spared, while those of the oppressors lost their firstborn.

This was indeed a victory celebration of times past. But it was more. Though unknown to the occupying Romans, the feast also foretold future victory. For at this time when the Jews remembered what miracles the

God of Israel had performed, they were assured he would again smite the enemies of the sons of Israel.

The Jews knew him as a just and mighty God. They were comforted in their own bondage to Rome by the promise of a Savior. They awaited patiently the fruition of their dreams—a dream kept alive through each succeeding generation. Like Moses, who had come out of the wilderness to deliver their forefathers from captivity, so the Messiah would come in great power and glory, setting free the captive people of Israel and uniting the twelve tribes into a nation set up to rule the world in peace and prosperity.

This man, Jesus—the one claiming to be the Son of God—how could *he* be the Chosen One of Israel? He was one of them—a simple carpenter from Nazareth. Though some were convinced by his profound teachings and miraculous deeds, others murmured among themselves of blasphemy.

Marcus stopped. He thought he recognized the old man sitting cross-legged off to one side of a "bargain" tent. Several children listened attentively as the old man told stories. Marcus moved closer, sidestepping a woman set on pushing her way to the proclaimed bargains. The merchant grabbed the young thief's sleeve and pulled him aside. "Move on, boy!" the old man growled.

Marcus, his attention held by the aged storyteller, took a few more mechanical steps, not really noticing the irritated merchant. He moved over to the side and listened. The old man's voice stirred a memory buried deep in his mind. *Who was he?* His eyes narrowed as he scrutinized the rugged, old face. Marcus studied the thick, white beard and the movement of the lips. He listened.

"And then," the old man continued, "he asked me

what he could do for me." He paused, looking into each upturned face. "You see, my children, the people following him had no patience with a blind, old fool such as I." He leaned down to them as they sat, intent on his every word. A bony finger went up. "But I want all of you to know," his voice lowered with intensity, "old Bartimaeus would not be denied." A smile swept across his face. "No sir!" he cried. "I just kept shoutin'." He raised his arms. "I cried out to the Son of David. The people told me to keep silent, but he heard me!"

His eyes grew large. "Someone near the middle of the crowd around him said, 'He calls for you.' Someone else took my arm and led me through the crowd to him. That's how I came to meet this Jesus you hear so much about. He is the reason I can see today!"

The old man sat up straight, his chest bulging with pride and gratitude. "Now," he said loudly, "I can see! I was blind, but the Nazarene healed me!" His voice grew louder, and the tempo increased as he chanted, "I WAS BLIND, BUT THE NAZARENE HEALED ME!"

He seemed to be shouting out against the religious leaders, especially those who had denied his healing. Tears formed little pools in the corners of his eyes, and he stood up quickly. He continued proclaiming his victory over blindness, and his gratitude to the controversial figure. Bartimaeus pushed through the crowds into the street. The children followed close behind, joining the jubilant dancing and taking up the chant.

Marcus watched the happy parade, unconsciously smiling in approval. He remembered the day Bartimaeus was healed and the story behind it. Now Bartimaeus seemed to be one of the happiest of men. The old man melted into the crowd, the children close behind, and Marcus moved on.

As the young thief weaved his way through the thick

masses, he pulled his hood up over his dark hair, and allowed the cloth to drape low over his forehead. He certainly didn't want to be recognized by Obeha or . . .

The crowd parted and he could see her. "Priscilla," he whispered. She was barely thirty feet away, busily dealing with a fig merchant. The man was obviously trying to overcharge for his inferior fruit. The thought infuriated Marcus. He clenched his fist and ground his teeth as he helplessly watched her paying the unreasonable price. Marcus sighed in frustration and vowed to remember that dealer and even things later. *If I am still alive*, he thought. He watched Priscilla place the few dried figs in her shopping basket and move on. He followed, pushing through the people and keeping a safe distance.

Priscilla stopped to look over some meat. The merchant brushed the flies away from the hanging leg, but Priscilla refused the cut. She moved away, the butcher calling after her.

Along the other side of the street and well back, Marcus followed, keeping her in sight. He watched Priscilla with a longing deep within. He fixed his eyes on her green cape and long beige robe. Her tiny feet barely touched the ground as she walked. The dark ringlets peeking from beneath the hood of her cape shone silky in the sunlight. Marcus was reminded of their first meeting aboard the ship. He winced at the thought of the grubby old captain and his crew. Quickly! She was moving to the steps of the upper city.

They ascended the steps and moved up a small street to the main artery through the upper city. Priscilla entered a small shop. As Marcus waited outside, he noticed they were close by the condensing station. His heart beat faster.

Priscilla came out, **her errand** completed. Marcus

turned away and drew the hood down further over his face. He stood there a moment, satisfied she had not seen him. The crowd was not as dense here as it was in the bazaar area. He must take greater pains not to be recognized.

Marcus glanced at the sun. "They should be here soon," he muttered to himself. A frown suddenly creased his brow. Priscilla was walking directly toward the condensing station. There was nothing to distinguish it from the other tax booths that had sprung up throughout the city, except for the four soldiers guarding it. Such tables usually required only one guard.

A man sat at the table recording the amount of collected tax from the individual record of each small collector. The pouches of coin were placed in the well-guarded booth, to be taken to the Fort of Antonia later in the day. There, it would be recounted, recorded again, and stored in Caesar's treasury.

Barabbas planned to steal the heavy bags in much the same way they had made off with Sosthenes' coin. They would wait until the bags had been loaded on the cart and then stage their robbery. He knew a detail of Roman soldiers would be sent to escort the cart to Antonia. To divert attention, he planned an insurrection at the Temple. Phinehas was assigned to bring the news of riot and bitter fighting to the captain of the detail. Barabbas was aware of the decree that had been issued from Tiberius Caesar himself ordering the instant quelling of riot and uprising at all cost. The fresh detail would be compelled to leave the loaded wagon with those soldiers who were tired from a long and boring day of guard duty. The thieves could then follow through with their well-rehearsed maneuvers and be off with the wagon.

Marcus watched intently as Priscilla approached the table. She stopped and leaned down, kissing the man seated behind it. Marcus' mouth dropped open. As she stepped back, Marcus drew closer, pulling his hood down. He looked at the man. His mind went blank. The very table the thieves had chosen to take was being served by Priscilla's grandfather! Marcus swallowed. The lump forming in his throat actually hurt. *Now what?* he thought. *What should I do?* He watched the two in conversation, wondering if they were speaking of him.

Within a few minutes, Priscilla moved on toward home. The old physician received another tax collector. He transposed the figures from the man's record book to his own, stamped the seal of Caesar on the page, and handed the book back to the collector. The slave who stood behind the big tax official stepped forward on cue and lifted two bags of coin onto the table. A man stepped from the booth, tagged the bags, and took them back into the booth with him.

Another tax collector was coming up the street with two slaves carrying two bags each. The man led them to the table, arrogance written across his every move. The haughty tax collector snapped his fingers at the first slave. The young man jumped toward the table and deposited the bags he held. The second followed quickly, then stepped back several paces. Marcus smiled at the look on Oshea's face. He read the distaste in the doctor's eyes, for he knew the old man's attitude toward such treatment.

The sound of hooves clicking along the pavement startled Marcus. He melted back into a doorway. The sound grew louder as the horses moved toward the condensing station. Marcus leaned against the doorway and peered from under his drooping hood. He reached up and pulled it back a little. Marching down the street were four Roman equestrians, outfitted in full dress uniform. Brass shone splendidly. Their mounts were magnificent horses, bearing identical white markings. Truly, Caesar and Judea's Procurator, Pontius Pilate, had made a point of impressing the citizens of Jerusalem. The regal quaternion began to canter on command as they approached the taxing station.

Coming up behind them was a wagon drawn by a white horse. The animal was large, possibly twenty hands, and gleamed from a recent scrubbing. The small cart seemed almost toy-like beside the massive animal. The young boy sat atop the wagon's seat, guiding his steed with confidence and ability.

Marcus was alarmed at the sight of them. The hour was imminent. Suddenly he felt sick to his stomach. Bubbles whirled deep inside. He breathed heavily, allowing the fresh supply of oxygen a chance to clear his thinking.

His mind raced frantically. How could he be a part of this with Priscilla's grandfather in the middle of it all. Yet Barabbas' warning was no idle threat. Marcus knew he would not be killed, but rather held captive to witness a sadistic ritual in the brutal slaying of those he loved dearly. If he didn't follow through with his commitment, Barabbas would stop at nothing until all of them were dead—Priscilla, the old doctor, and even Obeha.

The quaternion reined up at the condensing station and the soldiers dismounted. The man from the booth directed the lad with the wagon while Oshea watched the proceedings from his seat behind the tax table. Oshea opened his record book, and the captain reviewed it. There was some conversation. It seemed to Marcus that they were waiting for one final collector. No one moved to load the wagon, nor did Oshea and his employer attempt to finish up business. *Yes,* Marcus thought, *they must be waiting for a latecomer.*

The slight delay in the movement of Caesar's money meant little to Barabbas' plan, except the aggravation of waiting.

Marcus watched the Roman soldiers. He hated the arrogant manner in which they swaggered. He eyed the people in the street. The crowd was dispersing. He looked up at the sun. By his calculations he had been in the city about five hours. When he looked back down, a dark spot bounced around in front of his eyes. He closed them a few moments. When his vision cleared, he caught a glimpse of Phinehas standing on the far side of the street, about forty paces from the condensing station.

At the table, Oshea was growing impatient. Marcus concurred with the feeling. He, too, wished that final transaction would take place rather than prolonging the agony. He moistened his lips. He would have to go through with the theft and pray that the old gentleman would escape injury.

Suddenly he saw Barabbas emerging from the crowd to survey the situation. The man's disguise was excellent. Marcus himself would never have recognized him. Barak, too, was dressed as a cripple in ragged clothing. Marcus' eyes darted from the thieves to the tax table and back again. He swallowed hard. His mouth and throat were dry and cottony. He saw Barak lean close to Barabbas to confer with him. Barabbas motioned to someone behind Marcus. It was Garth, moving stealthily to the opposite side of the tax booth. The plan was already taking shape. He wanted desperately to warn the old man, yet he knew Barabbas was watching his every move.

At this moment activity around the table increased.

The man in charge of the tax booth leaned down to Oshea and pointed to some figures in his record book. They motioned to the captain. With a wave of his hand, he alerted his men to begin the transfer of the bags of money. As the eight Roman soldiers formed a line, relaying the money bags, Marcus glanced at Barabbas. The big man was looking on, unnoticed by the Romans. No one had ever made such a brazen attempt on the treasury of Caesar; therefore, the presence of the Roman guard was a mere token of precaution.

Garth had simply melted into the hustle of people, moving slowly, stopping to finger first one thing, then another. Marcus followed his movements. There was no doubt Garth was sly and cunning. He paced back and forth like a jackal, waiting to snatch his share of the fresh kill.

As the last of the bags was loaded onto the wagon, the young driver climbed up. Suddenly a shout could be heard echoing from far down the street. A tax collector was running, awkwardly lifting his robes and waving a bag of coin. "Wait! I must be recorded! Wait!"

As Oshea received the tax, the captain derided the breathless little man for his tardiness. The soldier turned on one heel and ordered his men to mount. Within seconds the wagon was ready for escort to Antonia. The foot soldiers who had been on duty all day fell into formation, readying themselves to move out.

Marcus glanced at Barabbas, then looked for Phinehas. Phinehas was nowhere to be seen. Marcus had barely mumbled a prayer for help, when the sound of Phinehas' screams chilled him. The knowledge that the alarm was false didn't relieve the uneasy feeling as Phinehas ran toward the four horsemen. "Riot!" he yelled. "There's a riot at the Temple!" He ran to the captain in charge and grabbed the reins, holding the horse at bay. "S-sir!" he gasped, as though he'd been running a long way. "They riot at the Temple!"

Instantly the captain responded to the convincing act. Without a word to Phinehas, he motioned his horsemen forward. He called to the leader of the foot soldiers. "Guard the wagon!"

"But, Captain, we've been on duty since dawn. My men need rest."

"Stay with the wagon!" he insisted. He urged his men on toward the Temple.

Many of the people ran to catch a glimpse of the happenings, causing more confusion. A few dashed by Marcus. He stood numbly, watching Oshea standing near the table. He wished the old man would follow the curiosity seekers. He had completed his assignment for the day, and Marcus hoped he would leave before he became an innocent victim.

The moment had arrived. Barabbas had his back to Marcus, but began to turn slowly. His disguise was perfect. He bent low and leaned on his crutch. A kerchief was wound tightly around his head, and he wore a patch over one eye. He looked at Marcus, then hobbled slowly toward the tax booth. The area in front of the table was clear now; only a few people milled around the edges of the street. Barabbas made his way to the middle, just ten paces from the table.

Oshea and the other tax man were busily engaged in conversation. The foot soldiers leaned wearily against the wagon. The young driver hopped down and ambled around to talk with one of the soldiers.

Perspiration oozed from Marcus' forehead. His palms were sweaty, and he rubbed them together. A sharp pain throbbed in his chest.

Barabbas hobbled on, closer to the wagon now. Barak moved along the opposite side of the street. Slowly, silently, he closed in on the target. Barabbas stopped and untied a small pouch from his waistband. Opening it, he pretended to count the coin.

This was Marcus' cue to move in. Rather, he stood im-mobile, watching the man count the coin a second time. He swallowed and glanced at Barak. Barak glared at him from across the street, and opened his coat to expose the gleam of his knife. Marcus looked to his left. Garth snarled his disapproval. There was no time left for con-templation. His breathing quickened as he darted into the middle of the street and slammed into Barabbas' side, grabbing the pouch as the big man went down. He then darted off, Barabbas yelling after him.

The guards turned to investigate the commotion.

Barabbas screamed. "The treasury money! That boy just took my tax money! He has stolen from Caesar!" One of the soldiers ran to Barabbas' side. Barak ap-proached as though to offer assistance. He called to the other soldiers. Garth edged around behind them.

Breathing heavily, Marcus rounded a corner, and ducked into a small opening between the buildings. He waited, his chest heaving. He peered around the edge of the building. No one had given chase. He looked again. Still no one followed. He leaned against the stone wall. His mind raced, wondering about Oshea. With luck, the old man might escape harm. He checked once again, but still no one came for him. The only sound he heard was the pounding of his heart.

After several minutes, he decided to ease back to see what had happened. He couldn't understand why no one had pursued him. Cautiously, he peered around the corner. He moved out, remaining close to the buildings and made his way back to the main street. A large crowd had gathered in front of the tax booth. The wagon was still there, he knew, because he could see the horse towering above the crowd. He crept forward. Everyone was jockeying for position to see what was going on.

Apparently the plan had failed. Marcus felt a surge of relief. Perhaps they were captured or even dead, and he was free of them at last! But he must be sure. Taking a place behind two large men, he crouched down to peer between them.

There in front of the two men lay Garth, a knife—his own knife—buried deep in his chest. Barak was being tied to the wagon, and Barabbas had been beaten and lay helpless. Marcus was glad Phinehas had gone to lead the crowd to the Temple.

Marcus' eyes swept the scene. The tax table was completely demolished and the head tax recorder lay across it, dead. Marcus grimaced. He searched desperately for Oshea. He shoved against the two men in front of him, trying to separate them so he could get a better view. Priscilla's grandfather was nowhere in sight. He leaned in and looked from side to side. Suddenly one of the men shifted and stepped aside. Marcus lost his footing and sprawled headlong into the center of the action, landing next to the lifeless body of Garth.

Barak jerked. "So there you are, you sniveling lamb!" He spat. The guard closest to him slapped him across the jaw with the back of his hand.

Another guard grabbed Marcus' wrist. "What has this one to do with you?" the soldier growled.

"He is one of us!"

Just then, Marcus heard a welcome voice. "Marcus? Is it you?"

As he looked up into the old man's face, the tears blurred his vision. God had heard his prayer.

CHAPTER
XVIII

Within hours, Marcus' circumstances had been reduced to those of a pig wallowing in the slop of its pen.
The young Jew lay helpless against the cold stone wall of
his cell. The chains that bound his hands and feet cut
cruelly into the flesh. He could open only one eye. The
other was swollen shut from the violent kick of a Roman
boot. He shivered as the cool, damp air drifted over his
half-naked body. He couldn't tell if it was night or day
for, in the darkness of the cell, there were no clues to
time.

Marcus tried to sit up. Even his bones ached. The
soldiers had beaten and kicked him in every part of his
body. He forced himself to a standing position. The
chains on his legs jerked violently. He screamed into the
darkness. Pain racked his ankles and he reached out to
ease the pressure. Immediately, his wrist chains
snapped. Marcus groaned. He squinted painfully, but
the darkness was bitter and kept the secret of his tor-

turers. He closed his eyes and sagged against the cold stone.

A voice cracked the night air, rousing Marcus from his stupor. "Sleep well," taunted the guard. "Tomorrow you will find relief—the relief only death can bring." He laughed heartily. All was quiet once more.

Marcus thought of Oshea who was alive and well. He thanked God for answering his prayer. Now he could die in peace, knowing those he loved were safe. His mind drifted in a haze of pain.

"You Jews," the voice interrupted contemptuously, "are ignorant barbarians. Romans are practical people. We live and die in a practical way." He continued to philosophize. "You live in a world of unrealized dreams and unfulfilled hopes. You view death with superstitions much like the Greeks. All of you are fools. You dream of a life beyond the grave. What mockery! Life is lived once and then nothingness." He jerked Marcus' chains. "And what shall your God do with *you* in this other life?"

Marcus held his silence. The gnawing pain in the pit of his stomach made him want to retch, but he fought for control. The Roman had scratched a sensitive area wedged in the back of Marcus' mind. God himself and the life after death his mother had spoken of, seemed remote and unreal. With pain throbbing even in the tips of his fingers, he found it difficult to comprehend a God who cared about one Jew in a filthy cell. Where was he now?

In one corner, a lone rat sniffed out crumbs of stale bread. He scampered across the cold stone floor, then wriggled through a large crack near the door. His gray-black tail slithered behind him and disappeared. Even the rat was free to come and go as he pleased.

The young Jew closed his eyes and listened. Somewhere, in the distance, a cart was being drawn across the stone street. Inside the jail cell, the breathing of the guard grew heavy. Marcus listened to the loud rasping of it. He opened his eyes again.

The darkness had mellowed to heavy gray. Slowly he turned his throbbing head. A sharp pain stabbed his left shoulder. There, chained to the other side of his captor, lay Barak. His large frame slumped against the dank, stone wall. He was unconscious and bleeding from an ugly gash on his forehead. The blood oozed out and ran down between his eyes, parting to either side of his nose and soaking into his mustache and beard. He was naked, except for a loincloth. The thick hair on his chest was matted and wet with blood.

Without warning, the night silence was broken by the scraping of metal against metal, and then the thud of a bolt. The outer door creaked as it swung open. A voice sounded, and heels cracked smartly against the corridor floor, awakening the guard. He sat up straight and jerked the chains.

Marcus groaned, swallowing a scream. Barak's eyes fluttered, then opened. His tongue emerged, thick and milkish, in an attempt to lick his swollen lips. He tried to focus.

A light shown under the door. The muffled voices of soldiers were heard in the long hallway. A key was inserted and the door opened. Instantly, the blinding light of flaming torches caused the three men to cover their eyes as the soldiers swarmed in bringing a draft of cold air with them. They removed the wall chains, relieving the guard of his bonds. "What's going on?" he asked.

"Can you believe those stupid Jews are going to get their way?" one of the soldiers answered. "Pilate is up at this late hour to hold execution hearings for the one called Jesus. You know," he laughed, "the one they call the Messiah. With his political career at stake, our glorious leader wishes to dispense with all possible problem cases." He squatted down and checked Marcus' ankle chains. "Tonight!" he declared. "Even at this late hour, he questions the one called Barabbas." Marcus looked up at the soldier. The man continued. "Yet one of their priests has stormed out of the Judgment Hall in protest of Barabbas' execution." He shook his head. "These Jews have a very odd religious custom. They can call for the release of the prisoner of their choice during the time of Passover."

"Rosh," Marcus mumbled.

The soldier looked down at the young Jew. "You know him?" he asked. "He is one of yours. But don't be angry. Seems likely this Rosh will get your leader off free. He is stirring the people to call for the death of the Nazarene," he smiled and nodded toward his comrades. "These Jews have so many leaders, even their leaders don't know which to follow." Everyone laughed.

One soldier pulled Marcus to his feet, while another lifted Barak. "Come," the Roman commanded, "you have an audience with Pilate."

In the large Judgment Hall, Barabbas stood before Pontius Pilate, his eyes glazed with hatred. A black metal collar had sliced his neck raw. The big thief seemed to feel no pain.

Pilate spoke. "Have you an answer?"

Barabbas looked at the Proconsul. "If I should die," he began, "others mightier than I shall rise against the oppressor and crush him!"

Off to one side, a soldier whispered loudly. "He speaks of Caesar! It is heresy!" A wave of murmuring swept through the hall.

"Silence!" Pilate commanded. He rose and stepped down from his high seat. With piercing eyes, he looked at the bloodstained face, reading the hatred. Barabbas held his stare.

Pilate sneered. "*You* are their leader?" he challenged. "A filthy wretch, without a penny and no command of knowledge, leads insurrections and daring robberies? We have your man who lured away our quaternion to the false Temple riot." He looked down at the chains that bound the big man and stepped closer. He reached out as though to touch the dirty thief, then withdrew his hand. "I dare not stain my hands," he taunted.

"Pig!" Barabbas spat. He lunged toward the Roman judge and Pilate stumbled backyard. "Pig!" he yelled again. His outburst was cut short by the guard who snapped the chain attached to the collar. The pain was unbearable. Barabbas fell to his knees and was dragged from the hall.

Out on the street, the three soldiers led Barak and Marcus to the steps of the porch surrounding the Judgment Hall. One of the three went into the hall for a few moments, then returned to lead the others in before Pilate.

The swelling in Marcus' eye had subsided slightly. He was able to see the man seated on the judgment seat before he and Barak were forced to their knees. The guard standing behind Marcus grabbed a fistful of hair and snapped his head back. "This is one of the thieving band at the condensing station, sir," the guard said. "He is worthy of death for insurrection and robbery attempted upon the tax belonging to Caesar."

The other guard grabbed Barak's hair and snapped the man's head back. Barak cursed and resisted, twisting his neck in an effort to jerk his head free. The big Roman's knee caught Barak low in the back. The thief gasped and slumped forward. As the soldier released his grip on Barak's hair, his face smashed against the marble floor.

At that moment, another man entered the Judgment Hall, bowed toward Pilate, and was told to approach the judgment seat. Marcus watched as the man spoke briefly to Pilate. Pilate pursed his lips and frowned, staring out into the vast hall. The messenger leaned over again. Pilate shook his head. The man slipped out silently, and the Procurator spoke. He stood and pointed a long finger at the pair. "Remove these men. I've heard enough. They are guilty of crimes against Rome, and against Caesar himself."

As Marcus was pulled to his feet, he caught a glimpse of the Nazarene entering the Judgment Hall. Marcus stared. He couldn't believe it was the same man. Jesus' eyes were deep-set and drawn with heavy, dark circles. The weight of the world seemed to rest on his shoulders. As he moved to the front of the Hall, he glanced at Marcus. A look of indescribable joy and sorrow emanated from his eyes. Marcus swallowed, wanting to call out, "He is guilty of nothing but love!" But his captor jerked him by the hair. "Come, pig!" The guard jerked again. "It is the dawning of the *day of death*," he laughed. Marcus looked back once more.

The sun pushed boldly against the morning sky, but failed to warm the crisp air hanging over the city. Priscilla moved quickly down the street. Her sandals scraped the stones and the hem of her robe swished daintily as she hurried toward the jail. The basket she carried contained a loaf of bread and some fresh fruit to strengthen Marcus for whatever ordeal lay ahead.

With a slight smile, she thought of the awkwardness of their first kiss. Her thoughts continued on to Bethany and her meeting with his sweet mother. It was wonderful how the older woman desired to share her only son. Her motherly instinct had swept Priscilla into the family unit as if she were one of her own. She was sorrowful over the older woman's death, yet felt it was best now. Phoebe would be suffering the anguish of a loving mother if she were to see Marcus in trouble.

Priscilla hurried on.

A squad of soldiers marched up the street. The handsome, young officer leading the men looked directly at Priscilla. His eyes fixed impertinently on hers. His smile was one created especially for pretty young women.

Priscilla dropped her eyes and hurried on.

The jail was only a short distance now. She reviewed the terrible hours before dawn. She and her grandfather had prayed and talked all night. The old man had wanted to go to Pontius Pilate and explain the situation to him. Pilate wasn't an unreasonable man, he had told her. In fact, he was sympathetic to Oshea for the miscarriage of justice that had befallen him at the hands of Gaius and his friends, years ago. Yet he couldn't convince Priscilla of the Roman Procurator's trustworthiness. He must consult with Obeha.

She approached the jail. Two Roman guards were posted at the large front gate. She stopped, checked her basket, then proceeded toward the two men.

"Halt!"

Priscilla stopped short. "I-I have come to deliver this," she said, pushing the basket under the guard's nose.

"What is this?"

"A loaf and some fresh fruit. It's for . . ."

"Ho, ho!" the guard bellowed. "Fresh fruit, is it?" The big man grabbed the basket and tore the cloth from it. "Look," he said, turning the basket so the other man could see, "it's fruit indeed!" He pulled out some grapes and popped them into his mouth, allowing the juice to dribble from the corners. "Ummm, fresh, too." He laughed, opening his mouth wide, displaying the half-eaten food. "Thank you, little woman, thank you." He laughed more loudly and handed the basket to the other guard.

"But, sir, that is for my . . . I-I mean, I have brought it . . ." She dropped her eyes to hide the tears.

The big guard stepped close to her, sliding his arm around her waist. "Now, now, little lady, don't cry." He pulled her close. She struggled. "Oh, ho! A fistful of tiger!" He looked at the other man feeding himself. "I . . ." A flashing of her nails stopped his lighthearted jesting. "I shall tame this one," he vowed.

"I am a Roman citizen!" Priscilla screamed.

The big man released his hold on her. He sobered. "You?" he questioned. "How have you found favor with Caesar?"

Priscilla ignored the question. "Give me the basket and allow me to make good my delivery."

The second guard handed her the basket. It now contained a half-loaf and two bruised grapes. She looked inside and a veil of anger spread across her face. She tipped the basket toward the first guard, her lips pursed tightly.

"Oh," he said in mock surprise. "Well, little woman, I don't know which of the prisoners you intended this for, but I can tell you now, he won't be needing it." He leered at her. "Today is the day of death for all who abide here."

Priscilla looked up in horror. The man's rotten teeth and the wiry hair springing from his nostrils reminded her of the captain on the boat from Rome. She burst into tears and ran sobbing up the street.

CHAPTER XIX

Only a short time had passed since Marcus had been thrust unceremoniously into his cell. Now, however, some light filtered in from a small, barred window high on the far wall. The half hour had crept by, seeming more like half a day.

Marcus was thankful that his companions were chained to the wall. They were in a vile humor since returning to the cell. Barabbas was slumped in one corner, feigning sleep. Barak, on the other hand, sat rigidly upright staring at Marcus.

"Today we die," he snarled. "I will be interested to see if you can die like a man."

As Barak loudly cursed their fate, the cell door opened, admitting a guard dragging Phinehas behind him. A second guard followed and pulled the door shut. He chained the stunned man to the wall next to Marcus, then stood and searched the dimly lit cell.

"That's the one." He motioned toward Barabbas,

whom the other Roman proceeded to prod with the shaft of his spear. Barabbas grabbed at the object poking his side. He cursed and spat, then opened his eyes.

"Pilate calls for you again," the guard said. "Let's move!"

They removed the wall chains but left the wrist and ankle binds in place. Barabbas submitted meekly.

When the three men were out of sight, Marcus whispered, "Phinehas, what happened?"

Barak leaned forward from the opposite wall. "Yes, fool," he gibed, "tell us how you managed to get yourself caught."

Phinehas glared at Barak then turned to Marcus. "As soon as the soldiers neared the Temple area, they suspected the hoax. There was no riot. Barabbas promised that Judas would bribe some of Rosh's friends to raise a stir with the Nazarene. But neither Jesus nor any of the lawyers were anywhere near the Temple." He drew a deep breath. "The captain of the quaternion grabbed me and sent the others back to the tax booth to see about the wagon." Phinehas shrugged his shoulders. "You know the rest."

"No, I don't," Marcus denied.

Barak strained against his chains. "He doesn't know what happened because the coward ran as soon as the trouble started!"

"I wasn't running from the trouble!" Marcus protested. "You knew the plan as well as I. I was to lure the soldiers, at least one or two of them, away from the scene of the robbery!"

Phinehas continued. "I almost got away when the captain himself brought me to the jail. The crowd was so thick we could barely get through. When we passed the Judgment Hall, I caught a glimpse of Rosh."

"That son of a sow!" Barak mumbled.

"Rosh had formed a gathering of Sadducees and the like to call for the execution of Jesus and the release of another prisoner in his place—Barabbas!" Phinehas paused dramatically. "We three are about to be crucified, and justly so. Barabbas deserves the same; yet Jesus shall take his punishment." He stared off into the darkness. "It's as though an innocent lamb were being offered up so this, the greater sinner, might go free."

Barak's lip curled. "He shall never go free!" he growled. "Barabbas has caused more uprisings and trouble for the Roman pigs than the three of us put together!"

Phinehas smiled wryly. "You forget, my obnoxious friend, Barabbas has Rosh working for him. The stage has been set." He shook his head sorrowfully. "From the beginning, this whole thing has been a plot to destroy Jesus—the one many are calling the Messiah."

Marcus frowned. "You mean Barabbas expected to be caught?"

Phinehas shrugged his shoulders. "I can't prove it. But I have heard plans . . ."

Barak roared in a frenzy of rage. "I should have killed the pig long ago!"

"If you don't believe me, stop and consider." He eyed the spot where Barabbas had been chained. "Why do you think they took Barabbas away? Why did he follow so willingly without putting up a struggle? And why has Barabbas been seen with Rosh so much in these past few weeks?" Phinehas looked inquiringly at the two men as they weighed his words.

"I suspect much money has exchanged hands. Rosh is very powerful among the leaders of the Sanhedrin, and those pious men have wealth almost equal to that of Caesar. That group would give their last gold piece to be rid of the Nazarene. He makes them see themselves as they really are—a generation of vipers!" He leaned back against the wall. "I would venture to say a large quantity of gold will line Barabbas' pockets before it's all over." He closed his eyes, exhausted.

Marcus studied the man appreciatively. This was a Phinehas he had not known. "But Jesus is an innocent man!" he protested. "And Barabbas is a known murderer!"

"You and I know that," Phinehas sighed. "Even the people know it. But their lust for the blood of the Nazarene will not be satisfied until he is dead."

A sound of voices preceded the three soldiers who stepped brusquely into the cell. "Time for your appointment with death," one of them intoned. "Looks like there will be only three crosses today," he said as the guards removed the chains. "I've seen as many as nine crucified at one time."

As the grim processional moved out of the cell and down the corridor, the guard mumbled to himself, "Yet, there may still be a fourth. They call for the death of the Nazarene."

In the Hall of Justice, Barabbas was receiving his freedom as Jesus was led away to be scourged. Pilate had found no fault with the man. He seemed incapable of violence or inciting great gatherings to riot. Yet the religious leaders had accused him of the most heinous of all charges—blasphemy—claiming to be the Son of God. It was a very serious accusation. When Pilate had questioned Jesus, he neither denied nor confirmed the charge. Indeed, the man had said nothing at all in his own defense. It was quite disturbing.

The Roman Procurator had called for a silver bowl and washed his hands, relieving himself of the whole affair and leaving the judgment to the people who waited outside the great hall.

As he dried his hands, he agreed to one more appointment before pronouncing sentence on the three prisoners being escorted from the jail.

Three Jews entered the Hall and approached the Procurator as he seated himself. "And what can I do for you gentlemen?" Pilate asked.

"We'll be brief, sir," Obeha said, beginning his plea. The old man and the mediator stood silently by, waiting their turn to speak.

In the outer chamber, the guards led the prisoners to the door of the Judgment Hall. They were met by a Senate aide. "You will have to wait," he stated flatly. "Proconsul is entertaining a plea right now and will see you shortly." His voice was almost effeminate.

"As far as I'm concerned, he can take his time!" Phinehas said.

"Silence!" shouted the commander of the guards, cruelly twisting the wrist chain and bringing a sharp outcry from Phinehas.

A second aide entered the hallway with a whispered message. It rippled among the Romans. The sound of it fell dully on Marcus' ears. "They have released Barabbas, and Pilate has given Jesus to be crucified!"

A guard came out into the corridor. "Which one of you is Marcus?"

Marcus frowned and hesitated, "I am he."

"Unchain him from the others and take him aside," the guard ordered. "Pilate reserves judgment momentarily." He waved a hand. "Bring in the other poor wretches now."

Marcus was led farther down the corridor where he slid to the marble floor and leaned against the wall. The guard shackled his ankles and moved a few paces away, seating himself. Marcus looked down the hallway. All was quiet.

A scuffling of boots and sandals roused him from his

stupor. He looked up to find the door of the Judgment Hall opening and a Roman soldier emerging, followed by a second and a third. They laughed and called over their shoulders to the man they led by a chain around his neck. "Come, O King, you must move faster! Your subjects are waiting!"

Marcus' heart stood still. The sight of the man sent a shiver through his entire frame. The chain around the man's neck and the lean nakedness of his tortured body caused Marcus physical pain. The guard behind Jesus jabbed him periodically, causing him to stumble. Blood from countless blows stained the upper edge of his loincloth. He paused, then was shoved roughly into a room directly across from Marcus. The young Jew could see him clearly as he stood in the middle of the room.

When Jesus turned, Marcus gasped. His back was laid open, exposing muscle and bone. Blood oozed from hundreds of lash marks crisscrossing his flesh. Marcus cringed, feeling in his own body the jagged metal pieces imbedded in the tips of the whip. He imagined the flesh being torn from his back, and knew the dreaded scourging would soon be his lot.

Another aide hurried down the corridor and turned into the room. "As you requested, Captain," he announced, "a crown for the King of the Jews!"

The soldier took the wreath, composed of plaited brambles and thorns. Each thorn was as long as a man's finger and sharp as a tailor's needle. The Roman pricked his finger and cursed disgustedly. He placed the wreath on Jesus' head, pressing it down and drawing blood. Jesus flinched as trickles of the warm liquid ran into the lines of his forehead.

Another soldier, who had left the room unnoticed, returned with a purple robe. "Look what I have found for our King—a garment befitting royalty," he mocked.

The soldier threw the garment around Jesus' shoulders, jerking him roughly in the pretense of straightening the robe. "Sorry, my lord. I was only making sure of the fit." He stepped back and bent to one knee. The gesture brought shouts of laughter from the onlookers.

"Hail, King of the Jews!" he mocked, then spat into the Nazarene's face. The spittle fell just below his left eye and ran slowly down his cheek like a tear.

The room was silent. The soldier glanced around defiantly. "Deliver to us a great pronouncement, O King!" he sneered. "Speak to us with your final breath!"

Jesus kept his silence. Marcus could barely see his face through his own tear-filled eyes. He moved his lips in a prayer as he watched the hollow exhibition of reverence.

"Pilate summons you!" an aide called sharply. "Hey, you! Pilate demands your presence!"

Marcus' jaw twitched. He could not tear his eyes from the drama unfolding in the opposite room. Finally, he could contain himself no longer and loosed a loud cry of outrage and frustration, "He is not guilty!" The scream shattered the sadistic ritual, and a dead silence settled over the crowd.

Jesus turned to gaze deep into Marcus' eyes. His look spoke of tender concern for Marcus—none for his own suffering. His eyes pierced Marcus' very soul, searching out the confusion and pain. Though no words passed between them, Marcus felt a surge of hope. The words of the prophet Esaias echoed in some dark chamber of his mind: *He was wounded and bruised for our sins . . . He was lashed—and we were healed! He was afflicted, yet he never spoke a word.*

Could it be true? Marcus reached out a hand, his chains clanging loudly against the marble floor. Jesus smiled faintly. *I am the only way to the Father.* Did he speak, or was Marcus imagining the gentle words that fell like a benediction on his spirit?

At that moment a blindfold was pressed over Jesus' eyes and he was led away to the slaughter. "Wait!" Marcus screamed silently. "I must know more about this man!"

With his gaze still fixed on the retreating figure of Jesus, Marcus moved passively down the corridor and into the Hall of Judgment to receive his own sentence.

Among the crowd, gathered like vultures, anticipating the verdict of the Procurator, Priscilla waited for her grandfather and Obeha. As they came down the marble steps, she observed that both men wore solemn expressions. She pushed through the masses, trying to reach them.

Suddenly a great cheer rose from the crowd. Priscilla looked back to see Barabbas on the portico, hands on hips, grinning triumphantly. The young woman watched as some of the people rushed to greet him. Barabbas clasped some of the outstretched hands, but his eyes were scanning the crowd. When he spotted Rosh, he raised a fist in silent tribute. The crowd roared and Rosh nodded, smiling.

"Priscilla," Obeha called.

Startled, she turned to see the two men approaching. She fell into her grandfather's arms. "Oh, Grandpapa, what about Marcus? What did Pilate say?"

"We did our best," the old man assured her. "Pilate seemed very receptive to our plea."

"Does that mean he will release Marcus?"

Obeha placed his hands on her shoulders. "My dear," he said, "who but God knows what that man may do? We can only pray and wait now, child."

Priscilla covered her face and sobbed soundlessly.

Jesus appeared in the entrance to the Temple courtyard, supported by guards on either side. The fickle
crowd stood in silent clusters to witness the agonizing
journey up to Golgotha where the crucifixion would
take place. Several people inched forward to see if a
closer look would confirm his identity. Even those who
hadn't thought about the Nazarene one way or the
other felt a sickening deep in the pit of their stomachs.
The man was scarcely recognizable, so cruelly had he
been tortured.

A low hum began at the front of the crowd and
flowed in waves toward the outer perimeter. The
Pharisees, Sadducees and the lawyers, along with the
scribes and other Temple workers shifted uneasily.

Suddenly Rosh, the leader in the cause to crucify the
Nazarene, revived the worn-out chant of the morning.
It began low and spread quickly among the edgy Temple
workers. Within seconds, the tempo accelerated, and
the volume increased. "Crucify him! Crucify him!"
Others, caught up in the hysteria of the masses, took up
the cry. The voices grew louder, permeating the chilly
morning air. "Crucify him!"

The tense crowd surged forward, some shaking their
fists angrily. Many in the crowd were silent. They had
witnessed his miracles and listened to his teachings.
They were curious to see what he would do now that he
faced death. Others vied for a more satisfactory
position—the better to view the grisly scene. Extra
guards and Roman soldiers were kept busy handling the
unruly crowd.

In the background were some faithful followers, remaining inconspicuous, but eager to know his condition.

One of the Roman guards waved toward a foot soldier
standing to one side. He motioned for slaves who

dragged the roughhewn cross into position near the portico where Jesus stood waiting, his head bowed in fatigue.

Two thieves, condemned to the same fate, had already been scourged and half-carried to the Place of the Skull. There, they awaited their final punishment, while Jesus was compelled to bear the full weight of the wooden beams upon his own shoulders. He struggled beneath the load and stumbled, but was brought to his feet by the clout of a Roman club.

The grim procession turned onto the dusty road outside the city's walls. Up ahead, a stream of smoke traced its way up into the crisp morning air. As they approached the slight rise of the hill, the craggy rocks and tufts of seared grass cast a ghastly pallor of death on the scene.

The enormous crowd encircled the site of the two crosses already standing in place, bearing their human burdens. The thieves hung limply, moaning in pain. Just then, the younger thief cried out. From every indication, he had received more than the customary number of lashes before being nailed to the crossbars. Every blemish was evident on the smooth flesh. The cutting edges of the whip had left great gashes across his chest and, as a cruel memento, had buried bits of the metal in the wounds.

Seven Roman guards surrounded Jesus, expecting a struggle. He was commanded to place himself on the cross lying next to his bare feet and he submitted mutely. The crowd on the hillside murmured in amazement. All who had ever been brought to this place of punishment had been forced to lie on the rugged wooden cross. Most of them were dragged, screaming, to the post or had to be knocked unconscious—all, except this Jesus, who remained strangely silent throughout the nailing.

When the soldiers had secured Jesus to the cross, they lifted it slowly. As it moved into an upright position, it dropped into the hole gouged into the rocky hillside. Now fully upright, the wooden beam settled into the ground, tearing the flesh of the man who slumped forward.

Priscilla and her grandfather, accompanied by a sorrowing Obeha, had followed at a great distance. They had waited until the very last minute, hoping to hear word of Marcus' fate. When none came, there was nothing to do but follow the crowd and offer whatever comfort was possible to ease his suffering. The pain in the young girl's heart was almost more than she could bear—that she must witness the torment of two whom she loved more than life itself.

On the hill, the three crosses stood in bold relief against the gray sky. Angry, dark clouds rolled in over the Judean hills. The air smelled of rain and death. Priscilla's legs could scarcely support her, and she leaned heavily on the two men beside her.

On the crosses, the thieves moaned intermittently and called for water or a sedative to dull the pain. The central figure was quiet except for an occasional word of comfort spoken to the faithful ones who stood weeping near his feet.

"Don't weep for me, but for yourselves," he said weakly. "If such things as this are done to me, what will they do to you?"

To one side the coarse Roman soldiers gambled for the only possession he had—a homespun robe.

The Jewish leaders, led by Rosh, boasted among themselves of their successful mission. Looking on at the dying man, they taunted, "He was so good at helping others, let's see if he can save himself if he is really God's

Chosen One, the promised Messiah. And we shall be the first to fall at his feet!"

"Yes!" shouted some in the crowd. "Save yourself and we will *all* follow you! Show us another miracle! Come down from the cross and save yourself!"

The soldiers, still casting lots for his garment, joined in the jeers. "Come now, if you are truly the King of the Jews, save yourself!"

The burly thief, hanging on the cross beside him, scoffed, "So you're the Messiah, are you? Prove it by saving yourself—and us, too, while you're at it!"

At that moment a faint voice carried above the clamor. "Stop it! Stop, all of you! Can't you see this man has done nothing wrong? We deserve to die for our evil deeds, but he is not guilty!"

Painfully, the younger thief rolled his head to look into Jesus' face. "Master, remember me when you come into your kingdom."

Jesus looked into the young face. "I promise you solemnly—today you will be with me in Paradise."

Priscilla and the two men left in her life had crested the hill just as the lightning bolt illuminated the three hanging on the crosses. She cringed at the sight of her beloved Master, bludgeoned almost beyond recognition—then searched the faces of the other two.

"Marcus!" Priscilla gasped. She reached out a hand to steady herself, and caught her grandfather's arm. "Marcus is not there!"

With renewed hope she turned to Obeha. His face reflected her joy. In pity they looked again at Barak and the younger thief, Phinehas.

"I must find him!" Priscilla exclaimed. With that, she broke away and moved quickly in and out among the clusters of people looking on. The earth rumbled and the sky darkened to night shades.

Marcus, too, was searching for his love. His quest had brought him to the foot of the crosses. He stood between Jesus and Phinehas, as though drawn by a power beyond himself. He gazed at the Nazarene, overwhelmed by the love that filled his being.

As his eyes moved to Phinehas, he leaned forward to catch the halting words of his friend: "I told you . . ." Phinehas gasped, "that I would be one of his . . . when he came into his Kingdom. Today . . . I shall be with him . . . in Paradise."

Marcus felt the cool tears running down his cheeks, but he was unashamed.

He turned to see Priscilla stumbling through the crowd and ran to meet her just as the storm clouds clashed, bringing the drenching rains. Her arms locked around his neck and he clasped her tightly to him. Their tears mingled with the rain, blending in a single stream of joy.

DEDICATION

To God be the glory!